A *Dream* FOR HANNAH

JERRY S. EICHER

HARVEST HOUSE PUBLISHERS

EUGENE, OREGON

All Scripture quotations are taken from the King James Version of the Bible.

Cover by Garborg Design Works, Savage, Minnesota

Cover photo © Garborg Design Works

A DREAM FOR HANNAH
Copyright © 2010 by Jerry S. Eicher
Published by Harvest House Publishers
Eugene, Oregon 97402
www.harvesthousepublishers.com

Library of Congress Cataloging-in-Publication Data

Eicher, Jerry S.
   A dream for Hannah / Jerry Eicher.
      p. cm.
   ISBN 978-0-7369-3045-1 (pbk.)
   1. Amish--Indiana--Fiction. 2. Young women--Montana--Fiction. I. Title.
   PS3605.I34H36 2010
   813'.6--dc22

                                           2009047454

Printed in the United States of America

10 11 12 13 14 15 16 17 18 / BP-SK / 10 9 8 7 6 5 4 3 2 1

One

Outside Hannah Miller's upstairs window, springtime had come. The earth was finally awakening from what had been a worse than normal northern Indiana winter.

Breakfast was finished, and her mother would soon call from downstairs for help. Her cousins were coming to visit this evening, and there was a lot of work to do.

As she secured her dark hair beneath the head covering she wore for work, Hannah glanced down at the paper on which she had scribbled the words of the poem. Surely she had time for another quick read, and that would have to do. Her almost seventeen-year-old hands trembled as she held the writing in front of her.

The words of the poem by E.S. White, written in 1908, gripped her again.

A Ballad of Spring

It's Spring, my Love.
Bowed down with care,
Your branches are stripped and bare.

Old Winter's past.
Its snow and cold
Have melted long and lost their hold.

The earth it waited
With bated breath for something more,
For life renewed called from its core.

It opens wide its arms.
For strength, for vigor, for its best,
It stirs its creatures to their nests.

All around it lies the warmth
Because the sun has drawn near,
Touching, caressing, there and here.

Arise, it calls.
The pomegranates bloom.
They yell that life has room.

Will you come, my Dear,
Hold my hand, touch what I bring?
Because, my Love, it's Spring.

Hannah paused as thoughts raced through her head. *Can this be true? Is there really such a feeling? Is this something I could really feel... this thing called love?*

Then, from downstairs she heard the urgent sound of her mother's voice, "Hannah, time to start the day."

"Yes, I'm coming," she called as she quickly placed the poem on the dresser, smoothed the last wrinkles out of the bed covers, and then rushed out of her room and down the stairs.

"The wash needs to be started right away," her mom said as she busied herself with the dishes in the kitchen sink.

"Yes, right away," Hannah said. After making one last check for dirty clothes in the bedrooms, she made her way down to the basement. The sparse room seemed dingy and damp, in stark contrast to the fresh spring day she had seen from her upstairs window. She'd much rather be outside, but the laundry must be done.

Hannah ran the water into the tub from the attached hose. When the water reached the fill line, she turned off the water and tossed in the first load of dirty clothes. With a jerk on the starter rope, the old tub started vibrating. The motor changed its speed and sound as the center tumbler turned, dragging the load of pants and shirts through the water.

As Hannah reached inside the washer to check the progress, the memory of the poem returned to her. Then she thought of James back in seventh grade. His grin had been lopsided but cute. He was a sweet boy—his eyes always lit up whenever Hannah looked at him. Was that the first stirrings of whatever this thing called "love" was?

Surely not. Such ideas! If someone could read my thoughts... "A *dummkopf,* that's what they'd say," she spoke aloud, smiling at her youthful memory.

Her hand dodged the tumbler's wrath, but still the tumbler caught a piece of cloth and whipped water in her direction.

Then her memory moved up to eighth grade. Sam Knepp. A thirteen-year-old girl just had to have someone to like. The other girls would have thought her a true *dummkopf* if she had no one. And so she had picked Sam at random. What other choice had there been? Sam sat across the aisle from her. He was sort of cute. He had freckles, red hair, and a good smile. But there was that horrible habit he had of opening his mouth when he was puzzled or surprised.

When Hannah told the other girls she liked Sam, they reacted with admiration. So she had made the right choice. Maybe she was not a *dummkopf.* Her friend Mary stuck up for her choice. Mary was blonde and sweet on Laverne, who was truly a wonder in the world of Amish eighth graders. He was easily the best-looking boy in the district. In fact Hannah would have picked Laverne had he not already been taken by Mary. For some reason, it didn't bother her that Annie, who was in the sixth grade, had her attention on Sam; blushing every time he walked by, but saying nothing.

No, Hannah decided, Sam didn't fit for her. Not really. Maybe Laverne would have been a good choice, but not as long as he was Mary's choice. Hannah supposed even now that Laverne and Mary would soon be dating.

"Hannah," her mother called from upstairs, "are you done yet?"

"Coming," Hannah called out. "This old washer is going as fast as it can."

"Well, hurry up. The clothing needs to be on the line soon. The sun is already well up."

"Yes," Hannah called out again, "I'll get it out as soon as I can."

Minutes later the cycle was finished, and Hannah quickly loaded the basket with the heavy wet laundry and made her way up the steps and out to the clothesline.

Outside, the glorious spring day greeted her brightly. Hannah turned her face skyward and almost lost her grip on the basket as she soaked in the warm sunshine. What a glorious spring it was going to be! It felt so good to be young and alive.

Hannah began pinning the wet clothes onto the line till they stretched out, heavy in the still morning air. Later the breeze would pick up and dry the clothes as they flapped in the wind. It was a beautiful sight to behold. Hannah hoped the wind would stay gentle until the last piece was fully dry, but with spring days, one was never sure. The wind could have a mind of its own.

She stood back and watched with approval the first of the wash begin to move slightly in the breeze. *Yes, this is going to be a wonderful spring*, she decided as she picked up the basket and turned to go back inside.

The sun was still out when the first buggies arrived for the evening's family gathering. Two buggies came in, one right after the other, and then two more arrived fifteen minutes later. Among the guests were Ben and Susan Yoder—Susan was Hannah's mom's cousin. Also in attendance were Leroy and John, brothers on her dad's side, and Mose, Leroy's brother-in-law. Other people who were in some way connected to the Millers had also been invited. Having a few outside guests allowed for some spontaneity while maintaining some of the structures formed by the natural family. Sam Knepp came that night because one of the cousins had taken the notion to invite him.

It amused Hannah to see Sam again, having just thought of him that morning. She noticed that he still had that habit of occasionally allowing his mouth to drop open almost randomly.

After a hearty supper, all the young people went outside to play.

Since so many younger children were involved, they had to choose a simple game. The game they chose was Wolf, which caused Hannah to consider whether or not she might be too old to join in. The game involved races run at full speed in the darkness. When all of the cousins and Sam announced they would play, Hannah decided to join in. After all, Sam and she were the same age. If he could play, so could she.

With that decided, the game was called to order, and the first "wolf"—her cousin Micah—was chosen. He picked the big tree beside the house for his home base, hollered loudly that the game had begun, and began to count. The children scattered to find hiding places before he counted to one hundred. Hannah decided to try to bluff the wolf by hiding just around the corner of the house.

At the count of a hundred, the wolf silently moved to the edge of the house, stuck his head around the corner, spotted Hannah, and howled with glee. He easily beat her back to the tree trunk.

"That was stupid of me," Hannah muttered as she joined Micah at the tree.

"They try that on me all the time," the wolf crowed in triumph. "Now let's get the rest of them. You go around the house that way, and I'll take the side you hid on."

Hannah imitated the wolf's trick, now that she was one herself, but the corner of the house produced no hidden sheep. The moon had already set by now, and the only light came from the stars. This corner of the house was particularly dark, absent of any light beams from the gas lanterns in the living room and kitchen.

Hannah felt her way along the house and, hearing a noise, she turned toward the front porch where she flushed someone out of the bush and found herself in a race back to the tree trunk. Hannah wasn't sure who she was chasing, but that didn't matter. The only thing that mattered was who got to the tree first.

Just as she passed the corner of the house, Hannah's world exploded into a deeper darkness than the evening around her. Sam, the one she had flushed from the bush, somehow collided with Hannah. He flew backward, and Hannah flew off into complete darkness in the other direction. Two other racers just missed her fallen body and dodged Sam who had now crawled slowly to a sitting position.

Young cousin Jonas, one of the children who had to jump to avoid Hannah's body, immediately ran to the kitchen door, stuck his head in, and yelled in his loudest little-boy voice, "Someone bring a light! There's been a hurt!"

Roy Miller, Hannah's father, reacted first. He grabbed the kitchen lantern from its hook and ran outside.

"What's going on?" he called from the porch, holding his lantern aloft, the light reaching out in a great circle.

"She's hurt! Over here!" Sam called. He now rested on his left elbow and pointed toward Hannah's still body.

As Roy approached, Sam slowly huddled closer to Hannah, both hands wrapped around his head. "Hannah," he whispered, "are you hurt?"

By the light of Roy's approaching lantern, Sam saw that Hannah was not moving. He took his hands off his head and gently pushed her arm but got no response. "You okay?" he asked again, tilting his head sideways to look down at her.

"Oh no, I hurt her!" Sam yelled as he jumped to his feet. He then stood speechless, his mouth wide open.

With the lantern in hand, Roy was now standing over the two young people. Glancing briefly at Sam, Roy reached for Hannah's hand and then focused his attention on Hannah's head, which had obviously taken the brunt of the hit as evidenced by a deep gash and wound to her left eye. Roy gently gathered Hannah in his arms and spoke to his brother, Leroy, standing beside him.

"Better take a look at Sam," Roy said with a motion of his head toward the boy, and then he headed to the kitchen with Hannah.

Hannah's mom met them at the door. "How bad is she hurt?" she asked, holding the kitchen door open.

"I don't know," Roy told her. "Let's get her to the couch."

Roy placed Hannah down gently and then stepped aside as Kathy got her first good look at Hannah's head.

"We have to take her to the doctor—now," Kathy said. "This looks serious."

"Are you sure?" Roy said. "Is it that bad?"

"Roy, just look at her eye and that cut on her head!"

Roy, for the first time, carefully studied his daughter's injury and then nodded. "Can someone run down to Mr. Bowen's place and call for a driver?" he asked.

"I'll go," Ben said as he headed for the door.

Hannah had become alert enough to barely moan but nothing more.

Ben returned minutes later, a little breathless but with news. "Mr. Bowen said it wasn't necessary to call for a ride. He'll take her himself."

"*Da Hah* be praised," Roy said, worried about his daughter.

Old Mr. Bowen drove his car up to the front porch. Roy helped the groggy Hannah into the backseat.

"Why don't you ride in the back with her?" Roy suggested to Kathy.

Kathy nodded, slid in next to Hannah, and held her upright against her own shoulder. With Roy in the front seat, Mr. Bowen pulled out of the driveway.

"Is she hurt badly?" Mr. Bowen asked.

"I can't tell," Roy said. "Her head seems to have...quite a gash in it. And her left eye doesn't look normal."

"I'll get you there as fast as I can." Mr. Bowen accelerated slowly on the gravel road and hung tightly onto the steering wheel. Once they reached the blacktop, he sped up considerably.

They reached Elkhart without incident, and Mr. Bowen pulled into the hospital parking lot. Roy quickly got out, opened the back door, and helped Hannah out of the car. He and Kathy took Hannah's arms and made their way into the emergency room reception area.

The attending nurse took one look at Hannah, brought a wheelchair for her, and then took her to an examining room to wait for the doctor.

An hour later Roy and Kathy were seated in the waiting room.

"Did they say how bad she is?" Roy asked again.

"The nurse said she'll be fine. That's all she said," Kathy repeated.

"Will she lose the eye?"

"No, surely not," Kathy said, though with some uncertainty.

"We'll just have to trust," he said, attempting a smile and squeezing her hand.

"I'll wait for you folks. Whatever time this takes," Mr. Bowen assured them.

"That awful nice of you," Kathy said. "We can call when we're done. This could take much of the night."

"The Mrs. understands," Mr. Bowen said. "I don't need much sleep myself anyway."

"It's still nice of you," Kathy said with a smile as she took a seat beside Roy.

A few minutes later, the attending doctor walked into the waiting room and motioned for Hannah's parents to follow him.

"I'm Dr. Benson," he announced to the couple as they walked down the hall. "Your daughter is resting now. There isn't much more we can do other than keep her under observation. We can't let her sleep for a while, of course."

"What happened?" Kathy asked.

"A bad concussion, that's all, from what I can tell. The bone structure of her skull has actually been damaged where the impact occurred. That's also what caused her left eye to protrude. We patched her up as best we could. Now nature will have to take its course. The eye, I believe, will return to normal now that we have taken the worst of the pressure off. We'd like to keep her here under observation for a day or two just to be sure."

"Yes, of course," Roy said. "I appreciate the prompt attention. She had us really worried. Will we be able to see her now?"

"Yes, the nurse will take you back. Do you have any questions?"

Roy and Kathy looked at each other, and Kathy said, "No, doctor, I don't think so. Thank you for all you've done."

The couple then followed the nurse into the elevator and two floors up.

Hannah lay in the bed, covered with white sheets and kept awake by a watchful nurse. The bed beside Hannah was occupied by another girl whose face was turned away from them. She moved slightly when they walked in but didn't turn in their direction.

"You're in good hands," Kathy whispered and squeezed Hannah's hand.

Hannah blinked slowly but made no other response.

"A little groggy," the nurse said and smiled. "We gave her something for the pain."

"We'd better leave, then, I suppose," Kathy whispered. "They'll take good care of you, Hannah. I'll come back tomorrow first thing."

Hannah nodded, and Kathy brushed her hand across her cheek.

At the doorway, Kathy glanced back quickly before she followed Roy out.

"She looked okay," Roy assured her.

"But here—all night by herself."

"They'll watch her. You can come back in the morning. Half the night's gone already the way it is."

"I suppose so," Kathy agreed.

Roy pushed the elevator button. They stepped inside when the doors opened and arrived at the waiting room to find Mr. Bowen had nodded off, his chin on his chest.

"We're back," Roy whispered into his ear.

He awoke with a start, grinned, and promptly bounced to his feet.

"How is she?" he asked as they walked outside.

"She'll be okay," Roy said, "but she's staying for a day or two."

"Sounds good for how she looked," Mr. Bowen commented. "So let me get you folks home. I suppose you're ready?"

"That we are," Roy agreed.

Mr. Bowen drove slowly on the way home, taking his time around the curves. When he pulled into the Miller's graveled driveway, he turned to Kathy in the backseat. "What's your driver situation for tomorrow?"

"I have no one," Kathy said, "and I have to go first thing in the morning, but I'll call around from the pay phone."

"No, just count on me as your driver until this is over," Mr. Bowen said.

"That's awfully nice of you," Kathy said, "but we don't to want to take advantage."

"Think nothing of it," Mr. Bowen assured her. "I'm more than glad to help out."

Two

Sunlight streamed through the hospital window when the nurse pulled open the blinds. Hannah, still groggy, looked around, uncertain where she was. The white-clad nurse sure wasn't someone she knew. Then Hannah faintly remembered loud noises, bright lights, her mother's whispered voice, and then someone who wouldn't let her sleep for a long, long time. Shivers ran up and down her body from the strangeness of it all.

"Are you cold?" the nurse asked.

"No," Hannah replied, "but where am I?"

"In the hospital, dear. You banged your head pretty bad last night."

The explanation made some sense, as her recollections of the previous evening continued to burst in on her tired and bruised brain. A stray sunbeam played on her face, and she squinted her eyes and moved to escape its brightness. The nurse didn't seem to notice and left, her step clipped and hurried. For the first time, Hannah noticed the English girl in the next bed. The girl had turned toward Hannah and now asked, "You're Amish, aren't you?"

Hannah nodded, not overly inclined to talk but not wanting to seem rude either. One never knew where that conversation would go with *Englisha* people.

"I thought so," the girl said. "My name's Alice. I live in town. My mom owns the dry goods store in Nappanee. You Amish come in there all the time."

Hannah nodded again.

"What are you in here for?"

"Hurt my head last night in a game," Hannah said slowly.

"Must have been a rough game."

"Not usually," Hannah said, holding her hand to her head. "It's just a running game, but I guess I didn't see the person coming the other way."

"Must have been a big person to put such a big gash in your forehead," Alice said, surveying the large bandage.

"*Jah*, a boy," Hannah said and made a face.

Alice grinned. "Your boyfriend?"

"No," Hannah said, horror in her voice. Her hand flew to her head in reflex. "Sam? I would say not." *Maybe in eighth grade but not now!*

Alice just grinned. "Sounds like the ones you usually end up marrying. Hate 'em and then love 'em."

Hannah's mind caught the vision of Sam's mouth dropping open and his freckled face turning fully toward her. *Nee, definitely not Sam.*

"Right, aren't I? Admit it."

Hannah would have glared at her if Alice had been Amish, but this was an *Englisha* girl, and so she smiled. "Sam's not my type at all."

"Whatever you say. I just hope it turns out all right for you." Alice paused, a startled look on her face, her eyes fixed on their doorway that led to the hall.

Hannah turned to look but saw nothing more unusual than the glimpse of a boy in a wheelchair slowly moving up the hallway. From the back of him, Hannah could tell little of what he looked like other than he had blond hair and looked *Englisha*.

"You know him?" she asked Alice.

Alice turned her face away, for what reason Hannah couldn't fathom. "Oh, a little," she said. Then suddenly turning toward Hannah, she said, "I've seen him around town."

"You looked surprised."

"Oh, it's nothing," Alice assured her. "Just seeing somebody I know—it's kind of unexpected in here. I mean, what are the chances of them getting sick at the same time you do?" Alice sat up suddenly, reached over, and pushed the call button. When the nurse appeared, she asked, "Can I go move around in the hall a bit? I think I need some exercise."

"Sure, honey," the nurse replied, "exercise sounds like a good idea. Let me go make arrangements for you," she said, disappearing down the hall.

"Just need some air," Alice said in Hannah's direction.

Before Hannah could respond, the same boy in the wheelchair appeared in the bedroom doorway.

"Can I come in?" he asked cheerfully.

Hannah wasn't certain as to what to say, and so she said nothing.

He smiled, gave the wheels of his wheelchair a push, and rolled between the two beds.

"Hi," he said to both of them, his head turning in one direction and then the other.

"Hi, Peter," Alice said. Then in Hannah's direction, she added, "He's the boy that just went by."

Hannah nodded in Peter's direction. He seemed awfully bold—the kind of boy her mom always warned her about. He had bright blue eyes and tremendous good looks. How tall he was, she couldn't tell because of the wheelchair, but his hair was, in fact, blond. She was also sure now that he looked quite *Englisha*.

"You going home soon?" he asked in Alice's direction.

"This afternoon," she said. "Mom's coming. Dad's coming too if he has the time. I should be up and about in a few days. Nothing serious, you know. Why it took them this long to figure it out, I'll never know."

"I'll be out tomorrow afternoon," Peter said. Then he turned in Hannah's direction and said, "You're Amish, aren't you?"

She looked at him without answering right away, reluctant to get into another *Englisha* person's questions about the Amish.

"I know you are," he said when she said nothing, "because your parents were in here last night. I saw them check on you. I'm Amish too. We live over in Goshen. What's your name?"

Hannah's attention was immediately gained, and her reluctance melted like ice on a hot summer's day. Amish made him safe, even if he was in *rumspringa,* which given his non-Amish appearance, he might very well be.

"I'm in because I had my appendix taken out yesterday," Peter offered, his eyes focused on her. "Like I told Alice, I should be here till tomorrow. You look like you might be out soon too," he added as he reached his hand out as if to touch her forehead in sympathy.

Although Hannah could only see his eyes, she felt a great weakness flood over her. *This boy is not an* Englisha. The thought burned inside of her. He was Amish and so much better looking than even Mary's Laverne back in eighth grade.

Then slowly, against her will, Hannah felt her face become warm. First her neck, then the flush spread over her face, yet her body shivered under the blankets. Peter had the biggest, sweetest smile she had ever seen. The sight took her breath away—the arch of his high brows, the warm expressive mouth, the quick blink of his eyes. Against the light hospital gown, his blond hair looked even blonder.

"Is your mother coming back anytime soon?" he asked. His blue eyes shone deeply.

Hannah looked into them and found no strength to answer.

Alice solved the problem by saying, "You are a bad boy, Peter." Her voice carried a deep sarcasm and broke the spell Hannah was under.

Peter laughed, a deep manly sound. "That's something coming from you. You're quite the judge."

Hannah caught her breath at the sound of his laugh. How could a laugh sound so delightful?

The nurse suddenly appeared in the doorway and said to Peter, "Visiting again?"

"Not anymore," Peter said as he turned his wheelchair around.

"Your mother's here," the nurse said to Hannah. Turning back to Peter, she asked, "Have you been behaving?"

He grinned at her. "Of course, I'm always a good boy." And with that, he wheeled himself out of the room.

Just then, Kathy knocked gently on the side of the door and said, "Good morning" to Hannah and, "Hi," to Alice.

To Hannah's surprise her mom seemed to know Alice.

"I had heard you were in the hospital," Kathy said. "A case of the winter flu...in springtime?"

"It turned into pneumonia," Alice said, "but I'm better now, and I'm supposed to go home today."

"I imagine you can't wait." Kathy patted her on the arm.

The nurse returned with a wheelchair just then and said, "She doesn't have to wait at all. Alice, your parents are here. You're being released now."

Hannah and Kathy waited while the nurse helped Alice gather her things and gingerly climb into the wheelchair. Hannah was sure Alice gave her a sideways glance as she left, making a point to not say goodbye. Why, Hannah couldn't imagine.

Hannah brought her thoughts back to her mother as Kathy told her, "Hannah, the doctor says you're doing well and can come home the day after tomorrow."

"I'd be ready to go right now," Hannah said with considerable passion. "I don't like this place."

"I know, but it's best to follow the doctor's orders. If you go home too soon, it could cause complications we'll regret."

Hannah nodded grimly.

"I brought you something," Kathy said, holding out her hand with an obviously homemade card.

"Oh," Hannah said, her face brightening, "a card."

"Yes, guess who from."

Hannah made a face. "How should I know?"

Kathy chuckled as she gave her the card.

Hannah eagerly opened the envelope, pulled the card out, and then shrieked. The card flew from her hand back toward her mom as if it were poison. "Not from Sam! I can't believe this. After he dared—" She pointed to her head.

Kathy laughed heartily and then said, "But Hannah, Sam didn't mean it. He was so cute when he brought the card over. You can't help but love the bumbling fellow. His mouth dropped open in that special way when I told him that I would be glad to give you the card."

"Oh, Mom. He's *not* cute when he does that. It's really pretty disgusting."

Kathy was still laughing. "I thought you liked him back in eighth grade. What happened?"

"I only liked him because we had to have someone, and there was no one else."

"We should always be careful of what we say," Kathy said in an attempt to quell her laughter. "You should at least look at the card."

"I already did."

"You sure?" Kathy held up the opened card so Hannah could see both sides. Sam had drawn a rough sketch of flowers. Half of them looked as if they were dead—the others on life support. Over the top he had written, "So sorry. Hope you get well soon. Yours truly, Sam Knepp."

Hannah shivered as she remembered the blow to her head and then the sudden darkness of last night.

"Take that away. Don't make me look at the thing." She turned her face away to emphasize the point and then relented at the look on her mom's face. "Well, take it home then. Put it in my room, if you must. Maybe I'll get more cards to hide this one behind."

"Well, be nice to him," Kathy said. "And by the way, who was that boy who left just as I was coming down the hall?"

"His name's Peter. He said he was Amish and from the Goshen area. He's in here because of an appendix operation. That's about all I know of him."

"I see," Kathy said. "He looks familiar. I think I know him from somewhere."

Hannah was tempted to ask from where but changed her mind, because her mom would notice if the color spread to her face as it surely would if she talked about Peter.

"Everyone felt bad about the accident," Kathy said. "Miriam said a couple of the parents talked with their children after we left. I hope everyone will be more careful in the future."

"Surely they didn't blame anyone for what happened to me. It wasn't anyone's fault."

"No, they didn't," Kathy assured her. "I suppose they just want everyone to slow down a bit, especially on corners."

"No one ever slows down when playing Wolf," Hannah said. "If you run slowly, the other person will beat you."

"Yes, I remember," Kathy said. "I used to play Wolf too, you know."

Hannah smiled at the thought.

"By the way, Isaac found blood on the grass." Kathy wrinkled her own face. "Why he would look, I don't know. But he had to announce his find at the breakfast table."

Hannah could easily picture her younger brother, with his plate of eggs and bacon, telling everyone about finding his sister's blood.

"That's like him."

"I thought Emma would lose it, but she's used to her brother's teasing," Kathy said. "My brothers were like that too. We just learned to live with them."

"Why couldn't I have just had sisters?" Hannah said.

"Same question I used to ask," Kathy said with a grin. "Well, I better go now. But I'll be back tomorrow to see you." Kathy got to her feet. "Will you be okay? They seem to have good care here at the hospital."

Hannah nodded, and Kathy kissed her gently on the cheek. "Be a good girl now."

As Kathy went out the door, Hannah wanted to cry, but choked back the tears. Alice's empty bed across the room didn't help much either. She had to be a big girl now, whatever that meant. She sure didn't feel very big.

By late that afternoon, Hannah lay awake despite the medicine that was supposed to make her drowsy. She watched the window as the last rays of the sun hung in the sky. They seemed to weakly work their way into the hospital room as if to say a last goodbye before the night came. Hannah's mind then wandered to Peter and those strange emotions she had felt earlier in the day. She wondered if she would ever get to see those blue eyes again.

Then suddenly she knew, as if the weak rays from the window were transformed into the bright light of the morning. What she was feeling must surely be love. The poem! She had felt this same way when she read the poem.

Hannah closed her eyes as the realization fully sank in. *Who would have thought this possible and so soon? Love at first sight. It really does happen. It has happened to me!*

"Peter," she said, moving her lips without any sound. She said the name again, "Peter," and it sounded even better the second time.

Will it feel like this forever? She turned the question over in her mind. *Will this last? Surely it will.* Hannah said his name again, the sound soft on her lips, and hung on to the memory of the moments when he had been by her bedside.

"So *this* is love," she said, closing her eyes and slowly dropping off to sleep.

Back at the Miller home, Kathy told the other children it was their bedtime and, after they left reluctantly, she turned to Roy and said, "I have to tell you something."

He glanced up, mild concern on his face. "You sound serious."

"I hope it's nothing," Kathy said quickly, "but when I visited Hannah today, there was a boy leaving her room as I came in."

"Hannah? A boy?" Roy wrinkled up his face. "Already? I wish she wouldn't get involved with boys. She's not old enough."

"No, she's not. But this boy is someone I recognize. I think he's in *rumspringa*. He has a reputation."

"But Hannah's a bright girl. She knows right from wrong."

"Yes, she's a bright girl, but she's still a girl. When I walked into the room, I noticed something different—not just her injury. A mother can tell these things. She had a serious flush on her face even as she felt the pain from her injury. Roy, this boy's name is Peter. He's Nathaniel's boy. You know, one of your cousin's friends."

"Even so, surely it won't go any further. She'll be out of the hospital soon. It's not like this Peter will be around her after this."

"From the look on his face, I wouldn't trust him very much. And just remember that she's about seventeen."

"Yes." Roy sat back in his chair. "That *rumspringa*. She hasn't started anything yet, and I hope she doesn't. Depending on the boy, this might give her ideas. If the boy's running around in town, she might want to also. I don't like it one bit."

"I know," Kathy said with a sigh. "The thought had crossed my mind…" Then a little smile played on her face. "Maybe you'd rather have her go out with Sam. He's sure sweet on Hannah. He even gave me a card to take to the hospital."

Roy laughed. "That boy? Well, he might at least be decent and a hard worker. His dad has his place paid off. He wouldn't be too bad a choice in that respect."

"She'll have to make up her own mind, but Sam would be better than someone like Peter," Kathy said.

"Yes, I agree," Roy said.

Three

Hannah awoke with the first rays of the sun and gently rubbed her head near the bandage. She turned her head as the door opened and the nurse entered.

"How are you feeling, dear?" the nurse asked.

"My head aches."

"I imagine it does after what you've gone through. It's about time for another pill for your pain. That ought to help."

Hannah watched the nurse check some monitors and then leave the room with a promise to return with her medication.

No sooner had she left than the wheels of a wheelchair appeared in the doorway. And just as Hannah had hoped, it was Peter.

"Hi," he said as he rolled closer. "They let me take a spin on my own, and I thought I'd stop by."

Hannah found nothing to say.

"It's sure a nice morning," Peter said, apparently not bothered by her silence.

Since he seemed so relaxed, Hannah simply laid back and let the pleasure of his presence wash over her. It soothed her head in a strange sort of way.

"Mom and Dad should be by this afternoon," he said with a gentle voice. "I'm going home soon."

When she remained silent, Peter asked, "Are you okay?" He tilted his head sideways, one hand slightly raised in her direction.

"Yes." She felt like she couldn't breathe but forced herself to smile. "I'm okay."

Is that what the other girls feel when they leave the singings with their boyfriends? Suddenly she felt more than a little scared and very uncertain of herself. *This is a boy.* The thought—like an alarm—went off inside of her, and Hannah didn't like the feeling.

Cautiously she looked down at Peter's feet. She froze when they moved, sliding around on the floor in search of support. Hannah glanced up quickly and saw a slight smile on his face. Halfway out of his chair, he extended his hand toward her. She sat as still as she could as he gently brushed his fingers against her hand.

"You'll be better soon. I know it."

Hannah was surprised to find her fear gone. In its place her heart grew warm. She felt strangely cared for. Hannah looked down again.

"It'll be okay," he whispered, and his fingers moved on her arm. "I heard the nurse say she would get you something."

She nodded but didn't look at his face.

"How old are you, Hannah?"

"Almost seventeen," she whispered and wondered why he wanted to know. *Does he think I'm too young?*

"I'm seventeen." He smiled and volunteered, "I started *rumspringa* last year. You're old enough for that…and I was hoping to see more of you."

Her heart pounded in her chest. Not that she wanted to be involved in *rumspringa*, even if her parents allowed it, but she did want to see him again. What would he say if he knew she didn't do *rumspringa*?

Well," he said, and his fingers left her arm, "I'm sure we'll see more of each other somewhere. I'll make sure of that. You're a really nice girl. I like you."

Before Hannah could find her voice, footsteps sounded in the hallway, and Peter quickly pulled away from the bed. He smiled at Hannah and then put a complete blank look on his face just as the nurse entered. She carried a tray with the pain medication and handed the pills and a glass of water to Hannah.

"What are you doing in here?" the nurse asked, directing her question at Peter.

"Visiting," he said over his shoulder. "She's Amish—like I am." Then he was gone out the door.

"Was he bothering you?" the nurse asked, glancing sharply at Hannah.

She shook her head, stared at the pills, and hoped her face wasn't telltale red. The nurse shrugged and helped Hannah sit up to take the medicine. As the pills went down, Hannah knew that something else had already taken the pain away faster than these pills ever would. She wondered how such a thing was possible. Was this how love worked? If it was, she liked it a lot.

The day continued, but Peter didn't make any more appearances. Hannah could still feel the effects of his blue eyes, though. After lunch the nurse returned, stuck her head through the doorway, and said, "Peter's being discharged now. Thought you'd like to know."

"Thanks," Hannah said since that seemed the thing to say.

A few minutes later, both of Peter's parents walked by her door. She assumed it was Peter's parents because they were dressed as the Amish dressed. A nurse with an empty wheelchair followed behind them.

"There we are," she heard the nurse say, her voice off in the distance. "All better and ready to go home."

A few minutes later they passed her door, Peter in his wheelchair, his parents on either side of him. Peter made no attempt to look at her—he faced straight ahead. As she watched the last of his wheelchair disappear, a strange feeling of emptiness settled upon her. The emotion was different from the pang of hunger, yet in a way it was the same, as if two different people tried to use the same buggy for different purposes. Hannah had never known that one could be hungry for something like words. Nor had she known that words could be so satisfying when spoken and could leave one so empty when they were gone.

Was this love too? She drew in her breath deeply. *I'm sure we'll see more of each other somewhere. I'll make sure of that.* She treasured the sound of those words. Could it be that Peter felt the same way she did?

That evening the hospital room settled into a hum of silence. People continually came and went by her door. Eventually even the comings and goings subsided. A nurse came in to check on her and seemed in a big hurry.

"You ready for the night?" she asked as she checked the monitors.

"I think so." Hannah managed a smile, and the nurse left.

The darkness outside was deep by now, and homesickness flooded Hannah. Supper would be over, and the family would now be gathered under the gas lantern in the living room. Miriam and Emma would go upstairs to their room soon, across from her bedroom. Oh, for her own bed and the familiar sights and smells of her own room. Hannah felt tears slip down her cheeks, but there was nothing that could be done. She would have to stay here another night. In the dim light of the hospital room, she finally dropped off into a troubled sleep.

The nurse woke her in the morning with the news, "You're going home today. The doctor signed your release. That's good news!"

Hannah smiled weakly and fought to clear the fog in her head. "Is Mom coming? Does she know?"

"We'll let her know when she comes in later this morning."

"I want to go home now," Hannah told the nurse.

Hannah waited impatiently until her mom and Mr. Bowen arrived for the official release, a little before lunch. The nurse pushed her in the wheelchair just as she had done for Alice and Peter. Mr. Bowen fussed over her at the car, wanting to make sure she was comfortable.

"I'm okay," Hannah assured him though she could still feel the deep throb in her forehead that even the slightest touch would cause.

Once they were home, Hannah headed straight for the couch in the living room. Everything looked the same when she glanced around, but it seemed like she had been gone a very long time.

"How long was I gone?" she hollered toward the kitchen.

"Only a couple of days," Kathy called back.

"It seems longer."

"That's normal, dear."

Hannah nodded grimly and laid back on the couch to rest.

Miriam arrived about the time Emma came home from school on her bike. They both rushed into the house, apparently aware Hannah would be home.

"She looks *awful*," Emma announced and then quickly placed her hand to her mouth. "Sorry! I shouldn't have said that."

"No, you shouldn't have," Miriam agreed. "She doesn't look that bad."

"So, which one of you is lying?" Hannah asked with a half smile.

"Stop tormenting your sister," their mother called from the kitchen, and so they both disappeared, Emma toward the kitchen and Miriam upstairs.

Hannah was still on the couch when Isaac and Roy came in from the fields. Isaac must have been curious because he opened the front door, stuck his head in, and made a face. Hannah made one right back at him. He closed the door and broke out into peals of laughter. Her heart sank, believing she must indeed look awful. With a feeling of despair, she ran her fingers over her forehead.

"Am I that bad looking?" she asked in the direction of the kitchen, her voice weak.

"I heard him laugh at you." Emma came into the living room. "Ignore him. That's what I'd do."

"But how do I *really* look? He's a boy, remember."

"You look just fine," Emma pronounced and disappeared back into the kitchen.

Hannah leaned back against the couch and groaned. Apparently her face would be disfigured for the rest of her life, well beyond any hope, at least from a boy's point of view.

Then the memory of Peter and his smile of approval returned. He had seen her in this very condition. With relief she relaxed once again and felt the tears of joy roll down her cheeks.

After supper, when Hannah had undressed and climbed into bed, she heard a knock on her door.

"Come in," she said and was surprised when both her father and mother entered. Apparently something serious was afoot. She held her breath while her dad sat down on the bed's edge, her mom beside him.

"That boy you met in the hospital," he said and cleared his throat, "have we any cause to worry about him? Your mom and I don't want you involved with boys like that."

"Don't be too hard on her, Roy," her mom said quickly. "She's just home from the hospital. Plus—nothing really happened. Perhaps we shouldn't bother her."

Her dad ignored her mom, kept his eyes on Hannah's face, and continued, "Your mom said his name's Peter. It's just that we're a bit concerned about this. Some boys just aren't right for you…or for us. Peter might be that type of boy. I think it would just be better, perhaps, if you stayed away from him."

Hannah caught her breath, not certain what to say, but her father needed some sort of an answer. "I'm not likely to see him," she said. "They live in a different district."

"So we have nothing to be concerned about?"

Hannah's mind raced. How was she to explain the feelings she felt in the hospital room? How upset would her father be if he knew?

"He said I was a nice girl," she ventured. If good feelings like this were such a bad thing, then what was one to do? Hide them? Deny they existed?

Her dad's voice cut through her thoughts. "That's just the problem. He shouldn't be saying things like that to a girl he doesn't really know."

"Why not?" Hannah asked in all sincerity.

Roy saw her innocence and responded forthrightly, "That is a very brazen thing to say…to a girl he has just met. It takes a certain kind of boy to do that. A kind," he said and then paused, searching for the right words, "that it would be best to stay away from."

Hannah said nothing.

Her father continued, "Hannah, I want you to remember something. Good men aren't made with just talk. It takes a lot of work to produce good character. This Peter may not have that yet."

Beside him Kathy tried to soften things a little. "We can't be absolutely certain of that, though. After all, we really don't know him either."

Hannah hung on to her mom's words.

"I think I'm pretty close to the truth," Roy said, glancing in Hannah's direction. "It would just be better if you have nothing to do with this boy. My guess is he won't be coming around anyway since you're still pretty young. But even if you were older…I would want you to stay away from him."

Hannah answered him with silence, averting her gaze to the wall. What else was there to say? She had no idea why things had to be so complicated.

Roy nodded and seemed satisfied.

"Just a warning," he said and smiled. "Hope it helps."

"We'd best go now," Kathy said.

Hannah watched as her parents left. The pain in her head was nothing compared to the pain of her broken heart. So the whole world must be bad. That was the only conclusion one could draw. For something that felt as good as her new love for Peter to be so wrong required a readjustment of major proportions. In the midst of her agony, she wished Peter were here. The memories of his voice brought back a desire to hear his words again. *I'm sure we'll see more of each other somewhere. I'll make sure of that.*

Gently she lay back on her pillow. "Peter," she said softly. Speaking his name out loud, the sound seemed to fill the whole room.

Four

Hannah spent the next several days mostly on the couch or in her bedroom as she continued to get better. Slowly she added some chores back into her routine. Then one day after breakfast, Hannah asked abruptly, "May I go riding, Mom? I miss being on Honey."

Kathy turned to look at her. "Are you sure you're well enough? You could risk reinjuring yourself."

"I'm much better," Hannah said. "I don't get dizzy anymore."

Kathy considered the request and then nodded. "Well, the ride might do you good. Honey misses you, I'm sure."

With no more present duties, Hannah left for the barn immediately, called for Honey in the barnyard, and slid his bridle on when he came. As she mounted him, she drew in deep breaths and let her eyes sweep across the open fields. How good it felt to be out of the house again. Honey was a faithful little beast, not given to any unnecessary excitement. Astride him, she was ready to ride anywhere. Hannah reveled in the joy she felt as the wind brushed softly against her face, stirring loose wisps of hair not restricted by her *kapp*.

"Come on, old boy," she said softly to the horse. "Are you ready to go?"

Just as she was ready to head for the open pasture, Hannah heard the sound of a horse's hooves on the pavement on the main road. She paused and waited to see who this was. No doubt it was one of the women-folk coming to see her mother.

When the single buggy appeared, Hannah was surprised to see

that it was driven by a boy. She was even more surprised to see Sam's red hair and distinct features come into view. What was Sam doing on the road at this time of the day?

She had no idea until he turned into their driveway. Then she realized he must be there to see her. Briskly he brought the buggy up to the hitching post, jumped out, and tied the horse. He saw her on Honey and headed toward her.

"Good morning," he said when he was close enough for her to hear.

"Good morning," she said, making no move to get off of Honey.

Sam rubbed his freckled face, a rueful expression on it. "I'm so sorry for what happened…with me running into you."

"It couldn't be helped," she said, wishing he would go away. *Where is Mom when I need her?*

"It was dark," he said, "and I couldn't see anything. I didn't mean to do it—especially to someone like you." He blushed and looked like he regretted what he had just said.

"It's okay," she said again and kept her eyes on Honey's feet. If she looked up, she just knew Sam's mouth would drop open. That would be a little too much at the moment.

"I just had a chance to slip away…between the field work," he said as an explanation.

At least he's conscientious. I guess that's one point in his favor. Still, he means nothing to me…in that way. Hannah glanced up and decided to at least be polite. She owed him that much.

"Mom allowed me to ride today. She wasn't sure if I was well enough, but I am." She was careful not to look Sam in the eyes.

A look of grateful surprise crossed Sam's face, but his mouth didn't drop open. Hannah almost smiled at the thought.

"Well, you should be careful," Sam said. "But it's plucky of you to be out and about so soon. Why don't you go for a ride and I'll just watch since I'm here anyway?" His freckles fairly vibrated on his face with eagerness.

Oh, great. Now he's impressed by my good wife qualities of being up and about so soon. Hannah made herself smile, although not in his direction. There seemed no option but to humor him since her mom still hadn't made an appearance. Hannah turned Honey around, let the reins out, and sped away. The open field of short stubble hay stretched out in front of her.

At that moment in the house, Kathy had come to the living room window. She glanced at Sam, who caused her to smile. Her hand reached for the living room door as if to open it, but then she paused when Hannah started across the field. She watched for a moment, shook her head in amusement, and left the window to go to the kitchen.

As Honey crossed the field and increased his speed, Hannah let him have more of the reins. Glad to be out of the stall, Honey laid deep into the gallop. His legs hit the ground in a rapid concussion of sound, and his breath soon came in sharp jerks. Even though she knew Sam was watching them, Hannah threw her head back, laughed deeply with the pleasure of the ride, and nearly lost her *kapp* in the process. She felt the cloth shift on her head and quickly snapped her head back down. With one hand she pulled the *kapp* forward and slowly tightened up the reins with the other. The end of the field rapidly approached.

"Slow, boy," she said softly. "There we go, Honey. Let's turn around."

Gently she brought the pony around, still at a trot, and then let him have the reins again for the return run to the barn. The wind caused tears to stream from her eyes, but her body felt refreshed right down to her bare toes. The barn came into view much too quickly as Hannah tightened the reins and slowed Honey to a walk by the board fence. Kathy stood at the window again, saw that Hannah completed the run, and stepped outside.

"Shall we do it again, Honey?" Hannah asked, still out of earshot of Sam. "Maybe you need to rest a little bit first?"

Hannah concluded that the pony did need a rest and urged him toward the gate. The water tank was there too. She intended to let him catch his breath and get a drink of water.

But unknown to Hannah, the horse was walking directly toward a hole, which had been dug by a recently deceased groundhog. The pesky critter had finally succumbed to Roy's .22 Long Rifle. A little dirt had fallen in around the top of the burrow, and a few small tufts of grass had grown across the width of the hole—ready and able to receive Honey's slim foot.

Into the hole the hoof dropped. If Honey had been at a run, he would never have been able to extract his hoof in time before the forward motion of his body snapped the leg. Now, however, he somehow sensed the threat and threw himself violently away from the endangered leg—his actions guided purely by his instincts to survive. He succeeded in saving his leg, but in the action that followed, Hannah lost her grip on the reins and was thrown through the air, striking the ground a few feet from where Sam stood. She then crashed into the gatepost, taking the full force with her right shoulder. Hannah felt a sickening crunch of bone and flesh against wood, and then everything went black.

How long she lay there, she wasn't sure. The time couldn't have been more than a few seconds. Honey's muzzle on her chest was the first sensation she felt. Her shoulder burned like fire. Through the haze of pain, she noticed that Honey trembled. He whinnied and jerked his neck up and down sharply.

"It wasn't your fault," she whispered. "I should have been watching where we were going."

Honey bobbed his head and nuzzled her chest again. He whinnied even louder.

"Honey, are you okay?" she asked louder and then winced when she tried to move her hand to touch his leg. "Oh, I must have hurt something!" Hannah allowed the weight of her body to settle back onto the ground. Her mom's hand appeared on the pony's neck, pushing him away and reaching for her.

"Hannah! Are you alright?" Kathy's voice was full of concern.

Hannah couldn't find her voice now that her mother was there.

"Hannah, are you hurt?" Kathy repeated.

"This hurts," Hannah said and pointed to her shoulder.

Kathy helped her gently to her feet and guided her slowly toward the house. Hannah winced with each step, each movement threatening to recreate the sickening sound deep inside her shoulder. Ahead of them, Sam's face was all worry, his mouth wide open.

"Sit on the steps," Kathy told Hannah. "Sam, can you go get Roy? He's in the back field."

Sam didn't need to be asked twice. He ran down the dirt lane toward the Miller's farming fields across the creek.

Roy noticed Sam and pulled the team to a halt, a surprised look on his face.

"Hannah hurt her shoulder while riding her pony," Sam called out and then waited as Roy responded.

"Is it bad?" he asked.

"I can't tell," Sam answered. "She was holding her shoulder."

"Well, I can't come in right now. I have to finish cutting the field. Just tell Kathy to go across the road and see if Mr. Bowen can take her to the doctor's office. Don't take her to the hospital. The bill last time was way too high. We can't afford any of that."

"I can finish the field for you," Sam offered.

Roy looked at him in surprise. "You have time for that?"

"I don't need to be back till after lunch."

Roy shrugged. "I'll go and see that they get off. That shouldn't take too long. Then I'll be back."

Sam didn't say anything but held out his hand to take the reins. With obvious expertise he climbed onto the hay cutter. Roy watched him drive the horses a few steps. Apparently satisfied the boy knew how to drive the team, Roy headed for the house.

"We have to get her to the doctor," Roy said after he took a quick look at Hannah's shoulder. "What's going on with you anyway?" he asked, half in jest to ease the tension. "All these accidents."

"It's that awful Sam," Hannah groaned, and even Roy had to grin.

"It's not funny," she retorted.

"Suppose not," Roy agreed. "Your mom will watch you while I get Mr. Bowen."

"What if the doctor says we have to go to the hospital?" Kathy asked.

"Ask him to do what he can…before you go to the hospital," Roy said over his shoulder.

"I'll do my best," she said. "Are you going to get Mr. Bowen?"

"Yes," he shouted back, well up the driveway already.

Mr. Bowen appeared within minutes. "Not again," he exclaimed and held the car door open for Hannah.

Hannah numbly nodded and climbed slowly into the backseat. Kathy was soon out of the house with the things she needed, and they were off. Roy watched till they were on the main road and then walked back to his hay field to relieve Sam.

"Is she okay?" Sam asked.

"They left for the doctor. She was walking by herself…so I think she'll be fine."

"I'm so sorry about all this," Sam told him.

"Well, these things happen," Roy said. "Thanks for keeping the team going."

"Glad to," Sam muttered and handed the reins over.

Roy climbed on and slapped the lines, and the whirling blades started up with the horses' first movements. Sam watched for a few minutes and then walked slowly back up the lane, got into his buggy, and left.

◈

An hour later the doctor held up the X-ray and said, "There's a nasty little break in the collarbone. The good news is we can tape you up, and you're out of here. Just take care of it for a few weeks, and you'll be okay."

"No cast for a broken bone?" Kathy asked.

"It's kind of hard to put a cast on the collarbone," the doctor, explained. "A neck support just rests on the collarbone, so that would make it worse. Sorry, but that's what we do in these cases."

◈

At home that evening, Roy found Hannah seated on the couch in silent despair. "You've got to quit hurting yourself," he said. "Can't you be more careful?"

"Well, if you'd keep that Sam away from me—"

Roy burst out laughing in spite of himself. "Sam had nothing to do with it this time, from what your mother says. She saw the whole thing."

"It was still him," Hannah muttered. Big tears gathered in her eyes and slowly spilled down her cheeks. "We were only walking—Honey and me. I don't know what happened."

"That's why we all need to be more careful," Roy told her. "These medical bills are getting expensive."

Hannah nodded numbly. "I wish I were a good girl," she whispered as her father's back disappeared toward the kitchen. "I try to be."

Five

One morning a week or so later, after Emma and Miriam had left for school, Kathy said, "I'm off to Nappanee. I've had to get some things for a long time already. I think I have a chance today."

"Can I go along?" Hannah piped up.

"You sure you're well enough to come along?" Kathy asked. "It hasn't been that long since you broke your collarbone. The doctor just took the tape off yesterday."

"I'm fine, Mom," Hannah assured her. "I really would like to go with you."

"Okay," Kathy agreed, "I don't want to keep you indoors longer than necessary, but you have to be careful."

"I will," Hannah said. "Surely I won't get hurt in town. After all, Sam won't be around…and I just need to get out."

"Well, get yourself ready. We'll leave in half an hour."

Hannah rushed upstairs to change her clothes and then met her mom out by the barn.

When Kathy opened the back barn door and called to the driving horse, Bob, to come in from the pasture, he lifted his head to look at them and must have decided a short run for freedom wasn't worth the effort. He slowly made his way to the barn and stood quietly while Hannah held him and Kathy threw the harness on. Bob neighed loudly, apparently hoping for a little grain as a reward for coming in so easily.

"Later," Kathy said and chuckled. "You eat too slowly. You can have grain when we get back."

Bob neither understood nor was used to the routine because he jerked his head back and forth a few times before settling down. Once Bob was hitched up, Hannah hopped into the buggy and held the reins while Kathy got in. Not that Bob would have made any problems, but there was always that moment between leaving the front of the horse and mounting the buggy steps when a horse could make a dash for it. With Hannah at the reins, there was no chance of that happening even if Bob had wanted to.

"Off we go," said Kathy, and she slapped the reins slightly to get Bob moving.

They drove along the main highway toward the town of Nappanee. Although the northern Indiana landscape slowly passed them by, the twenty minute drive into town passed much quicker than they expected. With the clip-clop of the horse's hooves on the road and the gentle sound of the buggy tires on the pavement, time didn't seem to matter. Peace settled over both the mind and soul.

Kathy drove carefully as they approached town. She maneuvered through the traffic lights and parked in front of the town's small farm supply store.

"I'll be right out," she told Hannah. "No sense you coming in. This won't take too long."

"I don't want to see anything in there anyway," Hannah replied, agreeing without regret. "I want to see the dry goods store."

"I figured so," Kathy said. "I'll still tie Bob, so you don't have to worry about holding the reins."

Hannah nodded and glanced along the dusty sides of the farm supply building. Several old trucks were parked out in front, and farmers went back and forth between them. A bright blue, spotless sports car was parked to the right, its rear end jacked up with overly large tires and shocks. No one seemed to be around the car, and Hannah wondered who owned it. As if in answer to her question, a side door to the loading dock opened, and out came a blond-headed boy, his features hidden to Hannah.

But as Kathy disappeared into the mill, the boy looked toward the parked buggy, and his face now became fully visible to Hannah.

Peter!

She drew in her breath, and her hands suddenly gripped the reins even with Bob securely tied to the hitching post. *Has he seen me? No, he mustn't. Not now.*

Quickly Hannah pulled her head back so that any view through the flexi-glass windshield would be blurred. Slowly she slid farther back on the seat, and her legs came up tight against the front edge. Even so she could clearly see Peter walk toward the buggy.

With bated breath she waited, knowing there was no escape.

"Hi," he said and reached out to touch the side of the buggy, his foot raised up to rest on the buggy wheel's hub. He smiled broadly. "I was hoping it was you when I saw your mom walk in." He nodded his head toward the mill doorway. "Is she staying long?"

"No," Hannah told him, "she'll be right back out."

"Then I'd best not stay too long," he grinned. "You're looking better than you did in the hospital. Are you okay now?"

Hannah just nodded, her voice gone. Peter didn't seem to be bothered by her silence. "I'm *rumspringa* you know. Did you see my car over there?" His head indicated the direction of the blue, jacked-up sports car. "She's a beauty—an old MGC with an incline six-cylinder engine all repainted and ready to go. Built in the late sixties. I got it real reasonable from a friend who works at the used car dealership. I'd like to give you a ride sometime."

Hannah found her voice and replied, "I couldn't do that. I'm not doing *rumspringa*. Dad's against all that, and I may never do it."

"That's too bad," he said smiling. "But what does that matter? A few more years and it will all be over for us anyway. Then we have to settle down like the old folks. Why not enjoy being young while we can? I can still give you a ride. A pretty girl like you...in my beautiful car. I would love to have you along at one of the Saturday night gatherings."

"I don't think so," she told him. "Dad and Mom wouldn't like it."

"Oh, so Dad's one of those? Old fashioned—is he? Plans to keep you from having any fun? That's too bad." Peter's brow furrowed as he pondered the situation. "Maybe you could sneak out? Yes? Let's see, I know where you live. Which is your bedroom window?" He paused, then looked at Hannah, and waited.

She felt her neck grow red. Her face, she was sure, burned quite brightly, but what was there to do? Peter had asked her where her bedroom window was. Should she tell him? A thousand questions chased themselves around in her head. *What would Dad say if he found out? Do I really want to see Peter that way? Would he really come for me?*

Hannah considered the safest answers. "I don't date yet...so why do you want to know where my window is...and what would we do anyway?"

Peter's face had been blank, but now he slowly began to grin. First appearing at the corners of his mouth, the grin spread sideways until his blond hair was accented by the boyish glee on his face. "I could park the car out by the road—where your dad wouldn't see me. Then I could sneak in the back way...by those bushes. Then I could throw some pebbles—or something like that—up against the window. You could come out. Wouldn't that be fun? We could go to a party."

Wondering how Peter knew so much about her place, she said in a low voice, "I don't think so. I don't want to go to a party...like that."

"Okay, we don't have to." His smile was still broad. "I'll just come in, and we can talk for a little while. That would be fun, right?"

Hannah drew in her breath. *I don't want to be silly and throw away my chance. He's a nice boy, and I want to feel in love again. But Dad said to stay away from him, and I should listen to him.*

He watched her intently and waited. "Your mother will be back soon."

"No, I don't think I can do it," she said quickly and dropped her gaze to the floor of the buggy.

"Okay," he said without any change to the tone in his voice. "But I will see you then...sometime. Right, lovely girl? Remember what I said in the hospital."

Hannah sat in stunned silence. Did that mean he felt the same way she did?

Peter turned and walked briskly back to the grain cart by the loading dock. With the cart in front of him, he disappeared inside just before Kathy came out the door of the mill. She walked to the buggy and glanced up to where a flushed Hannah sat. Kathy quickly turned to look back at the loading dock.

"Was that Peter?" she asked, suspicion in her voice.

Hannah felt her cheeks redden again and nodded.

"Did he talk to you?"

Hannah nodded again.

"What did he say?" Kathy stood by the buggy wheel now.

"Nothing, Mom. Just get in, okay?" Hannah said. Then she added, "Well, he told me about his sports car. It's the blue one over there."

Kathy didn't look convinced. "That's all he told you? From the look on your face, there must be more. You're as red as a beet."

"Come on, Mom," Hannah protested, already surprised that she wanted to protect Peter. "He did say some other things. They aren't important."

Kathy glanced up the street, apparently distracted by the urgency of her day's schedule. "Well, all right. But just remember what your father said. You're too young to be talking to boys this way—especially this Peter."

Hannah nodded. "Okay, but I didn't start this thing. He did."

"I know," Kathy said, sighing. "That's how boys are. I was just hoping you wouldn't learn that quite this soon."

Secretly Hannah wanted to say many things and ask many things, but she didn't dare. Hadn't her mother ever felt like this? Did it always feel this good to have a boy talk to you? Could this be an answer to a dream—a dream of having someone love you?

Kathy drove along the street, and Hannah kept her silence. When they came to the dry goods store and parked, Kathy looked hard at her. "You know I'll have to tell your dad about this."

"Please don't," Hannah pleaded. "Peter talked with me. I didn't start it."

"Dad must still be told. That's all I can say. It wouldn't be good if he found it out from somewhere else."

"No, I guess not," Hannah said, resigned to her fate. She followed her mom out of the buggy and into the store, all the while wondering why a good feeling like this caused so much trouble. The sight of all the wonderful things in this favorite of stores washed the unpleasantness of the earlier encounter away. Rolls and rolls of material lined the walls—colors of all shades, some so beautiful they took one's breath away. Hannah could see herself in any number of the colors, dresses cut to fit her size, sewn with her mom's expertise.

"I want this one," Hannah whispered, barely able to voice the words.

Kathy took a glance but shook her head. "You're just along today. Look all you want, but you have enough dresses."

"But this blue..." Hannah moaned.

"That's a very common color," Kathy said. "It's a 'no' for today."

That evening Kathy approached Roy with the subject of Peter.

Kathy motioned Hannah toward the couch. Emma stuck her head in from the kitchen, but Kathy waved her away. When they were alone, Kathy turned to Roy. "While I was in the mill today, this young man Peter—the one from the hospital—came out and talked with Hannah. He apparently works there. I thought you should be told."

Roy looked up. His face looked unreadable to Hannah.

"What did he have to say?"

"Well, he had his sports car parked there. I guess he told Hannah about it. He's *rumspringa*, of course."

"Anything else?"

"I don't think so."

Hannah held her breath as her dad turned toward her.

"Hannah, we can't keep you away from boys forever. I had just wished it wouldn't be this quick. You are still very young. Then there is the matter of which boys. Sweet talkers like Peter are not who they seem. They come and go as the wind. They leave a lot of broken hearts.

Good men are made through the trials of life. I guess I hoped you'd pick that kind of boy someday."

Hannah looked at the floor. She had expected an outburst for sure. And how did her dad know about the sweet talk thing?

Her dad continued, "I realize that *rumspringa* is perhaps coming up—even for you. I guess we can't keep you from that either, although I don't like it at all."

"You can't forbid her," Kathy interrupted him.

"I know," Roy told her. "That's not what I was thinking."

Now Kathy sounded surprised. "What have you been thinking?"

"I'll tell you some other time," he said. "Not right now, though. Let's let Hannah go to bed. I think it's our bedtime, isn't it? We'll talk about it later perhaps."

With that, Hannah left for her bedroom. She pulled up the window and breathed in deeply the night air. It was too late to see any sunsets but not too late to think about Peter and the day's events, and what her dad had said. Had he ever felt how she felt? Could men feel that way? She was sure Peter could. Very sure.

Dreamily she stood by the window and remembered. The night sounds filled her ears, and the thoughts of the day filled her heart. *I told him he couldn't come, but wouldn't it be wonderful if he did?*

"Peter," she whispered his name. What would it be like to go out with him on Saturday night? She wasn't sure how that would be, but it might be good to find out. She might like it.

What will I do if he does come to the window? She didn't know the answer. As she stood there breathing in the night air, she shivered—not because she was cold but because of her thoughts of Peter.

Six

Isaac sat between Hannah and Miriam and drove the buggy even though he was the youngest. It was a male thing, Hannah was sure. Isaac would probably fall out of the buggy in embarrassment if they were to pull up to the Sunday evening hymn sing in front of his friends with one of his sisters driving.

Hannah wished it was Peter driving the buggy—just the two of them, of course. She could imagine the feeling of how his words would wrap around her with comfort and strength. He wouldn't have to act all grown up like Isaac—who claimed the buggy lines so fiercely—because he was comfortable being himself.

"Expecting someone to ask you out?" Miriam teased.

Hannah blushed and shook her head. She knew Peter would never ask her out in the Amish way. He was into *rumspringa* and would hardly consider a visit to their calm Sunday night hymn sings worth his time. A bedroom window escape was Peter's real idea of a night out.

"I think Hannah's daydreaming about a boy," Miriam said in fun.

Hannah remained silent, used to her siblings teasing her.

"Sam's got his eye on her." Isaac slapped the reins and laughed. "But I haven't seen him around since Hannah's accident. Probably a good idea. That will keep the hospital bills down."

"You didn't see him, then," Hannah snapped.

Isaac kept his eyes straight ahead, but Hannah still heard his chuckle.

"We shouldn't be too hard on her," Miriam said. "She's had a rough time."

"With Sam, I would say so." Isaac gave up any pretense and laughed loudly.

"You're awful." Hannah made a face at him and then relented and grinned at the thought. What Isaac said was true, and if she wasn't careful, they would find out about Peter, and then there would be no end to the teasing.

"At least she still has a sense of humor," Miriam said as Isaac pulled into the driveway. He stopped at the end of the walk to drop his sisters off and barely waited till they were clear of the buggy before he took off. Hannah gathered her shawl quickly to keep it away from the wheel. The boy would learn the hard way to pay attention to how he drove.

Now if Peter had been driving—the thought brought a smile to her face—he would have waited till she was at the walk before he pulled the buggy away. She knew he would because he was Peter.

The smile on her face prompted Miriam to ask again, "You sure no one is taking you home?"

Hannah shook her head and kept her eyes on the sidewalk. Miriam would probably understand, since she occasionally dated. Yet Peter seemed such a sacred subject, one best left unmentioned for now.

They walked into the washroom and left their bonnets and shawls there. The girls then gathered in the kitchen, exchanging nods with a few others. As if by an unstated ritual, two of the oldest girls started to move toward the living room. The other girls lined up single file, followed the two leaders into the room, and took their seats on the benches. As Hannah sat down, she noticed right away that Sam was staring at her from across the room. She had felt his eyes on her from the time she stepped into the living room. As far as she was concerned, it was an entirely useless expenditure of his efforts.

Hannah was sure that a few of the girls had noticed his stare. She saw Annie glance in Sam's direction, but he wouldn't take his eyes off of Hannah. Did the boy think he could stare all evening? Why didn't he go for someone who liked him? She thought she knew the answer and didn't like it. *Perhaps it's because I'm better looking or maybe my ability to just get up and get going quickly after an accident. He probably thinks I'll make a good farmhand for that place his father will leave him.*

Hannah realized her face had turned into a look of disgust and caught herself in time. A look of disgust at the hymn sing was not exactly a welcome expression. Hannah relaxed her face and kept her eyes on the songbook page. *What an impossible boy.*

By nine o'clock the hymn sing was finished and the talk began, cut short at times when a girl had to leave to catch either her brother's or her boyfriend's buggy. Hannah kept a watch on Isaac, who sat in the back row with the younger boys. He was deep into conversation with his cousin and seemed to have plans to stay for a while yet. She turned to talk with Naomi Zook to pass the time.

When Miriam stood to leave, Hannah cut short her conversation and followed. On the way out, Hannah caught herself thinking that if this were Peter ahead of her, how wonderful the world would be.

In the washroom, Hannah found her bonnet and shawl. It occurred to her that maybe Sam had similar thoughts about her as he made his way to his buggy. What a strange world—and so mixed up—she thought as she pulled her bonnet strings tight.

At the end of the walkway, Isaac was parked with the buggy wheels turned away from the step. Perhaps he had visions of a girlfriend walking lightly down the walk toward him.

"He's got the wheels turned," Hannah whispered to Miriam.

Miriam laughed. "There is hope for him if he doesn't run us over before he learns."

Both girls climbed in, and Isaac burst out with the news almost before they took their seats, "Ernest Byler just took Betsy home tonight."

"I don't believe it," Miriam said in astonishment. "He's going on thirty or so."

"Well, it's true. I saw it with my own eyes. Betsy walked right by her brother's buggy and climbed into Ernest's. They must have had it planned like that—to try to sneak it by everyone."

"She's got to be close to thirty too," Hannah mused. "Who would have thought it? I didn't think either of them would ever get married."

"I guess the leftovers take the leftovers," Isaac proposed as an answer. "Everyone needs someone."

"That's not a nice thing to say," Miriam said. "Maybe they just waited for each other."

"It could be," he answered.

"I see you had the wheels turned for us." Miriam smiled at Isaac, her face faintly visible in the darkness of the buggy.

"Well..." Isaac seemed embarrassed.

"That's okay," Miriam said, patting his arm.

"You're not saying anything," Isaac said, turning in Hannah's direction.

"Just listening," she said. "After you ran us over, I thought that was nice. Thinking of some other girl perhaps?"

Isaac made a face at her.

"You shouldn't have any problem finding a girl," she said.

"Don't torment me," Isaac replied, groaning, and both sisters laughed.

"See," he said and slapped the reins, "it seems like you either get no one or you get too many. No one's my problem."

"Don't pay any attention to him," Miriam told Hannah. "He just wants you to feel sorry for him. He's got all the chances a decent boy should have. He's too young to make up his mind yet—which is good I suppose. That shows maturity."

Isaac rolled his eyes and slapped the reins again.

A few evenings later, Hannah stood by her upstairs bedroom window. The air, filled with the warmth of the late spring day, stirred in gentle ripples around her. The days were glorious and numbered, and she readily received the joy they gave. Each moment made her feel more alive than the last one.

On the flat northern Indiana horizon, the faint bubble of the full moon rose and soon would cast its deep glow across the sky. It would be another hour before the moon grew fully visible, but already Hannah could see low hanging clouds accented against the branches of the old tree that leaned over the house roof.

The thought of Peter came, adding even more fragrance to the scene. Would he actually ever come, climb up the tree, and drop from the branches? What would she do if he did?

She shivered and pulled the window shut. It slid softly in that way new windows in new houses do. As she turned the latch, Hannah paused. An object had struck the wall and rattled down the siding. Next she heard a ping on the window glass. Slowly she opened the window again. She saw nothing. Her eyes searched, but no form became visible by the tree or anywhere else in the open. Hannah glanced down the fencerow toward the road but saw nothing there either. Out by the barn, their dog, Shep, barked sharply. She almost told him to be quiet, but her voice would attract more attention. His bark was already bad enough.

Surely, she thought, *Peter's not coming. After all, it has been quite a while since I've seen him in town, and even then I warned him not to come.*

But if he did, would he know about the dog? That problem hadn't occurred to her. Shep barked louder, his bark urgent and aggressive.

Oh, I can't believe I am even thinking about this. I don't want him to come. I don't want him to come. She chanted the thought to herself but couldn't move herself away from the window. If Peter was out there, she wanted to see him. Surely he would be smart enough to avoid the dog. He was Peter, after all.

Hannah listened while the bark moved from the back of the barn to the front and then stopped. The silence was followed by a few short yaps. Nothing more happened. On the horizon the moon had slipped upward until it cleared the tree line. The warm glow of the moonlight revealed no signs of movement. She listened for long moments and then knew it was time to get to bed. Peter or no Peter, the morning would come quickly enough. Slowly she closed the window.

But the thoughts wouldn't stop. Even in bed with the covers tight under her chin, they toyed with her mind. What had the noise been? Would Shep bark over nothing? What if it was Peter, and he got chased away? Now he'd never come back. But what if he did actually come to the window? Would she let him in? Hannah shivered again. *I can't think like this! Stop it. Stop it. It's so wrong, and I have to be a good girl.*

With her eyes on the window and the moon's glow soon bright in the sky, Hannah drifted off to sleep.

At breakfast the next morning, her mom brought up the subject. "I wonder what Shep was barking about last night."

"I heard it too," her dad said. "It was probably one of the cows running around. The barking came from the barn."

"Was one out?" Kathy asked.

"I saw nothing while doing the chores," Roy said. "They are all accounted for. Did you see anything missing, Isaac?"

Isaac shook his head sleepily, apparently unwilling to make words this early in the morning.

"That's strange." Kathy glanced at Hannah. "Did you see anything? You're often up later than the others."

"I heard Shep barking," Hannah said and kept any emotion out of her voice. She had seen nothing, but they would not take it lightly if they knew who she thought it might have been.

Kathy glanced at her again. "Did you hear anything else?"

"Some noises on the side of the house," she said in the same tone of voice. "Then a bong and a ping."

"Well, that could be anything," Kathy said.

"That was probably a limb of that old tree brushing against the side of the house," Roy added. "I need to cut that limb off before it falls onto the house."

Hannah almost said, "No, don't cut it down," but caught herself in time.

"You had better not cut it yet, at least not right away," Kathy said. "The children like to climb around on the thing."

Hannah took a deep breath of relief and then said quickly, "Yes, it's real good to climb up on the roof with. Isaac still likes to use it."

Isaac didn't say anything.

"I don't know," Roy said. "You shouldn't be climbing around on the roof anyway. The limb could be a danger to the house during one of those wind storms. I think it needs to go."

"Whatever you think," Kathy acquiesced quickly.

Hannah said nothing. She figured there was no use, and besides her dad wouldn't get to the project right away. Perhaps Peter would come before that. Then she remembered and reversed her thinking. *I don't want him to come. I don't want him to come.* Those two trains of thought could sure confuse a person.

The next night the moon rose a little sooner and lit up the yard with its glow. Hannah stood by the window, unable to leave her post. The two thoughts in her mind chased each other around. *He's not coming,* she told herself. *It's much too light. If he does come and Shep chases him, Dad might catch him. I wonder if he likes me enough to come anyway.* The thought caught her fancy. *What if he wants to see me so much that he comes charging across the yard even if the moon is shining? What if he chases Shep away? Does he like me that much? Wouldn't that be something?*

Finally she knew that if he did come, she would climb out the window with him. There couldn't be that much harm in doing so.

With one last look around and no sign of Peter, Hannah closed the window and pulled down the spring-loaded shade. She got ready for bed and then put the shade back up for one last look around. There was no sign of anyone, but she could almost imagine there was. Peter was that wonderful. He would come soon, drop from the branch, and knock on her window, and they would go for a ride together in his nice sports car.

Hannah looked at the moon for a long time and studied the dark ridges that ran at crazy angles across the surface. Its soft glow seemed to agree with her. The world was right, and Peter would come soon—because he was Peter.

The moon rose later each night, and eventually Hannah no longer spent as much time by the window.

Today Kathy had both girls helping with peaches. The heat of the wood oven, carrying the heavy jars back and forth, and pealing the endless supply of peaches made for a very long day. There had been little time to think of other things.

Hannah hadn't forgotten Peter completely and paused tonight for a moment by the window. Her body and mind were equally weary as she looked out over the dark barnyard. At the memory of his words, faint pleasantness filled her, and then sleepiness overcame her. She climbed into bed and fell quickly into a deep, exhausted sleep.

⬧

A mile away, a blue MGC, with its six-cylinder engine, purred slowly along the dirt road.

"Why don't you go faster?" the passenger asked the driver.

"I'm not ready to get there yet," Peter told his cousin Lester.

"Scared, aren't you?"

"No, of course not."

"Then what am I along for?"

"I already told you. You need to feed the dog while I see the girl."

"So what keeps the dog from feeding on me?"

"Look, I've been feeding this dog every other night for almost a week now—ever since he chased me off. Please. He's not a vicious dog, just noisy."

"So you're trying to see this girl, right?"

"Yes."

"What's so important about her? I mean, there are plenty of English girls in town to see—like a certain girl I know of." Lester looked at Peter slyly. "Not everything is a secret, you know."

"This one is Amish. Now, we've already talked about it. Would you hush?"

"Well, there are plenty of Amish girls in town too. *Rumspringa* doesn't leave them behind, you know."

Peter paused for effect. "This one is different, okay?"

Lester looked skeptically in Peter's direction. The lights of the car cast too little light for Lester to catch a good glimpse of Peter's face. "How old is this girl?"

"About sixteen, maybe seventeen. About our age. Certainly not older."

"Have I seen her before?"

"I don't think so. I never did either till we met in the hospital. They're not in our district."

"So what's this girl like? What's so special?"

"Would you quit being so nosy?"

"What are you going to do when you get up to her window?"

"That's my business. Now just be quiet. We're getting close to their place."

Lester wasn't done yet. "I hope she knows what she's doing. I certainly wouldn't trust you."

"That's what's so cute about her." Peter grinned in the darkness. "She doesn't know what she's doing. She's got all kinds of stars in her eyes. Look, I'm just going to take her out for a ride. You'll have to wait around while we go for a spin."

"I don't trust you. I do declare!" Lester proclaimed.

"Come on! Would you just be quiet now and get that bag ready to feed the dog with?"

Lester grunted. "You'd better not get into trouble, or I'll tell on you."

"I won't. Besides I'm not doing anything wrong. Sure, she's only seventeen or so, but what's her dad going to do if he catches us? Give me a lecture on how it's a little early for a girl to do *rumspringa*? That's about all he can do."

"I wouldn't put much of anything past you. What's a certain English girl going to say—the one I saw you with Saturday night?"

"How's she going to find out? Besides, she doesn't have to know."

"I didn't say she did."

"Your voice said so. Look, just keep your mouth shut and feed the dog once we get there, okay? I'm tired of all this talk."

Lester grunted, apparently tired of the harassment, and then asked, "Why are we coming here in the middle of the week? To throw the regular crowd off the scent?"

"Now you're catching on." Peter grinned as the headlights of the MGC pierced the darkness along the edge of the dirt road. "Now, here go the lights," he said softly. "It's darkness from here on in." Peter switched off the lights as the car bumped along, its tires crunching on the gravel.

"You'd better not go too far without lights," Lester told him.

"I'm not. The house is just around that bend."

The MGC slowly pulled to a halt by the fence line. The two boys opened their car doors and cautiously got out.

"Bring that bag of food," Peter whispered to Lester.

"Why don't you carry it?" Lester asked.

"Because you're feeding the dog and I'm seeing the girl."

"I'm not going to carry it. I'll feed the dog, yes, but you can carry the bag." Lester stuck his hands in his pockets to make the point.

Peter looked at him and then calmly pulled the bag out of the backseat. He took the lead as they crept up the opposite side of the fence line, using the trees and bushes to hide their approach. The night was pitch black, and not a breeze stirred. Off to the left and across the open plowed field, a dog howled. What sounded like a bat squeaked by them in pursuit of an elusive insect. Apparently it missed its prey and swooped closer over the boys' heads.

"Where's this dog at?" Lester whispered.

"I've always found him by the barn."

They passed the silhouette of the house but couldn't see any lights through the bushes.

"Everyone's in bed," Lester said, his voice low.

"Good," Peter agreed.

"What if she's in bed?"

"That's even better," Peter whispered back. "She won't hear us, and I can wake her at the window. Now, would you be quiet?"

Lester didn't respond because a root had just caught his foot, and he crashed to the ground, his arms sprawled wide.

"You'll wake everybody up," Peter shot in his direction.

"I couldn't help it. Something tripped me."

"Shhh." Peter commanded, holding a finger to his lips.

Their breaths came in short gasps as they hunched over behind the fence. When no lights came on in the house, they continued toward the barn in search of the dog. They crossed the circle driveway and then paused again to listen.

"Okay," Peter said, "we'll slowly approach the barn, and when the dog comes out, I will do the talking. Whatever you do, don't run."

"What if he doesn't come out? Maybe he's in the house."

"Stop worrying and just be quiet," Peter said and stepped forward. Lester followed him without much space between them. The red side of the barn loomed up before them. Peter put out his hand to steady himself. The horizontal barn siding squeaked under his hand.

"Quit making noise." Lester's voice was tense.

"Where's that dog?" was Peter's response, and he ignored Lester's warning to be silent. A kerosene lamp flickered momentarily in the house and then went out.

Seven

The hour was late, but Sam Knepp tossed in his bed, unable to sleep. Life was passing him by it seemed. He felt like he needed to rush and do something. No doubt the day's hard fieldwork was on his mind. Farm life was demanding, no question about it. That's why he needed a wife before he became much older—a good wife, one that would stand him in good stead.

Without that, the years seemed to stretch out before him endlessly. Amish life was what he wanted. With the promised farm from his father, all he lacked was a good wife—a helpmeet.

Wearily he rolled over in bed, but the thoughts wouldn't stop. She needed to be strong and able to bear children because he'd need children, particularly boys to help on the farm. She must be able to help with the farmwork, especially when the children were young. With moral and physical stamina, she must get up at five each morning to do the milking, no matter the weather.

Many women, even Amish women, couldn't take it or—worse in Sam's mind—didn't *want* to take it. That was why Hannah was in his thoughts so much of late. Yes, she was still a little young, but so many other things were in her favor that he could overlook her youth.

Since their school days, she had been nice to him, smiling at him when he looked in her direction. But of late, things had changed. There had been that accident during the game of Wolf and the day Honey threw Hannah practically at Sam's feet. Those were not good ways to further a relationship. He frowned in the darkness but told himself not to be discouraged. Perhaps this might be God's way to bring them together. Shared sorrow, like the preachers said, made for shared hearts.

In his mind there was only one goal: to arrive at the point where the bishop married them and they exchanged the sacred vows. Then there could be no turning back. He would marry an Amish girl, and she would never divorce or leave him.

Hannah was the one for him. Of this, Sam was sure. He saw how quickly she had bounced back from the accident. Hannah had spunk. Besides that, she was a looker. Then, catching himself, Sam pushed that thought away. There were more important things in this world than physical beauty. Beauty faded away fast, the preachers said, and Sam had taken the lesson to heart. He would not allow good looks to play a big part in deciding who was to become his wife. That it played some part couldn't be helped. Hannah was a pretty girl, but God was responsible for that.

At that pleasing thought, he rolled over, shut his eyes tightly, and felt sleep creep slowly upon him.

In the pitch dark, Peter and Lester pressed their backs against the barn wall and into the contour of the building. In the house and to the left of their line of sight, the kerosene lamp kept flickering on and off. Thunder, which they had not heard before, now sounded in the distance. The wind stirred and whipped the leaves at their feet.

"Let's get out of here," Lester whispered.

"Be quiet. The dog will hear you," Peter hissed back.

"I thought that was what we wanted? That's what your bag of meat is for. Where's the dog?"

"Just be quiet. I've got to see this girl."

Along the fencerow, the wind moaned in the trees as it picked up speed. The weathervane on the barn roof rattled as it spun around to the southwest. The back door to the house unexpectedly creaked open, and there stood Roy in the back glow of the kerosene lamp. He turned a flashlight on and cast its beam first on the ground and then toward the barn. The bright beam raked the side of the barn.

"He's seen us. Let's run," Lester whispered shakily.

"No...the dog will catch us easily."

"Where's the stupid dog?"

"He's around here somewhere," Peter assured Lester.

The flashlight bobbed up and down as Roy walked toward the front of the barn, the gravel crunching under his feet.

Peter whispered, "He's not coming our way. Maybe he hasn't seen us."

Lester said nothing.

Roy opened the barn door on the side away from them just as lightning lit the sky to the south.

"He's coming out to check on the animals," Peter said quietly.

"Maybe he's coming for us," Lester said.

Peter chuckled quietly.

"I just want to get out of here," Lester whispered.

"We will just as soon as this man gets done with his animals and I can get up to that window."

"He's not making any noise," Lester managed to say.

"What do you mean?"

"In the barn. There's no noise. There should be."

Peter considered that as he listened. The wind had picked up around them. Its moans increased in the treetops down by the fencerow. The weathervane spun around again and creaked even louder on the barn roof. A roll of thunder followed dim flashes in the distance.

"That is strange," Peter ventured.

"He's up to something. If he catches us, my dad will tan my hide to a crisp."

"Would you just be quiet," Peter said in exasperation. "No one's going to catch us."

Peter's words were interrupted by a quiet insistent voice. "Shep, come here! Shep!" A shadowy figure came around the barn to the right of them. A flash of lightning revealed the distinct shape of a man. "Come here, Shep," he said. "Come here, boy."

Lester and Peter held still, their bodies taut against the barn's wooden siding. The flashlight beam in Roy's hand swept up and down the fencerow.

"Shep! Shep!" he repeated but received no response. "Where is that dog when you need him?"

Slowly Roy walked past the boys, his back turned toward them, his flashlight scanning up and down his property. When he found neither his dog nor anything else, he returned to the back door. As he opened it, the light from the kerosene lamp flickered into the dark yard. Lightning flashed still closer and was followed by a sharp roll of thunder.

"That was a close call," gasped Lester. "Let's get out of here."

"No, it wasn't," Peter told him. "He was looking for his dog. He has no idea we're out here."

"Let's keep it that way, then."

"We will, but I have to see this girl."

"You can see her by yourself."

"I will, but you're staying around to watch out for the dog. Otherwise, I could be up that tree when her dad shows up."

"What am I going to do?"

"I want you to stand by the tree while I climb up."

"No," Lester said insistently.

"Yes, you are. Now be quiet and follow me."

"I'm going home," Lester took a few steps toward the car.

"How are you going home? I have the keys," Peter reminded him.

Lester grunted in the darkness and knew he was hemmed in with no way out. "Then I'm going to wait by the fencerow," he said in protest. "If there's any trouble, I'll walk out, and you're on your own. I would rather be caught out by the car than here near the house. It'll look better. I'll say it was your idea and I didn't go along."

"Just be quiet and *wait*," Peter said.

A moment later, the two were at the base of the tree. "Wait here,"

Peter said as he reached for the first low hanging branch. "It looks like an easy climb."

Lester said nothing as Peter climbed upward. Lightning now flashed clearly on the horizon, splashing bright light in all directions. Only the shadow of the barn kept full illumination off the tree.

"Someone will see," Lester hissed.

Peter ignored him. Then suddenly Peter looked back and saw Shep approaching behind Lester, his eyes intent on the tree branches and Peter.

"The dog!" Peter hissed.

Lester moved quickly, though his hand was shaking, and reached behind him for the bag. His fingers found nothing but air. He wildly grabbed around and became more desperate when he only felt the grass on his palms. Where was the bag?

"The dog's going to bark! He sees me!" Peter whispered.

Lester tried again, his arms stretching wide in the search. A lightning strike finally did the trick, and he caught a glimpse of the bag just a few feet beyond his reach. On his hands and knees, he crept toward the bag. Behind him he heard Shep approaching. With a deep growl, Shep drew nearer.

"He's going to eat me," Lester whispered with a quaver.

"No, he's not," Peter said. "Shut him up with some food. Now! Quick!"

Lester desperately wished he'd stayed home instead of participating in this mad adventure and debated whether to run, to advance, or to wait this out. Shep took a step toward him, the hair on his neck straight up. The lightning cast crazy shadows on the lawn and made Shep look twice his real size.

"Good doggie. Good doggie." Lester managed to get the words past his dry lips. The bag was now between him and the dog.

Shep advanced another step and then paused. His head was right above the bag, its raw smells wafting into his nose.

"It's good stuff," Lester croaked from his parched throat.

Shep lifted his head and growled.

"I'll open the bag for you," Lester whispered and made a move toward the bag. The dog backed off slightly and waited. Lester opened the bag and pulled out some of the things Peter had brought along.

Shep looked up expectantly at him.

Lester pulled his hand out and tossed the tidbits toward the dog. Shep sniffed once and then lowered his head and began devouring the pieces of meat.

"What's going on down there?" Peter asked.

"I'm feeding the dog," Lester whispered back. Then the two heard a sound from the house. It was the sound of a window sliding open.

Shep stopped eating for a moment and looked up toward the upper story. Lester dug into the bag and threw everything he had to the dog. Shep wagged his tail, lowered his head, and chomped at the food again. After a long moment, the upstairs window closed.

"Let's get out of here," Lester hissed sharply.

This time Peter listened as he moved down the trunk of the tree as fast as he could. This took old Shep, who had just finished the last of the scraps, by surprise. For the first time he barked sharply.

"Shut up, old dog!" Peter commanded, now almost on the ground. His voice must have sounded familiar because Shep quieted down. Then he looked back and forth between the two boys and must have changed his mind—his barks began again, this time with urgency.

"Let's go," Peter said as he led the way rapidly down the fencerow to the car. Together they pushed the MGC a hundred feet before Peter jumped in and turned the key. With the car started, they drove off into the night.

"That was the craziest thing," Lester snapped when he felt free to breathe again. "I'm never doing that again."

"We'll see," Peter said calmly. "I still want to see that girl."

"There are plenty of other girls," Lester insisted.

"Well, yes," Peter concurred, "but not quite like this one."

"So, why didn't you say something to her when that window opened?"

"I don't know," said Peter thoughtfully. "I wasn't sure it was her window. I couldn't see too well in the dark. My first instinct was to freeze. What if it hadn't been her? I just can't mess this up. This may be my only chance, you know."

"There are all those English girls in town."

"Yes, but it's not the same. I want to get this Amish girl."

"You are a skunk," Lester said.

Peter only smiled and drove wildly around a curve as Lester hung on in the darkness.

Eight

Roy looked none too happy at the breakfast table. "There sure was an awful lot of fuss going on around here last night."

"I heard you go outside once," Kathy said quietly. "Did you see anything?"

"Shep was gone," Roy said with a wave of his fork. "There was no sign of him...but I was sure I heard something. I just don't like the feel of things around here right now. It's like something's going on that shouldn't be."

"You sure you're not imagining things?" Kathy asked.

"I could be," he acknowledged and turned his attention back to the food on his plate, "but Shep did bark a little later, after I was in bed. I almost got up again. Then it didn't last for very long. Something awfully strange is going on."

"I heard Shep too," Hannah said, thinking it would be best to volunteer a comment. If Peter was involved in any of this, she wanted her own part clear. "It sounded to me like he was chewing on a groundhog he'd dug up."

"There you go," Kathy said, jumping on the explanation. "It was probably just the dog."

Roy shrugged and remained unconvinced. "I just don't like it—that's all I can say."

Hannah kept her eyes on her bowl of oatmeal, not because she was trying to hide anything, but because she felt hope stir inside of her. Perhaps Peter had come...had tried to reach her window.

Miriam glanced in her direction. "I didn't hear anything."

"Me neither," Emma said, "but then our bedrooms are on the other side of the house."

"I didn't either," Isaac, for once, spoke up. "When I go to bed, I sleep. That's what beds are for."

"Yes, we know," Kathy said with a laugh. And then she looked to Hannah. Under her mother's gaze, she felt a flush on her face.

"Is there something wrong, Hannah?" her mother asked.

Hannah shook her head. "No." Her hopes to see Peter didn't quite qualify as something being wrong.

Kathy, using her mother's intuition about these things, asked, "You don't know anything more about the noises last night?"

"Not really," Hannah said unconvincingly.

When her mom didn't seem satisfied, she pressed on. "Hannah, if you do know something, you'd best tell us now. If we find out another way, it won't sit well with us."

Hannah didn't know how to answer.

Kathy watched her a moment longer and decided to act on a motherly hunch.

"Is this about a boy?" she asked.

Hannah came up with the best answer she could think of without lying. "Well, I could *wish* it was about a boy, couldn't I?"

Kathy laughed out loud. "You silly girl! I guess you're old enough for wishes like that, but remember you're still young. There's still plenty of time. Someone is out there for you."

"What are you talking about?" Roy asked.

Kathy said, "I think she was hoping it was a boy coming to see her."

"Who would do something like that?" Roy asked. "It's not even Friday night. Besides...I wouldn't let the boy who sneaks around into the house. She will do it the proper way—not with lights in the windows."

Hannah nodded, for reasons she couldn't quite understand, close to tears. A few slid down her cheeks, and she put down her spoon to wipe them away.

"Now, look what you've done," Kathy said. "You've broken her heart."

"It needs to be broken from ideas like that."

"That's not what I meant," Kathy said. "It's not that anyone would actually come. I'm sure Hannah wouldn't allow it. It's the *wish* that a boy might care so much that he'd want to come."

Roy looked skeptical.

"I wouldn't want it to actually happen either," Kathy assured him. "It's just the wish, I guess, that counts."

"Did you want me to come around to your window when I was dating you?" Roy asked.

"Well, you never thought of doing something like that," she said as she began clearing the table now that breakfast was over. Hannah got to her feet to help.

"That's not what I asked," he replied, waiting for an answer.

Kathy finally came over and gave him a hug. "You did just fine."

Roy grinned but shook his head. "I still don't think it's proper... or in order."

"I know that," she said, "and I'm sure Hannah knows it too." Kathy gathered up a stack of dirty dishes and headed for the kitchen sink. "Girls just have dreams sometimes."

Hannah felt stabs of guilt at her mother's words of confidence. Would she really go out with Peter or did she just want him to come to the window?

Her beloved poem had somehow awakened her to love, and she couldn't turn back now. Love was now her dream. And Peter was the object of that dream. He was a good boy, and she trusted him.

Hannah didn't have to wait long to find the answer to what she would do if Peter did come, for it was the very next evening a soft rapping sounded on her windowpane. Hannah had just come into her room, slipped off her shoes, and stretched out on the bed, weary to the bone from another hard day of housework. It felt so absolutely divine to rest, and so at first she didn't notice the noise on the windowpane. The taps were repeated, this time more insistently. She sat upright and swung her feet onto the floor. Her eyes went to the window where a shadowy figure crouched in front of the pane, his hand poised to knock again.

She felt a scream form deep within her, but no sound came out. The shadow moved and waved a hand. Hannah stood, her fear now mixing with excitement as she stared, undecided, at the window. The figure reached into a pocket and produced a long silver item. It used the other hand to cover the end, then a small flash of light appeared directed at the person's face. To her astonishment she saw the dimply lit face of Peter. She drew a sharp breath as her heart pounded. Peter had come to her window. In a flash, her decision was made, and she rushed to the window to raise the sash.

"Hi," Peter whispered and then moved away from the window to wait. "Come quick. You still want your ride?"

"You *came,*" she said.

"Of course," he said. "I said I would, didn't I? It just took a little while."

"But I told you not to come," Hannah said, now rethinking her decision. With Peter actually in front of her and the dark of night outside, she wasn't so sure of what she should do.

He ignored her comment but said, "I worked hard on this—now don't go spoiling it."

"How was that?" she asked.

"That dog of yours has been a great nuisance. I spent the last few evenings becoming friends with him."

"You went to all that trouble?" She found herself impressed. This was the Peter she knew, the Peter who cared for her.

"I wanted to see you," he whispered in the darkness.

"You did? Really?" she asked.

"Yes. Now come…or can I come in?"

"No," she said instinctively. That would not do at all. "We can talk here."

"It's pretty uncomfortable on this roof. It would be nicer inside."

She felt the emotion deep inside. *What should I do? What if my parents walk in?*

"Come on," he coaxed, "I won't stay long."

Hannah made no movement away from the window, and Peter made no attempt to force his way in.

"I went to all this work to see you. At least let me inside," he said.

Shep took it upon himself at that moment to bark.

"Oh, no," Peter said, "the dog."

"It's nothing," she said. "I can tell by his bark. It sounds friendly."

"Are you sure?"

"Yes."

"Will you go for a ride, then, in my car?"

"Where?" she asked.

"I'll take you downtown for a drive. We can just climb down the tree and follow the fencerow down to the road. We won't see anybody, and I'll have you back in no time. No one will ever know."

There was a pause as Hannah thought about it. The darkness made things look so much different than in the daytime. Why she wouldn't go baffled her at the moment. While trying to decide, she was very conscious that Peter was there, in the dark, his eyes on her face.

What harm could it do? For another moment she searched for reasons not to go and found only her parents' disapproval.

"I'll go," Hannah said.

Shep barked again, sharper this time. "Maybe you can get the dog to quiet down?" Peter asked.

"Yes," she whispered back into the darkness.

Peter reached for her hand to help her out the window. At his touch Hannah became more confident. Even more, she felt wanted.

Hannah followed Peter across the roof and noticed his carefulness lest he fall. Even on the tree, he climbed slowly and with great caution. But for Hannah the climb down was easy because of her years of practice.

At the base of the tree, Shep sat waiting and wagging his tail. He then followed the couple as they made their way to the fence. But Hannah turned and ordered him to stay. He sat obediently but offered a whimper of protest.

Hannah then followed Peter along the fencerow to where he had parked his car a ways up the road. The blue color of the MGC appeared even darker than in the daytime. She opened the door on the passenger's side by herself while Peter rushed around to the other side. She was already in when he slid into the driver's seat.

"She's a beauty, isn't she?" he whispered and turned the key.

The motor purred in the darkness.

"Don't drive too fast," she said, still nervous about her decision.

"You scared?" he asked, and although she couldn't see his face, she was sure he was grinning.

"Maybe, but just don't drive fast...okay? You said a *nice* drive."

"That it will be," he replied, laughing. "Let's go, then. I've wanted to do this for such a long time. "

As they got farther down the road, he began to speed up again.

"Not too fast," she repeated. The speed of the car made her feel more frightened in the darkness.

"This isn't fast," he said. "I could go a lot faster." But for her, he slowed down a little.

Hannah noticed he had barely slowed down for the stop signs posted at the last two intersections. Ahead of them the road dipped into a low spot, and the night made the lay of the ground look like a miniature canyon.

Peter pulled onto a side road and then into a secluded grove of trees, well hidden from the main road. There he turned the motor off and sat back against his seat. Over them the tree branches hung heavy and cast a pall on the ground even in the darkness.

"Why are we stopping here?" Hannah asked. "You said you were going downtown."

"Just a minute," he said as he slid over close to her. His hands reached out slowly toward her face. His fingers brushed lightly against her cheeks, and then his face drew closer until his lips touched hers. "You are a sweet girl," he whispered.

His sudden nearness overwhelmed Hannah. Under the great silence of the heavens so full of pulsating beacons of starlight, Hannah felt the power of unbidden emotion. Her eyes swept across the stars as her fingers touched his. *So this is what love is—this desire to be with him, to touch him. The God who had made the stars must be the very One who made a boy like Peter.* Yet, this delight also seemed to be mixed with guilt, she noticed with great astonishment. *Is love also like that? Is it always mixed with hesitation?*

"Something wrong?" he asked.

She shook her head, but she knew something *was* wrong.

His lips found hers again, and she tried to give in, to forget her mom and dad, her upbringing, the fact that she shouldn't be out here—and that she had climbed out of a window to be with this boy. Her dream of love rose before her, and a voice told her to enjoy the moment to its fullest now that what she had dreamed about had come to her. But at the same moment, she knew she couldn't.

"Something's wrong," Peter said when she pulled away. "What is it?"

"Take me home," Hannah said into the darkness. "I don't want this."

"Why not? We're not doing anything wrong." His fingers found hers in the darkness and caressed them, but she pulled away.

"Yes, we are," she told him. "Take me home."

"Don't be like your father, Hannah," Peter said with disdain in his voice. "Can't you see what they're doing to you? They want you to just throw your youth away, pine around in the house, and not have any fun at all."

"I thought this was love," she whispered, perhaps more to herself than to Peter.

"Well, it is," he said, laughing. "You don't have to be scared."

Hannah said nothing, and Peter didn't move from where he sat. But when tears threatened to spill, he must have sensed her distress because he let out a long low breath, started the car, backed up, and returned to the main road. With a flash headlights cut a clear path into the night air.

As the tears came, Peter said, "Hannah, don't go crybaby on me! And don't go telling your folks things. We didn't do anything wrong. I just kissed you."

"Just take me home," she repeated.

Nine

Roy awoke with a start. He sat upright in bed and listened. The house was silent, yet the uneasy feeling he'd experienced on and off all week had returned.

He got up, got dressed, and walked into the living room. Slowly he walked to the window and looked out. The night was moonless and dark though stars twinkled brightly in the sky. He opened the front door and glanced around. Nothing looked amiss. But according to his instincts, something clearly *was* amiss.

He went back to the bedroom and woke Kathy. "Something's going on. Something's not right," he said.

"Like what?" she asked sleepily. "Is Shep barking again?"

"No," he said, "something else. I don't know what. Would you get up and check the children's rooms?"

"Okay," Kathy muttered as she reached for her housecoat and put it on over her nightclothes.

As Kathy climbed the stairs, Roy went out to the porch again. He stood there and listened to the low hum of the night sounds and wondered what was wrong. Then, off in the distance, the headlights of a car cut into the night. From the movement of the lights, he was sure the car would pass their house. It was coming fast. Waves of light bounced around on their uneven gravel road. Yet, there was nothing unusual in that. Cars drove this road frequently, and they often drove fast.

It was when Roy heard the car abruptly slow down that his attention became focused. The tires slid on the gravel by their driveway, and the car came to a complete stop. The passenger door opened, and a girl got out. Roy couldn't make out who the girl was, nor did he hear any voices. But then he heard the squeal of tires on the gravel road as the car sped off. The taillights dimly lit the shape of the girl the car had left off. Even in the darkness that settled around her, Roy could tell she didn't move, as if she were frozen to the spot.

Roy, startled out of his surprise, moved with his first instinct, which was to get Kathy. He opened the front door and called to her.

She had just come down the stairs, her eyes wide with the news. "She's not here."

"Who isn't here?" he asked.

"Hannah."

"Look there," Roy said and pointed with his chin toward the road.

They stood together and looked at the form out by the road.

"Where did she come from?" Kathy asked.

"A car just dropped her off."

"It can't be Hannah, can it? She wouldn't be out without telling us."

"Maybe we ought to go and see," Roy ventured.

"But…she wouldn't do something like this—leave in the night… without telling us."

Roy took Kathy by the hand and led her down the steps and slowly out the driveway. They approached the still figure who was standing by the road with her back turned toward them. As they got closer, the unmistakable sounds of sobs became evident.

"Hannah," Kathy said when she was close enough to speak, "is that you?"

The only answer was yet louder cries.

Kathy walked up quickly, reached for Hannah's hand, pulled her tightly to herself, and asked, "What are you doing out here?"

"He just dropped me off."

"Who is he?" Kathy asked.

"Peter," Hannah sobbed.

"Why on earth were you with Peter?"

"He came to my window and offered me a ride."

"To your window?" Kathy was horrified.

Hannah's only reply was a sob of regret. "I'm so sorry."

"Tell me all about it," Kathy said after giving Hannah a few moments to calm down.

"Peter said…that he wanted to take me for a ride."

"And you went with him?"

Hannah nodded in the darkness.

"Didn't you know that's wrong?" Kathy asked.

"Yes, but I couldn't resist. It seemed like a harmless thing—just take a nice ride, he said, and then he would bring me right back. I thought it would be okay.

"Have you done this before?" Kathy asked.

Hannah shook her head.

"What happened then?"

"We drove a little, and he parked."

"He parked?" Kathy's voice echoed in the night.

"He said we would drive through downtown."

"What happened then—after you parked?"

Hannah's voice was weak. "He leaned over and kissed me—just twice, Mom. Really! I thought I'd enjoyed it…Then I couldn't. I don't know why. It was then that I told him to take me home."

"Did he bring you home then?"

"Yes, but he was really mad. He just dropped me off at the end of the lane, making a big fuss. I knew then I could never climb back into my room without you and Dad finding out."

"Is that why you're crying?" Kathy asked.

"Not just that." Hannah broke into fresh tears. "Oh, Mom, how can something like this turn out so terrible? I feel just awful inside. He wasn't nice at all. I thought he was so wonderful."

Kathy pulled Hannah to her again and said nothing as the two cried together.

"We had best go inside," Roy said, deciding to make his presence known. "We'll deal with this more in the morning. Right now it's time to get everyone to bed."

As Roy turned to lead them in, he thought he heard something in the distance, and his eyes caught a brilliant flare of light in the distance down the road. Red and yellow lights rose in a cloud of color that looked close. They soon died down and were replaced with a low hue that also soon faded.

Because they had just turned to walk toward the house, neither Hannah nor Kathy heard the noise or saw the lights.

Roy wondered what he had heard and what could have been the source of the lights. His instincts told him what they were, but he hoped he was wrong.

"Get Hannah to bed," he told Kathy when they were inside the house. "We will talk some more about this tomorrow. I need to go check on something."

Kathy nodded and headed for the stairs with Hannah in front of her. Pausing with her hand on the door, she asked, "Where are you going?"

"I'm taking the buggy. Don't worry." He turned only for a moment before he pulled on his work shoes.

"Do be careful," she said and followed Hannah up the stairs.

Roy rushed out to the barn, lit the gas lantern he kept there, and called the horse in. He worked quickly and soon drove the buggy out the driveway and onto the main road, the reins tight in his hands.

Officer Coons, from the Indiana State Police, had also seen the fireball. He quickly pulled his cruiser to the side of the road, made a U-turn, and drove in the direction of the flash. It didn't take him long to reach his destination and report in. "We have a one-car vehicle accident two miles west of 331 on the County Line Road. Have fire and rescue respond."

"Causality report?" the response came back.

"Unknown at this time," he said. "Exiting cruiser to examine the scene now. Does not look good."

With his flashlight in hand, Officer Coons jumped the ditch and approached the vehicle. Small fires were still burning inside the mangled frame of the car that was wrapped around a tree, but the worst of the fire seemed over. There was no sign of life that he could see.

He lifted his head as the clip-clop of horse's hooves approached. Although he was in Amish country, he had expected the sound of sirens, not horse's hooves at this time of the night. Although the accident likely happened because some lover boy was driving too fast on his way home from his girl's home, that too was strange. This was the middle of the week.

When the buggy stopped, Coons had to jump back across the ditch to deal with it. "Can I do something for you?" he asked.

"Name's Roy Miller," Hannah's father said, leaning out of his buggy. "I live down the road. My daughter was just dropped off by a young boy. I was wondering if this is the same one."

"What time was that?" Officer Coons asked.

"About twenty minutes ago."

"You have any information about him?"

"Just that his name is Peter."

"This one will be hard to identify by his name, I'm sorry to say. Hit that tree pretty hard." Officer Coons turned his flashlight in the direction Roy had just come from. Long black skid marks were clearly visible. "Looks like whoever this was was driving too fast. You know what kind of car he was driving?"

Roy shook his head. "I'm not sure. I never saw it myself. I think my wife mentioned a blue MGC once. The boy's been around my daughter before."

"One of those situations." The officer was sympathetic. "The color of the paint won't be much help either, I'm sorry to say, but we can look at the make of the car."

Coons' flashlight beam shone across the ditch at the wrecked car frame. The beam only partially reached before it faded away. The officer shook his flashlight to get more light and then brought the beam to bear on the rear of the car. Even from that distance, they could both read the distinct MGC letters.

"Sorry," the officer said. "Someone close to the girl?"

"No, they were just out for the first time."

"Did they have some kind of fight or something to cause him to be driving this fast?"

"Yes," Roy said with a voice that communicated his reluctance to make such an admission. "There was a disagreement. I only found out about it when he dropped her off."

"He still shouldn't have been driving like that," Officer Coons was quick to say. "Hormones, I guess, cost him big this time."

The wail of sirens came from the distance. The emergency vehicle's lights mingled with those of the trooper's cruiser.

"I should be going," Roy said, slapping the reins and turning the buggy around. As he passed the first rescue vehicle, he turned his head from the burst of bright lights.

When Roy returned home, Kathy was waiting in the kitchen for him. She had lit a kerosene lamp and set it on the table, its flickering light ghostly on the walls.

"What was that all about?" she asked, her voice hushed.

Apparently something about Roy's face, framed in the kitchen door, brought her to her feet, and Kathy sucked in her breath. "What's happened?"

Roy sat down, numb, and motioned for her to be seated. "I noticed something—a fire—when we were walking toward the house. You and Hannah didn't see it because your backs were turned. It looked like it could have been an accident, and so that was what I went to see."

"And?" Her question hung in the air.

"It was him," Roy said quietly.

"Peter?" Her hands went to her face.

"Yes," he said, "I'm afraid so. How are we going to tell Hannah?"

"What happened?" Kathy asked.

"There was an officer there already. From the skid marks, he thinks the boy was driving too fast. When I asked questions, he started asking me questions. Now that I think about it, I probably should have kept my mouth shut."

"You didn't tell him that Peter was out with Hannah?" Kathy tried to keep her composure.

"I'm afraid I did. I wasn't planning to, but the officer started asking direct questions, and it just came out."

"Oh, my," Kathy made as if to rise from the chair but sat down again. "What if this comes out? They weren't even dating."

Roy numbly nodded.

They sat there for a long time and said nothing. Finally the fatigue of the day took over, and they stumbled wearily to bed. Sleep came soon enough, and when the alarm went off, it was all both of them could do to get up.

Since he started his full-time factory job, Roy had to leave for work early. The farmwork was now limited to evenings and weekends. His ride always came by at five thirty.

"I'm sorry I won't be here for the talk with Hannah," he told Kathy as he ate his breakfast. "You could speak with her now but save the news for this evening. I could tell her then."

"I'd rather not wait," Kathy said. "I'll tell her."

Hearing his ride approaching on the gravel road, Roy nodded and dashed out the door, his lunch pail in his hand.

Kathy let Hannah and her sisters sleep in an extra hour before she woke them. She woke Isaac at the regular time, and he was now outside, busy with his chores. Hannah came downstairs first. Her head was throbbing, but even worse was the pain in her heart. Love had betrayed her.

"Sit down," Kathy said when she entered the kitchen. "We might as well wait till your sisters arrive. I don't want to have to repeat myself."

When Hannah looked up, showing the wounded expression on

her face, Kathy said, "They have to be told. You know that. And I'm afraid there's more—far more—than even you know."

Hannah's eyes teared up. Not understanding but nodding anyway, she clasped her hands together tightly under the table. She knew she deserved a good scolding and was ready for whatever punishment would come her way. With a deep breath, she calmed herself.

"Sit down, girls, for a minute," Kathy told Miriam and Emma when they appeared. "I have something I need to tell all of you."

Hannah looked up, and in an attempt to help her mother, she blurted out, "I'm so sorry." She looked down to her lap. "I know I deserve to be punished for what I did."

"What did she do?" Emma asked with great curiosity.

"Yes, what?" Miriam echoed.

"Now let's not make this harder than it has to be," Kathy said, her voice gentle. "Hannah has made a mistake, and it's hard enough already."

"I'll do anything to make it right," Hannah cried.

"It's not that, dear." Kathy put her arms around Hannah, tears now in her own eyes. "Something happened after Peter left here last night."

"Would someone explain what happened?" Emma complained. "Who's Peter?"

Hannah looked blankly at her mom.

"Hannah, Peter had an accident last night after he left here." Kathy had to force herself to look at Hannah as she continued, "Hannah, I have to tell you Peter was killed in that accident."

Hannah's face went white.

No one spoke until Hannah said, "He's dead? Peter's gone?"

"Yes. I'm afraid so."

"Just like that?" Hannah whispered the words.

"I'm so sorry." Kathy pulled her close again.

"But," Hannah struggled to make her voice audible, "you don't just die like that. I was with him last night. He can't be dead."

Kathy held her tightly, cushioning her sobs. Emma and Miriam waited speechless with sober faces.

"How did it happen?" Hannah finally asked when she had composed herself.

"The officer thinks Peter was driving too fast. He hit a tree. Your dad went down there last night."

"Why didn't you wake me then?" Hannah asked.

"We thought it best not to. It just didn't seem right."

"It's all my fault...that he's dead," Hannah stated numbly.

"No," Kathy said. "We don't know why these things happen. They just do."

"But I sent him away. If I hadn't made him angry, it wouldn't have happened. It was my fault."

"*Nee,* it wasn't. He drove too fast. That's not your fault—it was his. And as for sending him away, I think you know that was the right thing to do."

"It's still my fault," Hannah said as the tears continued to flow.

Miriam and Emma still had puzzled looks on their faces. Hannah would leave it to her mother to explain. Her voice was too choked to try even if she had wanted to.

"I did a lot of things wrong last night," she finally said.

Kathy then turned to Miriam and Emma and explained what had happened. Miriam went to Hannah and gave her a hug. Emma sat in her chair transfixed.

"She went out with a boy...through the window. Now he's dead."

"I know. It's all my fault." Hannah put her head in her hands.

"It wasn't your fault," Kathy said. "You have to stop saying that, or you'll never get over this."

"I never will get over it. I know I won't," Hannah insisted.

After a meager breakfast, during which Hannah barely touched her food, Kathy assigned them their duties for the day, Hannah included. Work would surely help soothe some of the pain.

Ten

By late that evening, Hannah had finally calmed down enough for Kathy to leave her alone in her bedroom. The tears had broken out fresh again after supper. Roy had wanted to speak with her but had decided against it when Kathy told him she'd gone through enough for one day. "Give her time," Kathy said.

Kathy came downstairs to join Ray in the living room. "When's the funeral?" she asked.

"Day after tomorrow. Do you think we should go?" he said, glancing up at her.

"Yes, I think we probably should," she said.

"What about Hannah?"

Kathy paused. "I'm not sure, but it may be the best thing for her. She's taking it really hard. Sometimes facing reality is the best route to take."

Roy nodded. "I think that's the best. Why do you think she's taking it so hard?"

Kathy gave the question some thought and said, "You know, I'm not sure I have it figured out yet. If he was her steady, it would make sense, but he wasn't."

"Do you think she loved the boy?" Roy asked.

Kathy shrugged. "It's hard to imagine so. She hardly knew him. She just saw him maybe two or three times."

"You don't think they've been seeing each other secretly, do you?"

Kathy frowned. "The thought has crossed my mind, but she isn't one to lie. I see no signs that she has started now. No, it must be something else."

Roy agreed but added, "We need to keep an eye on her. She's still pretty torn up. It won't help if she sees the story in the paper."

"What did they say?" she asked.

"Amish Boy Killed After Dropping Off Girlfriend," he said and kept his eyes straight ahead.

"Did the story give Hannah's name?"

"No, I mentioned no names to the officer other than my name, Roy. They can hardly trace it with that. I don't want Hannah's name attached to Peter's death. We know it wasn't her fault, but seeing it in print might not convince others—or Hannah for that matter."

Kathy sighed. "Perhaps *Da Hah* will have mercy. Seems like she's had it hard enough already. It *would* be hard on her if it comes out publicly."

"Perhaps there will be mercy," Roy said.

"Let's ask Him," Kathy suggested.

Roy nodded and lowered himself to his knees beside the couch. Kathy followed his example, gripped his arm, and listened to him pray. *Dear God, we ask for mercy and grace on this situation. Hannah has made her mistakes, and we ask for forgiveness for her and for Peter. Please be with his family as they suffer through this time. Their sorrow must be great, much greater than ours. In Your loving kindness, comfort them and give them peace. Amen.*

They got up from their knees, and Kathy made a quick trip upstairs. A peek in Hannah's bedroom confirmed that she seemed to be sound asleep.

The day of the funeral dawned cloudy with rain threatening, which Hannah thought quite appropriate. They had all gotten up early because there would be nearly an hour's drive to the district in which Peter had lived. Hannah ate breakfast in silence, and then they were on the road by seven thirty. Long before they even got close to the house, the road became lined with buggies. Vans, filled with what were clearly visitors, slowly passed them on the other side of the road. Nearer to the house, even the vans got in line and pulled along at the same speed as the buggies.

"It's going to be a huge funeral," Kathy noted.

"Quite large," Roy agreed. "A tragedy usually brings in more people."

Hannah tried to hold back her tears. How would she explain them? No one but her family knew she had any connections with Peter's death. Still the guilt hung heavy over her. Guilt almost more than she could bear.

When they finally turned onto the final road, the buggies had slowed down to a slow walk. Within a hundred yards of the field where they would park, the line moved haltingly, a constant stopping and starting.

"Drop us off at the house," Kathy suggested.

"You think you'll get into the house service?" Roy asked.

"Since we're not relatives, I doubt it. But they have a large pole barn out back. I'll wait for you at the house. Then we can head out there."

Roy nodded. Amish funerals were often conducted in two locations if the main building couldn't accommodate everyone. Separate preachers and preaching would be arranged with the secondary meeting kept informed of the progress in the main house. In this way similar schedules would be maintained.

Roy slowed the buggy to a halt and let Kathy out with Hannah and Emma. Isaac had driven a separate buggy with Miriam. As Hannah stepped down from the buggy, the usual sight greeted her—the long rows of men and boys attired in white shirts and black suits on each side of the driveway.

While the sight was the usual, the effect on Hannah this morning wasn't. She tried to maintain her composure as she followed Kathy up the driveway toward the house. The weight of so many somber and black-clad males was palpable in the air.

I'm guilty, Hannah cried inwardly as she fought back the tears. Other accusing voices joined in as the weight pressed in on her. *Yes, it's my fault Peter is dead.*

She felt so condemned. The best thing she could do to keep from crying out her guilt to everyone present was to keep her eyes on the ground and not show any undue emotion.

Hannah placed one foot in front of the other while she fought with her thoughts and her guilt. Surely relief would come soon after this day was over. This pain simply couldn't go on forever.

While they waited outside the house for Roy, Kathy greeted some of the women. Most of them were unfamiliar to Hannah, visitors no doubt, likely relatives of Peter's she had never met. Everyone spoke in short whispers, no in-depth conversations. Such talk would come later, but for now everyone stood silently and waited for the ushers to let them know when it would be time to go inside.

When Roy appeared, he motioned for Kathy to follow him to the pole barn and the secondary service. However, an usher stopped them and indicated they were to get in line for the primary service in the house.

"We're not relatives," Roy whispered to him.

"It was one of your cousin's friends, was it not?" the usher asked.

"Yes," Roy agreed.

"That's good enough, then." The usher motioned with his hand. "Most of the immediate relatives are already seated. There will yet be room."

Roy shrugged and got in line with Kathy and the girls. Hannah could see nothing of Miriam and Isaac. Wherever they were, they would find seats for themselves.

The service started without any songs as all Amish funerals did. The service began abruptly with the preaching as if to accent the suddenness with which death often comes.

Hannah sat numbly beside her mom and tried not to move. She listened to the preaching and hoped something would be said that would help. They were now on the third speaker, all of whom spoke, as Amish ministers do, without notes or a Bible. The love and mercy of God was mentioned, but the main points all three men made were about the evilness of sin and how God calls us before the judgment seat at unexpected times and in unexpected ways.

"The judgment day comes quickly," Minister Alvin said, "like the turning of a page or the opening of a door. We never know what lies beyond that door." He clasped his hands in front of him, holding them at chest level. His black beard, not yet showing any signs of gray, came down far enough to lightly touch his clasped hands.

"A holy God demands an answer for sin," he said as his voice gathered strength. "We cannot live as we want and then die expecting that He does not care. Our lives are as a vapor that today is rising, and then tomorrow suddenly it may be gone. Then comes the judgment. Today we have been given a warning in the life of one of our young people. We do not know what he found on the other side of that door. Perhaps he cried out to God and found mercy. How will we know until we ourselves arrive over there?

"What we do know is that time is still with each of us," Alvin thundered—his face intense, his eyes raised to the ceiling and focused on what could be eternity itself. "Time to repent, time to turn away from the world, time to come back to our families and the church, time to find God and good. The only question is: *Will we?* Will we take the warning? Will we heed the call of God? Will we listen to what He is saying?"

Hannah listened intently. Other than feeling a deep terror, her whole body felt numb. She was quite sure that she was worthy of being burned to a crisp on the spot. *If I hadn't made him mad, he wouldn't have driven so fast. Now nothing, for all eternity, can bring him back.*

Hannah couldn't have cried if she wanted to; she was too cold. Even in this room of more than 600 people, she shivered. Kathy glanced at her, concerned.

Alvin now came to the end of his sermon. "It is only by the mercy of God that any of us can ever stand before the Almighty God. If He had not sent His only Son, the beloved and holy Jesus, then all of us would be without hope. It is by the blood of Jesus, shed on that cruel cross, that our sins can be washed away. But we must all turn from our sins to Him. May God have mercy on us all."

With that Alvin took his seat, and Kathy pulled the shivering Hannah close to her. The ushers stood and began to escort the lines

of people past the closed casket. One by one they filed by until only
the family was left. Those seated inside the house returned to their
seats while those from the barn stood outside waiting.

Peter's immediate family, his father, mother, two brothers, and
three sisters, rose from their front row seats and gathered around for
their last goodbyes. More than a thousand people waited patiently for
whatever time was needed by the family.

The bowed shoulders and tears of Peter's family were not what
startled Hannah. This was a common enough sight among the Amish.
It was the English girl who rose with them to stand around Peter's
casket. Hannah—seated to the right of her mother—hadn't noticed
her before.

There was only one explanation for why a nonfamily member would
accompany the family at these last moments. He or she would have to
be either engaged or a longtime steady of the departed. Before Hannah's shocked eyes stood Alice, her hospital roommate. Alice stood
with Peter's family around the casket.

All morning no tears had gotten past the numb coldness of Hannah's body. Now the sight of Alice caused the dam to break. She
sobbed silently until her shoulders were shaking.

Kathy looked ready to take Hannah's hand and lead her outside lest
she distract the family at this tender moment. Already several heads
had turned in their direction. Kathy squeezed Hannah's hand, and
Hannah managed to choke back the sobs.

Somehow they got through the moment until the family found their
seats again. The ushers then formed lines to move the people out to
prepare for the trip to the graveside service. Hannah found herself able
to get to her feet, but as they left the house, the tears began again.

Roy noticed Hannah's distress from across the room on the men's
side, and he headed immediately for the horse and buggy. He hitched
up and pulled the buggy in line, and they were soon on their way home
with the still weeping Hannah in the backseat.

Eleven

Surrounded by the majestic mountain ranges of northwestern Montana, the Greyhound bus pulled hard in the curves as black smoke poured out of its tail pipe. Jake sat in the back, his regular seat for three days now. At the last stop, while seated in the restaurant with his straw hat on the table beside him, he realized he had to make a decision soon. Enough time had been spent on this bus. Enough troubles had muddled through his head, and only taking action could bring back a feeling of sanity.

Back in the bus, the memories flooded his mind, memories he wished to forget—summers in the hay field, autumns setting the oat shocks until his arms burned, mornings getting up at five to milk, and, of course, memories of Eliza.

He let his head rest against the back of the seat. The whine of the motor, as it tackled another steep incline, barely registered with him. He could only think of Eliza. In the summer, her face turned bronze from her work outside on the farm. In winters it turned a golden blush—softer but as beautiful a face as he had ever seen.

He had never looked at another girl after meeting Eliza. There was simply no need. She was perfect. Her smile left him dizzy. Yes, Eliza was the one girl for him.

But now he had to struggle to force his thoughts of her to cease. He forced himself to look at the mountains passing by. He gazed at the glorious splendor, but it was all in vain. No mountains, however awesome, could compete with the memory of Eliza.

Yet, there was a chance, he told himself, if he could only find a way to forget her now. And that would mean a new start. And so he had boarded the Greyhound and would simply go until he figured it was time to stop. His ticket was good for fifteen days of bus travel, for wherever he wanted to go. But this was it. He would get off at the next town. Perhaps there he could find his new start and relief from his pain.

Surely a town would appear soon. He glanced out the window as the smatter of houses thickened. *Where am I?* He quickly pulled the map of Montana out of his backpack and searched. He hadn't been paying attention, and so he couldn't be sure where he was on the map.

The Greyhound slowed as more houses appeared, sputtered with one more valiant effort, and then leveled off. This was obviously a main street of some town of which he had missed the name. He saw a few passengers in rows ahead of him get their things together. They clearly knew where they were.

When the bus pulled up to the station, several passengers got off. So did Jake, leaving his straw hat on the seat.

At the bottom step, he paused. There may be Amish communities even in Montana. He might need the hat after all. He made his way back through the bus and squashed the hat vigorously onto his head. This might be a new life for him, but he would not leave his old life entirely behind—only the memory of Eliza Brunstetter.

He stood and looked around for the name of the town. Somewhere on the building there ought to be a name. His eyes found it quickly, and he spoke the word out loud, "Libby." What a strange name for a town, but it would have to do. His mind was finally made up.

Resolutely he picked up his backpack and headed for the depot.

At the ticket counter, the attendant was very helpful. "The Sandman Motel," he said, "is the best place to stay. Are you staying long?"

Jake nodded and then asked, "Any jobs available in the area?"

"Well, now," the attendant said, "about the best place to start would be the Forest Service. The Kootenai National Forest is close by. They are always looking for adventurous people. You look like you might be up for an adventure."

He grinned weakly. "I don't know about that, but I will need a job. Where is this Forest Service office?"

"Right down on highway 2, going south out of town. You'll come to the motel first and then the Forest Service office building."

"Can I walk there?" he asked.

"Sure. It's not that far."

"Suits me," Jake said. "Thanks for the help."

Jake felt good about his decision. In fact, he began to laugh a little. Who would have thought that it would be in Montana when he could laugh again. With brisk steps he turned south as directed. To his right, across the plain where the town was situated, there rose those majestic mountains, their heights soaring skyward. He paused for a long look. This certainly wasn't the flat farmlands of Iowa. Somehow those mountains called to him.

Guided by the sign's gaudy bright letters, Jake easily found the Sandman Motel. The West was definitely different, he decided. Inside, his feet jerked to a halt at the giant grizzly bear head mounted on the wall. The mouth was wide open. Its white teeth were exposed in an angry snarl.

The man behind the counter laughed. "New in the area, I take it."

Jake nodded. "That I am. How much per night to stay here?"

The man quoted him the rate, a number he thought was too high.

"What are your weekly rates?" he asked.

The man shook his head.

"I'll take a room for one night, and then we'll see from there."

"Sign here," the manager said after he handed back the paperwork, "and write your license plate number here."

"No car," he said. "Came in on the Greyhound."

"Just your name, then."

For a moment he hesitated. Then, glancing down, he signed his name slowly on the indicated line—Jake Byler.

"So where is the Forest Service office?" Jake asked after the man handed him the key.

"Just down the block. Can't miss it."

Jake nodded his thanks. "Think I'll go up and see them once I get settled in."

"The best of luck to you, then. They're looking for young men this time of the year."

"That's what I heard." Jake picked up his backpack. "Thanks again."

"No problem. Let me know if you need anything."

"I'll do that," Jake said and went out the door to find his room. The hotel room was nothing fancy, but it would do. He opened the closet door and hung up his few items of clothing. Then he set off for the Forest Service office.

⊠

"Most certainly, young man," the smiling, uniformed Forest Ser-vice representative said. "We do have a few immediate job openings if you're willing to do lonely work."

"I'm willing. What's the job?" Jake asked. "Would it by any chance be on those mountains?" He pointed west out the window toward the range of peaks topped with snow.

"Oh, the Cabinet Mountains?" The uniformed man grinned. "You *do* want loneliness, don't you? Well, at present there's a position open on our eastern ridge fire lookout post. Almost to the top of the mountain… nice cabin there. As long as you work there, it can be yours. We rent them out in the off fire season."

"Sounds good," he nodded. "How do I apply for the job?"

"No questions about pay?" The representative lifted his eyebrows.

"No. I'll take the job," Jake said.

"Not so fast," the representative said, laughing. "All applicants have to fill out an application. Fill this out," he said, handing Jake a clipboard with official forms attached, "and we'll go from there."

Jake took the clipboard with him, pulled the pen out from the top, and found a seat by the front door. Carefully he wrote his name on the top of the application. When it came to his former occupation, he wrote in *farmer*. When he was asked for the phone number of the closest living relative, he wrote in the number of the Sandman Motel and a name from home. He hoped the man wouldn't notice.

He handed in the completed form, and the representative took it with a smile. "Well, this looks great. We'll need to take your measurements for a uniform. Let me process this—we have to do a background check on you—then come back tomorrow, and you should be all set. We'll give you some basic training, and in a few days you should be on your post. Where are you staying?"

"The Sandman Motel."

"Write the room phone number down, please."

He copied it onto the paper thrust toward him and carefully kept his eyes from the completed form beside him. If the Forest Service representative noticed the same numbers on each paper, he chose not to mention it.

Kathy woke Hannah the next morning at the usual time. The girl's mood was still subdued, but she seemed a bit better. But was she ready to resume a normal life?

Hannah seemed to anticipate the question. "I can do breakfast, Mother, just like always," she said without any emotion.

"Are you sure? I can manage without you for a few mornings. You've been through a lot."

"No, I want to help," Hannah said. She took her apron out of the closet in the hall and fell into the regular routine of breakfast preparation. She heated the water for oatmeal while Kathy fried the bacon. As soon as there was enough grease from Kathy's pan, Hannah heated the egg skillet.

Kathy glanced at Hannah more than once and then let it go. With her doubts pushed aside, Kathy proceeded with the day's work, occasionally and silently checking on Hannah. She seemed to still be a bit numb and performed her tasks as if she felt nothing.

By evening Hannah's dullness began to worry Kathy. Tears were one thing, but the silence that hung over her daughter, like the ice from a glacier, troubled her even more.

After everyone had gone to bed, she brought up the subject with Roy. "Hannah's not doing well. She just walks around like her world has ended."

"What do you think we should do?" he said as he set his Bible aside.

Kathy sighed. "I might try talking with her some more, but I'm afraid I won't get anywhere. She's lost in her own world, a world of guilt for something that really wasn't her fault at all."

"At least try," Roy suggested. "It's really strange that she's taking it so hard. I know she shouldn't have snuck out with him, but it was only once. That is, if that was the truth."

"You're not doubting her, are you?" Kathy asked.

Roy sighed. "Let's just say, I have no reason to doubt her…that I know of. I haven't heard anything…talk and such. If she had gone out with him, someone would surely have seen them."

"They could have stayed away from people," Kathy said. "Surely she's not lying to us?"

"The only thing that makes me wonder is the ruckus the few weeks before. Shep did a lot of barking. Maybe something was going on. Even then, that's hardly enough to get so deeply attached to a boy."

"Maybe she just fell hard for him," Kathy said. "But I still think guilt is at the bottom of this…that and her lost love. And I don't mean the boy…her idea of love."

"Could be," Roy agreed. "But guilt? Why is she feeling guilty? She barely knew the boy. She talked to him at the hospital and once in town. Then she sneaks out with him—once that we know of. And then she did the right thing when he wanted to take liberties with her. How can that cause such intense guilt?"

"I have no idea. It's beyond me, really. I just know the girl is troubled and we need to give her some help."

"We can pray," Roy said as he reached for his Bible. He opened the pages, found the passage he wanted, and read it out loud, "Call unto me, and I will answer thee, and shew thee great and mighty things, which thou knowest not."

"You think that He has an answer for us?" Kathy asked.

"I think we ought to believe that God will do what He says He will do."

"Well, let's call on Him then," Kathy said.

Roy nodded. "Yes, we can do it now in prayer, but let's do it during the day whenever we feel the burden to do so. God is not restricted to set times of prayer."

Kathy nodded in agreement as she knelt by the couch. Roy did the same by his recliner.

Twelve

When, by the end of the week, Hannah was still not herself, Kathy decided it was time for a long talk. Miriam had taken the buggy into town, Isaac was outside choring, and Emma was in school. The wash was on the line, flapping slightly in the mid-morning breezes.

Hannah had helped with the household chores as she usually did but seemed emotionally numb. Between the two of them, the house settled into silence.

"We need to talk," Kathy said as she pulled two chairs up to the kitchen table.

"I don't want to talk, Mom," Hannah said, her voice flat. "It won't do any good."

Kathy ignored her. "We have to start somewhere." She paused, uncertain how to start. "Can you tell me how you're feeling?"

Hannah's voice was still flat as she said, "Just dead inside, I guess. I'm to blame for Peter's death. I know I am."

"No," Kathy protested. "It was wrong for you to sneak out, but it wasn't your fault Peter drove away too fast. He did that on his own."

Hannah hung her head, but Kathy saw no sign of any tears.

"You weren't out with him more than you told us...were you?" Kathy asked.

Hannah shook her head.

"You're sure?"

Hannah nodded this time.

"Then I just don't understand why you're taking this so hard," Kathy said. "It's so strange to me."

"It's also my dream," Hannah said in a monotone, not looking up.

Deep in her own thoughts, Kathy almost missed this explanation but glanced up when she realized what Hannah had said.

"Your dream? You dreamed he would die?"

Hannah shook her head. "My dream of what love would be like. If I hadn't had it, I wouldn't have gone out with him, and Peter would still be alive."

"But," Kathy said and then paused, "a lot of people have dreams of what love is like."

"Do their dreams get people killed?" Hannah asked.

"No," Kathy said, "of course not."

"Then why did mine?"

"Tell me about this dream," Kathy said.

Hannah didn't know how to begin. Her eyes, already clouded over, became even darker.

Kathy waited.

In the silence, Hannah finally spoke, "I read this poem about love."

Kathy raised her hand to stop her. "Hold it right there. A poem— you read a poem. Can you get me the poem so I know what you're talking about?"

"Yes," Hannah said and rose to run upstairs to her room. She returned quickly and gave the piece of paper to her mother.

Kathy read it slowly.

"Well," she ventured when she was finished, "there's really nothing wrong with it. Idealistic, yes, but we all want someone to love us like this. What happened after the poem?"

Hannah looked relieved that her poem had survived her mom's scrutiny. She took a deep breath. "I then started thinking of who could fit this love that I wanted."

"You mean who could give it to you?"

Hannah shrugged. "Something like that. Mostly who it could be."

"And you came up with Peter?"

Hannah stared at the wall. "Not that I just picked him. I had feelings for him—feelings that seemed to be what the poem was talking about. So I was certain he was the one."

"So you think that if you hadn't had the dream, you wouldn't have snuck out with him?"

Hannah nodded. "I would have listened to Dad, but I thought the dream must have been right and Dad was wrong."

"Love between a man and a woman is wonderful," Kathy admitted. "We just have to put right and wrong *first*...before our feelings about love. You must remember that."

"I don't want to dream anymore," Hannah stated simply, still without any emotion.

"You must wait and let God bring you the right person," Kathy continued.

"I suppose so," Hannah said, her voice indifferent. "Following the dream didn't do me any good. I don't want to feel that way again."

"I don't think that's the right attitude either," Kathy protested. "Love between a married man and woman has many wonderful feelings."

"It's more trouble than good," Hannah said, a little emotion creeping into her voice.

Kathy decided the conversation had gone far enough in this direction. "What about your relationship with God. Are you bitter toward Him?"

"No," Hannah said, "just sick of myself."

"Maybe this is an opportunity to renew your dedication to Him," Kathy suggested. "You gave your heart to Him when you were younger. Now might be the time for a fresh commitment."

Hannah agreed with a nod but said nothing.

"Maybe even baptism," Kathy ventured. "What about a new—perhaps more mature—beginning with God and then with the church?"

"Do you think God wants me...after this?"

"Of course," Kathy said. "He loves all of us."

"Maybe if I told Him I would stop dreaming, He might forgive me. What do you think?"

Tears stung Kathy's eyes. "You shouldn't be thinking things like that—not at all."

"I'm an awful person," Hannah said. "I wanted what I wanted, and now Peter is dead."

Kathy got up and put her arm around Hannah's shoulder, but Hannah didn't return her hug.

"I will tell God I am so sorry," Hannah said, her eyes still blank. "Then He might not blame it all on Peter."

Kathy stroked her face gently. "Hannah, you shouldn't be thinking such things. Peter is in the hands of God. He will judge righteously. You must not think that He won't."

Hannah just whispered, "I'm so sorry."

Kathy held her, expecting tears to start at any moment, but they didn't. That seemed even worse to her, but how to help her, that was the question. "God will take care of you," Kathy said, releasing Hannah. "I'll talk to your dad about this. Perhaps he knows what to do."

"You don't have to bother Dad," Hannah said as she rose from her chair. "He has enough on his mind."

That alarmed Kathy again, and she considered Hannah's words as she began mixing the ingredients to make the bread.

They bumped along on the rough forest road as the jeep climbed the mountain. "It's beautiful up here," Jake's escort said, his voice enthusiastic. "We'd all love it more if it weren't so lonely."

Jake nodded and agreed for the sake of agreement. His basic training was over, and he was in the forest green uniform ready to go to work at his outpost. His hair, though, he wore in the traditional Amish fashion. That would not change.

His escort shifted into first gear, and the jeep lurched forward again. *That's something I wish were possible, a driver's license*, Jake thought as they bounced along. For now he doubted he would ever veer that far from his heritage and so would have to depend on others to drive him around.

"Beautiful," he said out loud to make conversation. Below them was the full expanse of the valley in which Libby, Montana, was located. The view cheered him like little had in weeks. Again he felt this was where he was supposed to be. He was sure of it.

"Ever been to the mountains before?" his escort asked.

"Nope," he said.

"Where're you from?"

"Iowa."

"Kind of flat, right?"

He grinned. "Mostly cows and farmland."

"You'll like this, then."

To this Jake nodded. As the jeep bounced violently again, his escort swerved away from the edge of a sheer drop-off.

"We're fine," his escort reassured him and jerked the wheel toward the other side of the mountain.

Jake only smiled, refusing to be afraid.

"I had a talk with Hannah today," Kathy said to Roy as they settled in for the evening, the stillness of the house all around them.

Roy glanced up from his Amish newspaper. "Yes?"

"The girl is really troubled," Kathy said. "She needs something more than what we're giving her."

"We're praying," Roy reminded her.

"It may require doing something more," Kathy said.

"Did you find out what's causing her sense of guilt? It still seems much too great for the circumstances."

"Partly," Kathy said. "It has to do with what she thought was love. Now I think she's become disillusioned with the idea of love."

"That could happen—considering her crush on Peter," Roy allowed.

"It's more than that," Kathy said. "She thought it was the real thing. She's a young girl, Roy. I remember being her age and wanting to love someone—and have someone love me—in the right way."

"Did you tell her that the right way involves a decent boy…not just someone who can sweet-talk her?"

"No, not today," Kathy said. "That's another conversation. Her heart is what concerns me at the moment. It's not just broken—that would be one thing—but she has lost hope. That's what seems so serious to me."

"She can find a good Amish boy anywhere," Roy ventured. "It shouldn't be that hard. She's good-looking and capable. I don't think she has anything to worry about."

"That's not what I mean," Kathy said. "Plenty of boys will want her. Her own feelings are the problem, and I don't think this is something that will just go away by itself. The girl is truly hurting."

Roy acknowledged that with a turn of his head. "Did you ask her about joining the church? Maybe this would be a good time. It might help in the healing process."

"I did, and she agreed."

"Well, then, let's try that. She can join the next instruction class."

"I think she needs something more than even that," Kathy said gently.

Roy stopped, his hand halfway to the paper, and waited.

"What would you think about sending her to my sister in Montana for a visit?"

"Yes," Roy said, nodding, "that small Amish community they helped start a while back. They're still not that stable, though, are they?"

"They have a minister and bishop now," Kathy said. "Anyway, Betty keeps writing all the time…about how beautiful the country is out there."

"Poor too," Roy added.

"Yes, but they also can't get much hired help. It's just too expensive. Betty mentioned in her last letter how surprised they've been with the demand for the riding horses they have. Betty started it as a sideline, but so many tourists stop there during the summer it could almost keep someone busy full-time."

"And you're thinking Hannah could help?"

"Yes, free of charge, of course, unless Betty thinks they can pay her something. But, as you said, they're poor. I would be happy if Hannah could just work for her room and board. Then, if this helps her get over her depression, we would be more than paid back."

"What kind of help would she receive there that we couldn't give her here?"

Kathy wasn't sure how to explain it but tried. "A change of scenery, a different church, maybe. A chance to meet new people. Oh, I don't know. It just might be the thing to do."

"When are you thinking this would happen?"

"There's another van load going up in two weeks. Some ministers plan to visit, plus several other couples who are just curious are going along. Mr. Bowen is taking them."

"You have it all planned out, then?" Roy said with a knowing smile.

"Not really," Kathy said, "just thinking out loud. What do you think?"

"I think we should see if she wants to go. If she does and if there's room in the van, I don't think it would cost too much for her share. How expensive are the motels on the way out?"

"I think Betty said they space the drives each day to stay at Amish or Hutterite communities in the evenings. It's about a three-day drive, two nights, she said."

Roy nodded. "Maybe this is the answer. Ask Hannah in the morning."

"I will," Kathy said, glad to have agreement on the matter.

Thirteen

This was to be Jake's first full day of fire watching. He stood on the fire deck in his forest-green colored uniform, the state of Montana insignia attached firmly above his left shirt pocket, and breathed in deeply the brisk morning air. *What a life,* he thought. One he'd never dreamed he'd see.

He raised his binoculars to his eyes and took long sweeps up and down the slopes and the valleys in search of possible fires. The beauty of the mountain range took his breath away. He continued his watch over the terrain, and at mid morning he noticed a slim column of smoke. Was his mind playing tricks on him?

As he brought the binoculars to bear on the base of the forest floor, as he had been trained, there was no mistake. He saw the clear lick of red flames spreading along the hillside. This was no contained campfire. Jake hurried inside, clicked the microphone on his radio, and stated, "Fire station zero-seven-five to base. Zero-seven-five to base."

"Zero-seven-five, come in," came the response.

"I have a small fire, two o'clock to my station. Appears to be about two miles out."

"Roger that, will be right on it," the voice on the radio responded.

Jake watched through his binoculars as the flames licked the base of a large tree and caught the lower branches on fire. From there it spread quickly upward until the whole tree was engulfed.

He swept his binoculars sideways, toward where he figured the help would come from, and caught sight of a dust cloud. It slowly materialized into a pickup truck with fire-fighting equipment. When the vehicle arrived on the scene, two men scrambled out, quickly cut a perimeter around the area, and lit backfires that burst out in streaks of flame.

An hour later, only a small section of burnt woods was visible in his lens. As the truck drove back toward town, Jake kept a careful watch on the slopes. At the end of the day, he had seen no other fires.

◈

When her mother approached Hannah the next morning with a suggestion that she visit Aunt Betty in Montana, Hannah was surprised that she found it agreeable. They discussed it as they washed the breakfast dishes and put them away. Miriam and Emma were sent outside to work so Kathy could speak with Hannah in private.

"Maybe it would help me forget," Hannah said hopefully.

"You need to heal," Kathy said. "I don't think forgetting is as much of a problem."

"I just never want to dream again," Hannah said as she carefully lifted the breakfast plates into the cupboard. "Never again."

"We all have to love," Kathy said. "What you felt was natural."

"Not in the way I did," Hannah replied. "That was so wrong. Do you think God will forgive me in Montana? Perhaps better than He can here? Perhaps He'd be closer to me near Aunt Betty's mountains?"

"He's close to us right here," Kathy assured her. "But we want you to go because we think it might do you good…and Betty could use the help, I'm sure."

"Keeping house?" Hannah couldn't think what other work might be there.

"No," Kathy said. "It's Betty's horse-riding business that you would be helping with."

Hannah's eyes brightened for the first time in days.

"I'll write Betty today," Kathy said. "She'll get the letter in time to write back if for some reason she doesn't want you to come. But I'm sure she'll want you. You'll be working for room and board so there shouldn't be a problem. In summers they really get busy with the rides on the farm. They have just the two horses, if I remember correctly."

Hannah felt relief for the first time in days.

"When will we know for sure?" she asked.

"I'll ask Mr. Bowen this morning. He should know if there's still room in the van."

They continued with the dishes in silence. The only sounds were the swish of the soapy water and the occasional clink of dishes. Kathy left around ten to talk with Mr. Bowen. She returned with the news that two spots were still available in the van, one of which Hannah could have.

***

Betty's letter arrived the day before the van was to leave. She expressed great delight in the idea of Hannah's visit.

So it was that Hannah boarded the van early on a Wednesday morning and headed for the distant land of Montana.

Kathy had read the letter aloud to the whole family.

> *Christian greetings from the mountain lands of Montana.*
>
> *We have received your welcome news of Hannah's desire to visit. Of course, she can come. With her skill with horses, she can take care of the riders all summer. We might even get another horse. The extra income would be welcome, of course. As you know, money is tight around here. Thanks again for your offer of Hannah's help. We will put her up to the best of our ability.*
>
> *With love,*
> *Your sister Betty*

***

The van was loaded with Hannah's suitcase, and she was settled on the backseat. Beside her were Lois and Elmer Zook and Lois's sister,

Ruth, all of whom Hannah knew well from her church district. Elmer and Lois, it was rumored, were interested in moving to Montana.

Minster Alvin, the one who preached at Peter's funeral, sat in the passenger seat beside Mr. Bowen. His wife was in the row behind him with her sister and her sister's husband.

Occupying the third row was an older couple whose son and his wife had moved to Troy, Montana. They were lonesome to see their grandchildren and wanted to see the West again. With them was Naomi, the wife's widowed sister, who offered Hannah a ready smile when she climbed into the van.

There followed two days of hard driving, as much as Mr. Bowen could take. He drove up through Chicago and then west onto Interstate 90. During the second night, Mr. Bowen almost couldn't make the designated stopping point at one of the Hutterite communities north of Billings.

With Minister Alvin's encouragement, Mr. Bowen persevered, and they finally arrived exhausted. He requested that he be allowed to retire early, and he even turned down a supper the Hutterites had quickly prepared at the common eating hall.

"I need sleep more than food," Mr. Bowen explained. The hosts willingly acquiesced and showed him to a room reserved for visitors. They invited the married couples to stay in small cabins while Hannah stayed with one of the young girls who introduced herself as Jane.

"I hear you're from Indiana," the girl said.

Hannah replied, "Yes, we live just outside of Nappanee. I'm going to spend the summer with my Aunt Betty in Troy, Montana."

"Is she Amish?" the girl asked.

"Yes," Hannah said. "She's part of a small Amish community in the mountains. She has horses she rents out in the summertime. I'll be helping her."

"Not a lot of mountains around here," the girl said wryly, "except way off in the distance."

"It is pretty flat," Hannah agreed. The big sky had awed her during the drive. She saw great sweeping views of grasslands that seemed to go on forever outside the van window. "Big sky country, right? Is that what you call it?"

Jane nodded.

"Have you lived here all your life?"

"I was born here," the girl said, "and I stayed here. Where else is there to go? You have to have a good reason to travel since the colony pays for it."

A piece of embroidery on the dresser caught Hannah's eye. On the bottom of the piece, the name *Jane* was stitched in fine, exquisite lettering.

"Did you sew that?" she asked. "It's beautiful."

Jane nodded. "Mom taught my sisters and me. They're all married now."

"You do nice work." Hannah ran her fingers lightly over the embroidered piece. "Do you have horses in the colony?"

"Lots of them," Jane said. "The boys ride them mostly for work."

"Can you girls ride them too?"

"Yes, when there's a chance. Some of the girls like to ride, and some don't."

"Do you?" Hannah asked. "It looks like you could ride here for days and never stop."

"Sometimes," Jane grinned. "We girls are kept pretty busy with the housework. We all have daily chores. There's not much time for things like horseback riding. Well," Jane said, motioning with her hand, "maybe we should get to bed. You must be tired."

Hannah agreed, and they turned out the lights. Outside the window Hannah could see the expanse of the open sky, now flooded with stars. The sight so drew her, she had to get out of bed to gaze at it for a long moment.

"It's beautiful," Jane whispered from her bed.

"Yes," Hannah said, "very beautiful. I hope the mountains will be as wonderful."

"I wouldn't know," Jane said. "This is about as good as it gets."

"Perhaps I should stay here," Hannah teased.

Jane laughed, and Hannah returned to her bed. Moments later she was under the covers and fast asleep.

The morning sun had risen in its glory. Its light streamed full against the side of the Cabinet Mountains. Jake was up early and at his post although signs of fire at this hour were unlikely. Only later, when the mist rose from the ground, could he spot the haze of smoke from any burning fires. An occasional campfire could still smolder from the night before, but he was now trained to notice those differences.

Around mid morning an English girl, accompanied by who he assumed to be her family, came up the trail. Part of his job was to give short tours to hikers who stopped by his station. This was an effort in public relations that was well worth its weight in gold, his supervisor had told him.

Jake was at ground level at the moment the group appeared. Perhaps that was why the full impact of her face wasn't lost on him. They were already close when he first saw her, and he jerked back, the similarities so shook him. She could have been Eliza's sister, but that wasn't possible. This was an English girl.

Unable to take his eyes off her, he blushed with feelings of shame and anger. Memories he had tried to keep buried rushed back with their full strength, undiminished by time or distance.

With great effort Jake managed to croak out a "good morning" to the tall, clean-shaven man in the lead.

"Good morning," the man replied as he extended a muscular hand to Jake. "Are you open for tours?"

"Certainly," Jake said. "Would you like to climb the tower?" He wished intensely this guy's daughter wasn't with him. His day had just been ruined.

"I do," the man announced. "Anyone else up to climbing the tower?"

Jake hoped they all would go and he could be away from her face and the intense look in her eyes. When she shook her head, he knew his wish wasn't to be granted. She had decided to stay on the ground along with who must have been her sister and mother.

Awkwardly Jake stood there, but they ignored him while they conversed among themselves. Her closeness and her indifference to him only added to his feelings of anger. From where he stood, he could see the side of her face. It had the same curve to it, the same outline of the lips, and the same long dark eyelashes. Only slight differences kept him from the obviously impossible conclusion that someone else had also left the Amish.

Only he hadn't left the Amish, Jake reminded himself. At least he hadn't in his own mind. He was just trying to get away from the pain, not the life he once knew. In fact, the old life was what he really wanted—a life that had all come to a halt that Sunday evening when Eliza broke the news to him.

In her father's house, where they had sat on the couch so many times over the years, she had told him. Words were spoken while the gasoline lantern hissed near the ceiling. She had simply and without any expression of regret said that it was over.

"But the wedding is in three months," he had managed to get out of his parched throat.

"I know," she had said. "That's why I am calling it off…while there is still time."

"But I thought we cared for each other," Jake had said.

"We do," she said, still without any emotion, her eyes avoiding his now tearful ones, "just not in this way. I'm sure you will find someone else—someone better suited to you."

Later he was thankful he had had enough sense to leave when he did. He found his horse in the dark and drove his buggy out of her driveway without any lights on. It wasn't until he was halfway home that he even noticed he had forgotten the lights. Two weeks later she dated his cousin for the first time.

The tramp of feet interrupted Jake's thoughts as the men descended the tower's wooden stairs. "It's a nice view," the man announced to the women.

"We can see it from here," his wife told him with a smile. "We're perfectly alright."

As the group headed back down the trail, Jake noticed that one of the young men whom he had assumed was a brother took the girl's hand in his in a clearly unbrotherly gesture.

He glanced away from the sight. The hurt in his heart cut even deeper, and his anger smoldered against the unfairness of it all. *I'll never trust a girl like that again*, he told himself. *Never*.

Fourteen

The next morning, Mr. Bowen insisted on leaving the Hutterite community early. Rising early, the travelers were able to eat breakfast at the eating house with the first round served to the men. Ham, bacon, eggs, and pancakes were all eaten at the long communal table. Hannah had never seen such a thing in all her life. *Different,* she thought, but she supposed it worked if you grew up with the custom.

The sun came up as the van full of Amish passengers drove away from the colony. Billings was an hour away, and two hours beyond that, the mountains started. Hannah sat transfixed, watching the view through the windows of the van. The scenery was so different from Indiana. Mountain after mountain appeared from the flat country and faded away, and then more appeared even taller than the ones before.

Sometime in the early afternoon, Mr. Bowen took the Thompson Falls exit off of the Interstate and drove up highway 200. From there they drove the west side of the Cabinet Mountains on highway 56 and arrived in Troy by four thirty.

"Do you have the directions to your aunt's place?" Mr. Bowen asked Hannah as he pulled to a stop in front of the town hall. Its gray stone front was offset by the colors of the American and Montana state flags flapping in the breeze on a tall flagpole.

"Yes," Hannah said as she handed the paper to him.

Mr. Bowen studied the directions and then proceeded north out of town. A mile or so later, he turned into a driveway and past a mailbox fashioned like a mini log home with *Mast* printed plainly on the top.

The house looked rustic with its unpainted, rough-sawn log siding. The barn had the same kind of siding. Two horses stood at the rail fence nearby.

Hannah wasn't sure this was her aunt's home. She hesitated, and Mr. Bowen asked her, "Do you think it's the right place?"

Alvin said, "There are no electric or phone lines around. It could be the right place...unless the English live rough around here too."

"I doubt it," Mr. Bowen ventured and said to Hannah, "Why don't you go to the door and see if this is the right place."

Hannah climbed slowly out of the van. Once she was out of the van, the full smell and feel of this new land hit her. She could hear the rush of water flowing heavily and fast in the distance. Trees were everywhere. Through the branches were the outlines of mountains surrounding her on all sides. Timidly she walked toward the house.

To Hannah's great relief, her Aunt Betty opened the door, just then, her white apron dusted with flour. "I thought I heard a van drive up, but with all the sounds around here, you can't be sure. We're so glad you're finally here! Where are your bags, Hannah?"

"In the van. We weren't sure this was the right place."

"Oh, it surely is," Betty said. "I know we don't look like the Amish places back East. But this is the West, and things are a bit different. It took a little getting used to for me too. But we just love it now. Welcome to Montana." Betty wrapped her arms around Hannah in a tight hug.

Betty then approached the van and shook hands with all of the others in turn. "I'm so glad to see all of you. It seems as if it has been years since we've had visitors although I'm sure it hasn't been. If you had the time, I would start with the questions now, but I guess they can wait till Sunday. I suppose everyone is in a hurry to get to their places so I won't hold you up."

"Yes," Mr. Bowen ventured, "I should get these people dropped off. It's been a long trip for everybody."

"I suppose you're exhausted yourself, having to drive so far," Betty said.

"I am," Mr. Bowen agreed, "although today's drive wasn't quite as long as yesterday's."

Naomi smiled from her seat in the second row. "He did real well. I haven't had a better driver in a long time."

Mr. Bowen nodded his thanks.

"Well, like I said," Betty repeated, "you can tell me all the news on Sunday."

She turned to Hannah as the van pulled out and gushed, "So what do you think of the West?"

"I haven't had much time to think of anything else," Hannah said. "It's absolutely beautiful—so different."

"Do you think you'll like it?" Betty asked without much apprehension in her voice and wrapped Hannah in another big hug. "It's so good to have you here."

"I'm glad to be here. It's so big...all around." Hannah motioned with her hand.

"That it is," Betty agreed. "God must have really used His imagination when He made this country."

"You think so?" Hannah asked, stirred by the thought.

"Yes," Betty said confidently. "As I have said to Steve, the East is made for the practical people. You know, for the ones who make the money. It's for those who keep the country running, but the West is made for people who *dream*."

Hannah gasped. "But I didn't come out here to dream. I came to help you."

"I'm sure you will," Betty said. "Now let's show you your room, and then we can look at the horses. Supper is waiting to be made after that. Dreaming will be on your own time."

Hannah frowned. "There won't be much dreaming for me. I came out to get over dreaming. I want to be practical—to work and help you. That's what I came for."

"There will be time for both," Betty said as Hannah picked up her suitcase and followed Betty inside. "Now, let's go inside, and you can see your Uncle Steve and your cousins."

Jake decided that it was time to update his folks on where he was. They had all gone to the Greyhound bus station to see him off, but he had been clear from the start that he didn't know when he would be back or where he was going.

He recalled his mother's tearful final words to him, "Just stay in the Amish communities."

She would want to know by now what bishop he had reported to. The fact that he had not done so yet would not be welcome news, but there was still time to do something about that. Since he arrived he had learned of a small community of Amish in Troy, just west of Libby. He hadn't yet made any attempt to join a church service—partly because of his job, but mostly because he didn't want to be reminded of anything to do with Eliza.

The gathering of his kind on a Sunday morning could bring back a rush of unwanted memories. He wanted to forget, but he also wanted to stay Amish. Jake wasn't sure how to make that all work together. He had kept his Amish clothing but didn't wear them on his job. He imagined that could be explained satisfactorily. Although as a member of the church, he might be required to make a "confession" because uniforms were not allowed by most bishops.

Jake truly wasn't sure if wearing his uniform crossed the line, but he considered a confession a serious matter, one that would require him to admit his error and beg forgiveness of God and the church. Afterward the church would take a vote. As grave as that might be, it would be much better than a "knee confession," which was required for more serious offenses.

Jake had been baptized in preparation for his wedding, and the thought of that now sent bitter feelings through him. Yet, it was time to let his parents hear from him.

He got out his paper and pen and wrote.

Dear Mom and Dad,

I arrived in Montana and have been working for the Forest Service since then. The work is wonderful, and the scenery is beautiful all around here.

His pen faltered. Did he have enough courage to tell them what they really wanted to know? He gripped the pen tightly and tried.

There is an Amish community close by, but I haven't been there yet. I have no plans to become English. Just thought I'd mention that. Please understand that I need some time alone. If Deacon Henry asks about me, you can tell him that.

Again he paused and wondered if he had said enough. He decided he had not and continued to write.

If I would decide to come home today, I would look exactly the same.

Those were code words for his haircut, and they would know what he meant. Few identifying features are as guarded by Amish males as their haircuts. Clothing can be changed in a few minutes, but cut hair takes months to grow out.

Thanks for your understanding on this matter. I will try to be at church at the Amish fellowship in Troy this Sunday.

Then Jake signed his name, addressed the envelope, and dropped it into the outside box where it would be taken into Libby later and sent out in the mail.

❖

Hannah woke the first morning of her stay in the West and felt more rested than she had in a long time. It was still dark outside when Betty called from the bottom of the stairs, "Time to get up, Hannah."

She answered in a muffled voice and got dressed quickly. She had lit the kerosene lamp on the dresser in her room but noticed no light in the hall. She figured the light was supposed to stay in the room and so she blew it out and managed to find her way down the sawn-log stairway without tripping. Hannah opened the stair door into the living room and found it dark except for the light from a gas lantern hissing near the kitchen ceiling.

"We get up early around here in the summertime," Betty informed her from the kitchen. "Winter's a little different. Now it's breakfast at five thirty. Steve has to be up by dawn because his ride to his job on the mountain comes at six."

Hannah rubbed her eyes, washed her hands at the sink, and got busy without much instruction from Betty. Her mother's sister seemed to have much of the same breakfast routine. Hannah cracked eggs into the pan on the stove and then flipped them at exactly the right time, which brought a look of admiration from Betty. "Your mother taught you well. She always was the best cook around the house."

"She tried," Hannah acknowledged. "Well it looks like you're learning," Betty said as she lifted the bacon out of the pan. "As soon as it's daylight, I'll show you how we do the horseback riding. I'm sure you noticed the horses yesterday, but with the English riders, it's a little different. You have to follow a set of rules with them in case of injury and such. We have to be careful."

Hannah nodded as she lifted the last of the eggs out of the frying pan.

Steve came through the kitchen door and took a chair. "Breakfast smells good," he said. "Good morning to you, Hannah."

"Good morning," Hannah replied, realizing at once she was very glad she had come.

"The children eat later," Betty said. "Kendra is old enough to start getting up earlier, but I just haven't started that yet."

"How old is she?" Hannah asked and searched her memory from the evening before. "Ten?"

"Eleven," Betty said. "She just turned eleven this month."

Steve glanced at Hannah from across the table. "You are about seventeen, aren't you? Any boyfriends yet?"

"Steve," Betty said, scolding him, "don't start that with her."

Neither of them noticed that Hannah had turned pale instead of the expected blush of red at the remark. They took her silence as a no. There was no boyfriend, and, of course, they knew nothing about Peter. Her mom wouldn't have written such news.

Steve chuckled. "We have several boys around here—all who are still single. There aren't as many choices as there are back East, but, still, they are a bunch of decent fellows. What we really don't have are many girls to select from. That's always a serious problem for the boys, of course."

Betty finally noticed Hannah's pale face. "Now look what you've done," she said. "You've scared the girl with these stories of our savage boys."

"I'm sorry," he said, laughing. "I'm just trying to give her some warning. You don't have to be scared, Hannah. Trust me. They don't bite."

Hannah was unable to find words, and so she said nothing. In one way it was a relief to know her mom and dad had told no one about Peter. But in another way, a great loneliness rushed over her. She wished someone did know. She wouldn't feel so alone then. Out here no one knew about Peter, the accident, or her guilt. Hannah pressed back the tears and decided it would be best to keep things so. She wanted a fresh start, after all.

Fifteen

By nine o'clock, two cars were already in the driveway.

"Looks like you'll have on-the-job training," Betty told Hannah. "I had hoped to give you more instructions first, but you'll just have to follow my lead now."

"I'm nervous," Hannah said.

"Don't be," Betty said. "It's not really hard. You read them the rules, saddle the horses, give them a map of the land, see that they mount safely, and send them off."

"I'll watch you," Hannah said.

"I'll stick with you for a few mornings, and then I'm sure you'll be fine on your own," Betty assured her.

With Hannah in tow, Betty headed for the barn. "Good morning," she said cheerfully to the two couples getting out of their cars. "Ready for some horseback riding?"

Everyone nodded and smiled.

"Well, it's first come, first served around here," Betty said. "You let me know how many horses you want and for how long."

"They were here first," the couple in the jeep admitted. "We'll see how long they take and then come back. There are things in town we can do."

"What are the rates?" the couple in the blue Mazda asked.

Betty told them.

"We'll take an hour, then, with both horses."

"I'm so sorry, we only have two horses," Betty told the other couple. "It takes fifteen minutes to saddle up and go over the basics, and then they take their hour."

"We'll be back," they said and headed back toward Troy.

"Okay, now for you," Betty told the other couple. "Let's see. First here are the rules." She rattled them off and asked about prior riding experience. Both claimed to have had some.

Hannah watched closely as Betty saddled the horses, adjusted the stirrups to fit the man and the woman, and finally directed them to the trail toward the mountain.

"We sure could use another set of horses," Betty told Hannah as they watched the two go around the bend.

As if to confirm her words, another vehicle pulled into the driveway. Hannah saw they were another young couple, this time with two children. When the man rolled down his window, Betty asked them, "Are you looking for horse rides?"

"Yes," the man said, "my wife and I were hoping to go riding. We also need a place for the children to stay for the time we're out. An Amish riding stable seemed like just the place. We used to do a lot of riding before we were married. It brings back good memories for us both."

"We would be glad to accommodate you," Betty said, "but we only have two horses, and they are both out at the moment."

"When is the next available time?" the man's wife asked.

"I don't know for sure," Betty told them with some hesitation. "We serve our customers in order on a first-come basis. The horses are already spoken for during the next hour. Then another couple has reserved them after that. I could take your names for after the second couple has finished."

"That's too bad," the man said. "Maybe we'll check back in a few hours—maybe after lunch."

"That would be fine," Betty said. "I'm so sorry."

As the car pulled out, Hannah asked, "Why don't you buy more horses?"

"That's what I was saying all last summer, but I just couldn't take care of the riding stable with two more horses and the housework too—not with the children, I can't. Kendra is of some help but not enough yet."

"Well, I'm here now," Hannah told her, "for all of the summer at least."

"Let's see how the rest of the day goes first," Betty said, nodding. "Then I'll talk about it with Steve tonight."

The rest of the day went as it had started, without sufficient horses to meet the need. Hannah caught on to the routine quickly. By late afternoon, Betty let her take care of the last riders of the day—the couple with the two small children who needed babysitting while the parents were out riding. With delight Hannah entertained the children in the barn by teaching them to play the simple Amish games she had learned as a child. When the parents returned in an hour, the eyes of the children shone, as did those of their parents.

"This has been a perfect ending to the day," the man told Hannah. "We are so grateful to you for babysitting the children." They paid Hannah the requested fee as well as a generous tip for the time she had spent with the children. She held the money tightly against her side and waved as they drove off.

When Hannah showed her aunt the extra money, Betty said, "You did real well for the first day, and they paid you for babysitting too."

"It was a lot more fun than cleaning houses," Hannah said.

After supper Betty talked with Steve in the living room. They put their heads together under the light of the gas lantern, Steve with a notepad where he scratched figures every few minutes. Thirty minutes later they had apparently made up their minds.

Steve followed Betty out to the kitchen and announced to Hannah, "Good news. We're going to buy two more horses. Even if they aren't busy all the time, it will still pay off."

"When?" Hannah asked, glad that her presence was already helping out.

"Saturday," he said. "That's the first chance I have. I shouldn't take off from my regular job for this. That would be expensive."

When Saturday arrived, Steve set out early with his horse and cart for Troy to make some phone calls. He returned before lunch to report success. By two o'clock that afternoon, a horse trailer had pulled into the driveway with two horses.

"These are perfect riding horses," the driver assured Steve. "I picked them out myself this morning. They are gentle and safe for anyone."

"What are the names?" Steve asked.

"This is Mandy," the driver said, stroking the neck of the smaller mare. Turning to the other horse, he said, "And this gelding is Prince."

Prince jerked his head at the sound of his name as if he knew he was being talked about. Hannah approached him cautiously and reached out to stroke his neck. He lowered his head as if to oblige her. She gently touched him, her eyes searching his.

He neighed, a soft, friendly sound.

"I think he likes you," the driver said.

Hannah felt as if her heart was too full and could say nothing for a long moment. Prince was like her pony, Honey, only bigger and stronger. Even Prince's face had the same contour and gentle lines.

"Looks like love at first sight," Steve said with a wink.

Hannah stroked Prince's mane. She knew with what she had already seen of him that this was a special horse.

"His name fits him," she finally managed to say.

"That it does," agreed Steve.

"Well, take care," the driver said. "It looks like everything is in order. You shouldn't have any trouble with these horses, Mr. Mast."

"Thanks for bringing them," Steve said as the driver got in his truck and pulled out of the driveway.

That same afternoon Jake Byler arrived at the home of Bishop Nisley. After a few inquiries, it had been an easy matter to find the bishop's residence. The Amish were enough of a novelty in the area that the locals seemed to know where they were located.

After the preliminary introductions, Jake had been invited to stay for supper, after which the bishop took Jake into the living room for further conversation. Jake had already guessed that Nisley was just a young bishop, in age as well as experience. This pleased him, and he expected easier treatment from a younger bishop who might not be as well versed in the rules of the church.

"So you are from Iowa?" Bishop Nisley asked.

Jake smiled inwardly. He realized that a strange Amish boy, even in full Amish dress, does not walk into an Amish community without questions. It was important that he answer those questions satisfactorily. If he had arrived on the Greyhound, straight from home, that would be one thing, but he had walked in.

Jake nodded. "Kalona."

"Is that an old church community?"

"Quite old," Jake allowed. "I was born there."

"Your grandfather's name was Simon Byler—Bishop Simon?"

Jake nodded.

"I've heard of him. He was made bishop in his late twenties, wasn't he?"

Jake nodded again, surprised at Nisley's knowledge of Amish history. Perhaps he had misjudged the man slightly.

"He was living until a few years ago, wasn't he?"

"Yes, he died in the fall of the year," Jake replied. "Now five years ago, I think."

With his lineage apparently established to Nisley's satisfaction, the bishop moved on. "How long have you been in the area?"

"A few weeks."

"This is the first that you have tried to contact us?"

"Yes." Jake decided not to explain further. It might be best to let the bishop probe where he wished.

"Why not?" The bishop didn't hesitate to ask the obvious question.

Jake took a deep breath. "At first I didn't know where any Amish churches were, but I promised my parents I would find the nearest one."

Nisley wasn't satisfied. "We're not that hard to find. Most everyone in town knows where we are."

"I know," Jake said. "I found that out when I started asking. But, you see, I really didn't want to start asking any sooner."

Nisley liked that, Jake thought. It probably sounded better to him than excuses. Amish boys weren't expected to lie.

"Are you a member at Kalona?" he asked.

"Yes," Jake answered.

"Your bishop will want to know where you are. Was there a good reason for not showing up here sooner?"

Jake felt his face blush, but he wasn't about to tell the bishop about his reason for leaving. Yet some explanation needed to be given.

"You see," Jake started, "I told my parents I needed some time away—to visit other places. They know and understand. I'm not try-ing to get away from the Amish. It just took a little while before I could contact you."

Jake's red neck was all the evidence Bishop Nisley needed, and he grinned. Obviously there was some personal issue involved. A wild Amish boy doing things against the church rules usually didn't feel much shame about it.

Nisley nodded his encouragement. "Well, I'm glad that you have come. Hopefully we'll see more of you while you're in the area."

Jake, greatly relieved, agreed. "I'll try to come down every other week at least."

"Where do you work?" Nisley asked.

"On Cabinet Mountain for the Forest Service."

Nisley gave Jake another long look and then asked, "They have to wear uniforms, don't they?"

Jake nodded and hung his head. *This one*, he thought, *will do me in for sure.*

Instead, to his surprise, Nisley let it go, apparently deciding that was a matter for his home bishop to rule on.

Sixteen

The next morning was Sunday and the need to get up early wasn't as urgent, and so Betty didn't call Hannah until six thirty. Already wide awake by then, Hannah got up, dressed, and made her way downstairs.

Betty was preparing breakfast at the stove, and so Hannah pitched in to help. Kendra soon appeared and began to set the table.

"So, are you worried about your first Sunday service?" Betty asked.

"A little," Hannah admitted. "I hardly know anyone but your family."

"Oh, you'll get to know the others fast. We're a small group and real friendly-like. We don't get visitors from the east that much. In the summers there are more, of course, and we always look forward to all of them."

"At least there will be a whole van load of other visitors, and so no one will notice me," Hannah said over the bacon.

"They'll notice," Betty allowed. "You are the only young girl—at least from what I saw in the van the other day."

"I'm not out here for *that*," Hannah said with emotion in her voice.

"Never say never," Betty chirped. "You might see someone you like."

Kendra grinned from ear to ear, but Hannah said firmly, "I'm not into that right now. No boys for me."

"Whatever you say," Betty said, unconvinced. "Just let me know if you need further information on any of the boys after the service."

Steve entered the kitchen with a morning greeting and, since breakfast appeared ready, quickly called for the morning prayer, and the meal began.

By eight thirty the Masts pulled their buggy into the driveway of the home where the service was to be held. The log siding was the same as what was on Betty and Steve's place, and Hannah wondered if everyone built with logs in Montana.

There were the usual lines of black hats and white shirts as the men and boys stood in front of the barn. The women headed up the wooden boardwalk that served as the entryway from the lane.

Hannah stepped carefully lest she trip on the rough edges and fall in her Sunday clothing. That would serve to announce her arrival in a way she least wanted. She would then, forever after, be remembered as the girl who had arrived from Indiana and had fallen flat on her face the very first Sunday.

The singing started in the usual manner as the song leader announced the number and then led out with the first bar. Hannah quickly recognized the lines and felt perfectly at home as the sound of their voices rose and fell together. Hannah kept her eyes on the floor, though, and made no attempt to look around. There were boys over on the other side of the room, and she had no desire to look at them. But that resolution lasted only until she began to feel less conspicuous. When a strong bass voice led out in the praise song, that old familiar song that is sung at every Sunday service, she glanced in his direction.

The man was someone she didn't know, obviously a local. Listening to the resonance of his nice voice somehow made her feel even more at home. She had indeed arrived among her own people.

Hannah knew she also was being watched. From where, she wasn't certain, and so she slowly searched the room. The bench two rows back from the men's front line had at least six boys on it—young boys about Isaac's age and not likely to pay her much attention. The boys on the front bench were even younger.

Further back she saw a rugged boy who looked like a logger. His arms had scars all over them. Beside him sat a younger boy, thin with a pinched face as if he hadn't seen too much good food in his lifetime. The one to his left looked like the logger's brother without the scars.

So far, so good, Hannah thought and felt herself relax. *If this is all there is to get over in the West, I won't have to fear reawakening any dreams.* A feeling of thankfulness swept over her as her gaze settled on the next two boys. God had made the road easy. Still, she couldn't identify the soothing bass voice. *Whose is it?*

As if to answer her thoughts, the singer led out again, his voice full and powerful. It seemed the voice was that of some boy beside the last one she could see. It was then that a wave of horror swept over her. Surely such a sound couldn't come from the voices of the locals she had seen. There was too much vigor, emotion, and feeling to it. Hardly ever had she heard the praise song sung this way. This singer was the maker of dreams. His voice wrapped around the room, powerful and rich, until the last notes of his lead blended with the voices of the others as they joined him. She felt a chill run through her body. *Who is this boy?*

A hefty man sat directly in front of the singer, blocking Hannah's view of him. The man's shoulders were strong and broad, those of an outdoorsman.

The sound of the next line filled the room again.

Did she want to see? *No*, she told herself, *I do not. Or do I? But it can't be avoided, and surely*, she thought, *after I've come all this way, God won't ask me to face a trial beyond my strength.*

The hefty, broad-shouldered fellow paused as the little boy next to him thumped him on his knee to tell him something. All in one motion the man bent sideways to listen, and the singer behind him became visible. Only one thought seared Hannah's mind in that one instant. *It's Peter.*

Hannah froze. In her sheer panic, she was unable to even drop her gaze, yet she knew she must control herself. This was church. Everyone could see her, and a strange girl in a strange church especially couldn't cause a scene.

This *couldn't* be Peter. She forced her eyes to look to the floor. Who then was it? Could it be his brother? She must know, and to know she must look again. Hannah raised her eyes slowly. With her heart beating wildly, she found his face again in the sea of boys and men, still visible over the hefty man's shoulder.

He was in the middle of a new lead, his face intent and focused. She stared for a moment, then slowly turned back to the songbook, and tried to resume her composure. It wasn't Peter or his brother. Her mind had played tricks on her.

Older by a year at least, he looked more somber. Peter's face never looked like that. The hair was much the same color, the outline of the face similar, yet the tilt of the head was different, and his jawline was more pronounced. Other differences became evident as she dared sneak another glance at him. He had the same wild good looks, though, and that was enough to unnerve her.

What a dummkopf *I am*, Hannah told herself. *This isn't Peter. There will never be another Peter. I must remember who I am and what I've learned. I must not dream about anyone again.* Her eyes firmly fixed on the floor, she didn't raise them again until the ministers filed down from upstairs and the preaching began.

◈

Jake had the distinct impression that someone watched him while he led out during the praise song. Being asked to lead the song as a visitor was not that unusual, but surely some people would wonder. Whatever the scrutiny, they would assume by his clothing and bearing that he was a member from some Amish church and thus qualified to lead out. Also he had arrived in Bishop Nisley's buggy, which would help. In any event, Jake decided he wouldn't worry about it. The request had been made, and he would comply and lead out in the singing. He had done so frequently at his home church.

Eliza had always told Jake that his voice was nice. That was the only thing that bothered him now, but he pushed the memory aside. She was not here, and he was determined that he would not be haunted by his memories of her.

Jake started another line and felt somehow that the watcher was not just a curious local. The intensity of the interest he felt was too much for that. Jake wanted to look around and see who this was. Yet, if he looked around during the middle of the song, it might break his concentration. Instead, he kept his mind on the page in front of him, keeping the rhythm and timing of the song in his head. The last line of the song would come soon enough, and then he could look.

He gave his all to the final lines. With its haunting, stirring cry, the last line of the last stanza pulled at one's soul. It was as if the agony of a martyr's impending death and final victory were called out for all to hear.

As the last note died away and as he settled onto a more comfortable spot on the bench, Jake allowed his eyes to lift and scan the room. He could see no one around who might have caused the sensation of being watched. All eyes seemed focused on the floor. The big broad back and suspenders of one of the locals were directly in front of him. To his left and right were the young girls, but none of them were old enough to have expressed what he felt.

That was when the local man shifted his position again. This time he stood up to take his son outside. The boy cried as if in pain and obviously needed to be taken outside lest his cries disturb the service. As the man stood, Jake saw what might have caused his feeling of being watched. Her hair was black, her skin delicate, her appearance cultured, her face somber, and her eyes were directed to the floor. What struck him the most was that this girl was beautiful but not anything like Eliza.

Jake wished she would look up and then hoped she wouldn't. *This is all wrong*, he told himself. He would just end up comparing this girl to Eliza. He wanted none of this, and yet…why was he drawn to her? He had no answer.

Finally, he decided he didn't want to know and turned his attention to the next song, which had just been announced. Girls would simply not be on his list of things to be concerned with, beautiful or not. *There is a summer of work in front of me. Why should I ever trust a girl again? Just because she's attractive? An ugly one might be better*, he thought bitterly and joined in with the song.

"I forgot to tell you we usually leave early," Betty whispered to Hannah right after the noon meal of peanut butter sandwiches, jam, pickles, and coffee.

"Sure," Hannah said and followed Betty to the washroom where they found their bonnets and shawls in the pile of women's wraps.

Hannah held the washroom door for Betty as they went outside and waited at the end of the board sidewalk till Steve pulled up in the surrey.

"The buggies look the same as at home," Hannah said.

"Oh, I suppose you're a little home-sick, aren't you?" Betty asked, her voice sympathetic.

"Yes, but not too much. I surprise myself," Hannah tried to laugh. There were actually worse aches in her heart than homesickness, but she tried hard to keep the pain off her face.

In the backseat of the buggy with Kendra and two of the children, who chatted merrily away about the day, Hannah almost could forget about Peter and that boy who had looked like him. Betty, however, didn't plan to leave the subject of Hannah's homesickness alone.

"Did you see anyone? Some boy perhaps…who reminded you of home?" Betty asked. She turned around from the front seat and gave Hannah a hopeful smile.

Steve chuckled. "Don't you women think about anything else?"

Hannah blinked hard and tried to smile. *How does Aunt Betty know?*

Betty noticed Hannah turn pale and raised her eyebrows in surprise.

"Hannah, are you feeling okay?" she asked.

Hannah simply nodded. There was no way she would tell Betty about Peter or his look-alike with the wonderful voice.

"She's tired, Mommy," Kendra offered as an explanation.

"Are we working you too hard?" Betty asked.

"No," Hannah said and laughed heartily this time. The thought of being overworked at Betty's place was ridiculous. "Guess it's just, you know, my first time in a new place."

Hannah didn't think Betty looked convinced. Likely she would bring the subject up later.

"So, did you get to talk to all the visiting men?" Betty asked Steve.

"Mostly," he said. "It was just good to have a visiting minister here. Ours are fine, but having others brings a fresh perspective, especially if they're from one of the established communities."

"I like our young church," Betty said.

"I do too," he agreed rather quickly. "I guess we don't have the problems some of them do."

There were a few minutes of silence, and then Hannah took a deep breath and gathered her courage. "Who was the boy who led the praise song?"

"I don't know," Betty said. "That's the first time I saw him. Do you know him, Steve?"

"No," Steve said, "he came with the bishop, and so he must have some stability. His name's Jake, Jake Byler, I was told. Beyond that no one seemed to know anything about him."

In the backseat, Hannah felt great relief flow over her. She would not have to see the boy every Sunday while she was here. He was also a visitor.

As they pulled in the driveway, Hannah felt Betty's eyes on her. She glanced up and smiled sweetly, but Betty had that look in her eye her mom always had when something didn't seem right to her. Clearly Betty was determined to get to the root of the matter.

Seventeen

It was already ten o'clock, and Betty was walking slowly out to the mailbox. The morning was well on its way and promised clear skies and warmth. Hannah had the first two horses out on the trail with what looked like competent riders.

Betty was amazed at how fast Hannah had caught on to how she wanted the riding stable run. She had already known how to saddle a horse, of course. The rest she had picked up quickly. Now Betty was sure the summer would be a good one for all of them, and they could certainly put the extra money to good use.

As she neared the mailbox, the thought crossed her mind, *Why did Kathy really send Hannah out here?* The thought had been in the back of her mind for a while. She paused and glanced toward the barn. Betty knew Kathy and how she thought. There was often a deeper reason than the one given—that it would do Hannah good to spend the summer in Montana. To send her daughter so far away, the reason had to be a good one. Betty determined then and there she would find out that reason, especially after yesterday. Hannah had acted so strangely on the buggy ride home.

Betty turned her concentration to the mail. Betty reached for the envelopes and held the letters up to the sunlight. *Here's one for me from Kathy, one for Hannah from her mother, and one for Hannah from—that's strange, it doesn't say.*

Puzzled, Betty turned the letter over. There was nothing written on the back, only their address on the front with Hannah's name on top. The writing was distinctly male with clumsy scrawls—possibly a young man.

So there is more to this than I was told. The conclusion seemed certain. *That's why Hannah is out here. She's running away from a boy.* Betty's mouth fell open at the implications. Maybe Kathy and Roy don't want her seeing him and are hoping she will forget him with a summer out West. *That must be it.* That's why Hannah refused to show any interest in the boys yesterday. She's being true to her love. Betty smiled at the thought. *My, and I'm in the middle of it. Oh, I have to be true to Kathy and Roy's wishes, but this is going to be hard.*

She held the letters tenderly. *Oh, what words might be in a little letter like this—dreams of love and yearning to see each other?* She shivered. *Stop it, you goose,* she told herself. *You have to be on your sister's side of things. Hannah must not see this letter.*

Betty walked quickly back to the house but couldn't decide. Should she throw the letter away? Perhaps she should hide it until Hannah's feelings had begun to weaken. Perhaps her affection for this forbidden boy would decrease. *Oh, it's too much for a poor soul like me. I'm just a simple goose. What am I to do?*

Hannah solved the problem when she appeared suddenly in front of Betty. In her fixation on the letters, Betty hadn't been paying attention to her surroundings. Now there was no time to hide anything. If she slipped the suspicious envelope behind her back or into her pocket, Hannah would see.

"Mail!" Hannah exclaimed. "Anything from Mom?"

Betty made one last desperate attempt and said, "Did you send the other two horses off yet?"

"Yes, they just mounted and left." Hannah waited expectantly.

"Well, there is one for you from your mother and one for me from your mother too."

Hannah held out her hand, a big smile on her face.

Betty wished with all her heart she knew which was which, but she did not. The result was that she had to look, and when she did Hannah also saw.

"Oh," Hannah said, "I have two letters? Who is the other one from?"

Betty looked at her with a sorrowful expression. "I think you probably know."

Hannah's face only showed confusion. "What do you mean?"

"You had been seeing someone secretly, and your mom doesn't like it."

Hannah's face paled. "Did Mom tell you?"

"No," Betty said, "I guessed."

"You guessed? That's not possible."

"Yes, I did. Look at that letter. Isn't that the handwriting of a boy? A clumsy one, I must admit, but most boys are clumsy, especially when they're in love. Now I may be a dumb goose, but I can figure that much out. I can also guess that's why you're really out here. Your mom wants to get you away from someone of whom she doesn't approve. Now isn't that right? That's why you weren't interested in any boys at church yesterday."

Hannah's mouth fell open.

"I'm right, am I not?" Betty asked, her voice triumphant. "Now the question is how can I help your mother out? I thought of hiding the letter, but you didn't give me a chance."

"Ah," Hannah cleared her throat and answered, "I can't really tell you why I'm out here. There is a reason, but it's best kept quiet. If Mom ever tells you, then that's okay. But until then, I can't say. And, as far as this letter being from a boy, I have no idea...Well, yes, I do have an idea. It's probably from Sam." Hannah looked more closely at the letter, "Yes, that's who it's from."

"From Sam?" Now Betty was confused. "He likes you?"

"I think so," Hannah said, numbly.

"So that is why you're out here," Betty affirmed and now quickly reversed her opinion. "It's you that wants to get away from Sam, and your mother wants you to take him."

"No, it's not like that," Hannah said.

Betty had no plans to be wrong twice in a row. And she would most certainly side with her sister. An inspiration came to her.

"Look at your letter, and see if I'm not right," Betty said.

"Which one? Sam's?" Hannah asked. "What will that prove?"

"No, your mother's."

"What will that show?"

"Just open it." Betty put all her eggs into this basket, her lips firmly pressed together. She had to be right.

Hannah slowly opened the letter and read out loud, "Dear Hannah, we are all missing you. Our weather is nice and sunny."

Betty interrupted her and said, "Keep reading. There must be something about your Sam."

Hannah scanned the page and then turned it over and read, "Who do you think I saw the day after you left?"

Betty's face had a big smile on it. Hannah kept reading, "It was Sam. He looked so sorrowful when he asked for your address that I gave it to him. If he writes, at least send him one letter back."

"See?" Betty was giddy. "There it is. Your mother wants you to see him. I knew it."

"I don't think it means what you think it does," Hannah protested.

"So what does it mean, then?" Betty challenged her.

"He's got a crush on me. That's all. I don't like him. Not in the least."

"But you're trying to get away from him, right?"

"No," Hannah said, "that's not why I'm here."

Betty held up her hand. "Hannah, child, I know how it is. You don't have to tell me. It's okay. But I think you really should consider this young man. If your mother likes him enough to give him your address, then I'm all for it." Betty was greatly encouraged by her obvious deductions and continued. "I'm guessing you liked him in school," she proclaimed in another stroke of genius.

"Yes," Hannah said, angry now, "but that was when I was much younger!"

"My, my," Betty said, "such an outburst! You do have it bad. I really think you ought to consider what your mother wants. Parents often know what's best for their children."

"Look, it's not what you think," Hannah said, trying to calm herself.

"Just remember," Betty said, "consider your mother's wishes."

Before Hannah could speak again, the first riders returned on the path.

"Now I have work to do," Betty said, "and you do too."

With that Betty left Hannah standing in the middle of the yard while she bustled toward the house.

Hannah watched her go and then walked toward the riders and took their horses from them as they dismounted.

"Wonderful ride!" the lady gushed. "Your horses are so well behaved."

"We try to keep them so," Hannah said with a smile as she wished humans were as well behaved.

The man produced his billfold and gave Hannah a generous tip.

"Thank you," she said, "but you don't have to do that."

"Oh, it was worth it," the lady said and then took the man's hand as they turned and walked to their car.

Hannah puzzled all day about whether to tell Betty about Peter, the real reason why she was in Montana. Perhaps Betty needed to know. In the end, Hannah decided against it. Things were best left alone. But if her mom ever wished to share the news with Betty, that would be okay.

In the meantime, there was the letter from Sam to deal with. She still hadn't opened the envelope. The last riders of the day arrived at three thirty, and when they returned an hour later, Hannah had a great urge to take a ride, especially as she looked at Prince. He was almost as nice as Honey. She stroked his neck and then turned to go into the house.

She found Betty in the kitchen and asked, "Will you come riding with me? I haven't had a chance yet, and the horses still have energy left."

"No, I'm afraid not, dear," Betty said. "I never was much of a rider."

"You don't know what you're missing. It's never too late to start."

Betty laughed. "That's easy for you to say. Just don't stay out too late and stay on the trail."

Hannah took off at a run toward the barn. She led Mandy inside, unsaddled her, and led her through the gate to the pasture. Prince neighed to join her.

"Now, now," Hannah told him when she got back out, "you and I are going for a ride. Isn't that going to be fun?"

He jerked his head up and down as if in agreement with her.

Hannah swung up and onto Prince. She led him up the trail and into the wooded hills. The beauty of it overwhelmed her again. Away from the buildings, the land rose to reveal the town in the distance and behind that the Cabinet Mountains. To the north were more mountains surrounding her with their vast ruggedness.

Already well into late spring, they were no longer snowcapped. Summer had almost come, even to this northwest corner of Montana.

Hannah came down to a wide river, the Kootenai Betty had said, and pulled Prince to a stop. Here was the source of the sound of rushing water that occasionally reached her ears when she was at the barn. By Eastern standards, it was a huge river. The hardy pines that grew everywhere descended the riverbank, in some places right up to the edge of the water. The water rippled past her with vigor and seemed to be in a great hurry to get where it was going. Steve had said the headwaters were in Canada. Hannah wondered how such a thing was possible. Water flowed in front of her that had begun as a small trickle in the mountains of Canada, from a mysterious place she had never been. Now it was here, and it went on from here to unknown places, propelled by a power beyond itself.

She patted Prince on the neck and leaned into his mane. The smell of horse soothed her mind. "Well, what do you think, old boy?" she asked him out loud.

He lifted his head toward the river and neighed sharply.

"Do you have friends around here?" she asked him and laughed.

He jerked his head back and forth and arched his neck.

They continued on, and before long the trail opened up to reveal a flat plateau along the bank. Although the rock-strewn riverbank was steep, where the foothill started again it was flat. The land was level for a long stretch into the distance. "Ah," she exclaimed, "let's go, Prince!"

He seemed to understand as she gave him his head. Hannah bent low on his neck to avoid the wind and then rose in the stirrups and rode with complete abandonment. Prince's hooves pounded on the trail, his stride smooth as he galloped in great bounds.

She shouted aloud in sheer joy, her heart opening itself wide. Out here it seemed as if there was no evil anywhere that could touch her. For one glorious moment, she could forget that anything or anyone else existed besides her and Prince and this wonderful world.

Hannah drew Prince in and laughed until the sound of her voice made her remember that there were indeed problems that needed to be faced, and this might be the exact place to start. The letter from Sam had still not been opened.

"Well," she told Prince, her voice still ringing with happiness, "that was very good. Now let's just stand here and let me look at some of my troubles."

Hannah pulled the letter out of her pocket. She shook the paper so that the contents slid to one end. For a moment she thought, *Why not just throw the thing away without reading it? Why spoil this joy?*

Prince stretched his neck out toward the ground and blew his nose.

"See," she told him, "that's what you would do, wouldn't you?"

But what would her mom want her to do? She had given Sam her address. Did she also think it was a good idea that Sam wrote? Betty was sure Kathy did, but was it really true?

Hannah could ask, she supposed, but that didn't help for now. Besides, asking would be foolish. Her mom might not want to tell lest it influence Hannah's decision. That would be like her mom, which also meant that Betty could be right. Hannah had never asked her mom how she felt about Sam. It was a horrible thought, but what if her mother *did* approve of Sam?

Hannah wished she could forget the whole thing, but boys somehow just didn't seem to go away. She had to admit it would be wonderful to be loved, but in the right way this time—not like with Peter and that dream. Love needed to be done the right way. But what was the right way? Her parents' way? Someone they approved of? That was an even scarier thought. Could it be that perhaps Sam should be examined closer, open mouth and all—especially if her mother thought so? She laughed out loud at the thought. Out here, seated on Prince, with the mountains around her, Sam's open mouth did not seem so serious. She supposed he kept it shut sometimes.

"Maybe," she said, chuckling to Prince, "but I don't know." Prince twitched his ear as if a fly had landed on it, but a glance around didn't reveal any flies.

With a sigh Hannah tore open one end of the envelope.

Eighteen

The sun had set behind the Cabinet Mountains. Jake sat in his cabin with his meager supper of canned bean soup. He desired greatly the taste of his mother's home-baked cooking. She would be appalled if she could see what he was eating now. Jake grinned at the thought.

The day had seen its share of visitors come past his outpost. Most of them were younger or middle-aged hikers. Occasionally a vehicle made the climb to his cabin with an older couple who simply wanted to enjoy the view. He made time for all of them and invited them to climb the tower if they wished.

Those had been his instructions. "We are employees of the public, and so show them every courtesy," he had been told. "Only in the event of a crisis and the tower is needed, is it to be off limits to the public."

Today there had been no fires to report, but Jake was still tired. He wasn't sure if it was from all the people who had come by or just a result of all his recent troubled thoughts. He stretched his legs out on the kitchen chair. Before him was the notepad on which he intended to write to his parents again. It was high time he did, plus there was good news to report. He had found and visited an Amish church.

Pushing his fatigue aside, he started.

Dear Mom and Dad,

Greetings in the name of Christ our Savior. I am happy to report that I have found an Amish church, and I attended there on Sunday. I spent the night at the bishop's house. His name is Nisley. He knew my grandfather and took me in very well.

On Sunday morning, they even asked me to lead the praise song. They are just a small group but very friendly. I have plans to attend there at least every other Sunday. Hopefully this will be okay with Deacon Miller, if he should ask. You know what I mean.

The peanut butter tasted strange. Not that it was bad or anything. Maybe they don't use the same syrup as back home. They have a bunch of boys in the young folks but not many youth activities.

> *Your son,*
> *Jake Byler*

Jake twiddled his pen. A great desire came over him to ask about Eliza. Did he dare? No, he better not. It could result in embarrassment. If anything had changed, they would have let him know, hoping it might just bring him home.

She's probably already planning her wedding, he thought, and fresh anger surged through him. *How could she do something like that? Did she care nothing for me? What of all the times she said she loved me?*

He rose from the table, walked over to the window, and looked at the valley. His thoughts were not on its beauty. Absently, after only a few moments, he returned to his letter, sealed it, and took it to the drop box in the office.

Hannah sat in the saddle on Prince and slid her fingers into the envelope. Carefully she extracted the letter, holding it away from her as if it were a serpent. Prince shifted his weight beneath her and lifted his head high into the air.

"Easy, boy," she said. "Let's see what this says."

The letter began with "Dear Hannah."

I suppose you will be surprised at a letter from me. It's just that I couldn't keep myself from writing to you.

I wondered how it would be with you gone. I miss you a lot already. I saw your mother in town and asked for your address. I hope you are doing well. Montana is a big state, I think. Don't get lost in it.

I would very much like to write more to you while you are gone. Would this be okay? It might make the time go faster for me, and if you would write what you are doing that would be interesting as well.

> *So long,*
> *Sam Knepp*

"There it is," Hannah pronounced loudly as if Prince could understand. "The monster himself. Now what shall we do with him? Mommy's love and Auntie's perfection—yet shall he be mine?"

She threw her head back and laughed at the idea. Out here things like this letter didn't seem as serious. *But life out here is different than back there, isn't it?*

Hearing her sigh, Prince turned his head as if mildly interested.

"You have no idea what's going on, Mr. Prince," she said. "Your little horse life is not complicated at all. Just go when you're told and eat when you're hungry, hmmm? What a life!"

Prince lowered his head as if looking for grass, and Hannah turned back to her thoughts. *Oh, to dream or not to dream? That is the question, now, isn't it? Yet, no more dreaming for me. No more wonder boys who charm me. Now it's time to do what's right and take the path that Mother wants.*

"Well, Mr. Prince," she said, "are you going to write the letter? Of course not," she said, answering herself. "That falls on me, the one who needs to do penance for her sins. Oh, if I had never strayed from the path, then this would not have happened to me." She sighed again. "But I must bear my burden and follow the best I can."

Then to her surprise, a tear trickled down her face. Prince neighed as if in sympathy.

"You understand," she said as she looked down to pat him on the neck, "even if I don't."

Suddenly Hannah noticed the sun was much lower in the sky. It was time to go back. Not in the mood to gallop, she still urged Prince into a run to save time. He cantered along as she rode smoothly. Hannah wished her life was as smooth, but there seemed little that could be done about it. When the wide plain narrowed down to the riverbed, she had to slow down and take the rest of the way at a walk.

❖

"Where were you?" a worried Betty called out from the kitchen door as Hannah came in.

"Putting Prince up," she said. "Time got away from me. I was sitting on Prince…thinking some things through."

"Any decisions?" Betty asked, her curiosity bubbling to the surface.

"I'm going to write him back," Hannah muttered.

Betty was not to be deterred. "Would that be to Sam?"

"Yes, Sam."

Betty gushed, "Oh, your mother will be so happy. Does Sam have a lot of money?"

"He's going to inherit the family farm," Hannah said without emotion.

"That's nothing to sneeze at," Betty proclaimed. "You don't have to look down your nose."

"I'm just writing a letter," Hannah said. "That's all."

"You never know," Betty said. "Little things can lead to bigger things. Remember your mother likes him."

"I'll try," Hannah said halfheartedly as she headed for her room upstairs.

She found her writing tablet and began her letter.

Dear Sam,

I am in Montana, of course, on Betty's little farm. They

have purchased two new horses since I've arrived. Business
is that good. I suppose you would know all about that. I
certainly enjoy myself, and the little church is nice. Friendly
people and all…

When she came close to the end of the letter, Hannah told Sam
what he really wanted to hear.

I guess writing would be okay for now. I don't know how
often I can, but I will try.

Then she signed it simply, "Hannah."

After that she couldn't resist. Carefully she drew a little smiley face
after her name. *That will do it,* she told herself.

In her mind, Hannah saw Sam's mouth drop open—just as plain
as day. She sobered a few minutes later. Something would have to be
done about that. Perhaps the boy really could be trained.

For the first time, that night Hannah dreamed of Peter. She found
herself in a moonless night again but with an awful roar in the air.
She was with Peter on the roof of her home in Indiana as leaves and
branches flew all around them. In the distance great flashes of light
came and went. She clung to the roof in terror while Peter bravely
walked around and beckoned for her to come to him. She tried to find
the courage, but the strength to move wasn't in her.

In a swirl of motion and without having climbed off the roof, she was
suddenly in his car. They sped along a gravel road as the wind whistled
through the open car window. She was rigid with fear, clutching the
handlebar above the window. "Stop, stop," she screamed.

"Be brave," Peter said, laughing. "Hang on." He drove even faster,
and now blue and yellow lights were everywhere as they raced along
in the night.

Her father's face appeared through the windshield, telling her to
come home, but she couldn't get Peter to stop the car. Her father called
her name loudly while Peter laughed.

Hannah struggled, her muscles like water, and finally got herself awake, sure that her cries had been heard by someone in the house. Her hands trembled under the covers, and she knew she needed to do something to calm herself.

Finally she got up enough courage to slide out of bed and lower herself to kneel on the floor. There, as the night air from her open windows blew around her, she begged God to forgive her and never let her dream this dream again.

"I will listen to Mom and Dad from now on. I promise," she whispered, believing the words spoken out loud were better than just thinking them. Surely God heard spoken prayers more clearly than just thought prayers.

"Just give me the strength to walk away from my own ways and the desire to do things Your way. Help me, please."

She stayed there until she felt sure God had heard, and then she climbed back into bed and fell asleep.

◈

Sam received Hannah's letter three days later. He gingerly pulled the letter out of the pile of mail his mother had left on the kitchen table. He took a long and deep breath. If this was from whom he hoped… Well, then he was a man now and must act accordingly.

"Is somebody writing to you?" his mother called from the sewing room. Sam could hear her ironing board squeak.

"Yep," he hollered and left it at that. He wanted to see the letter first. Perhaps it contained bad news, but at least she had written. He cut the envelope open and slid out the paper.

It *was* from her. That was good. The gentle feminine sweep of the words on the paper told him so. Her name at the end confirmed it. He rubbed his forehead and took another deep breath. That Hannah would write to him shouldn't come as a surprise, he told himself. He had asked her to write, and, of course, she would. Yet deep down, he knew he had tread on sacred ground, held out his hand to a beautiful blossom, strained for it, and had now touched it.

"Is somebody writing to you?" his mother repeated from the sewing room and stuck her head through the doorway. "I guess someone did." She answered the question herself when she noticed Sam with his head down, his eyes intent on the words.

Sam read quietly as his mother's face disappeared. Hannah had written all about what had happened—her trip to Montana, Prince, the new horse, and her work. At the end of the letter, Hannah finally wrote the news he really wanted to hear—she was, indeed, going to write more, and he could write to her.

The smiley face Hannah had drawn struck him to his heart. Sam thought long and hard. A girl now wrote to him. Not just *any* girl— Hannah Miller—the one from school who used to smile at him but afterward would have nothing to do with him. The world almost changed colors in front of him. Hannah Miller was writing to *him*.

Sam walked to the sewing room. His mom had the ironing board open and a stack of ironed clothes on one side. On the other side was a basketful of clothes still needing to be ironed.

"Hannah wrote to me," he said.

"Hannah Miller?" she asked and raised her eyebrows.

"Yes," he said with a pleased look on his face. She might as well share in his triumph.

"How did that happen?" she asked.

"I wrote to her first," he said and shrugged as if that were all the explanation necessary.

"It is just the one letter, though?" his mom said, asking the obvious.

"No," he said and let the pleasure show even more, "we are writing."

"Really?" she asked. The implications of writing were unspoken but clear. "Are you sure you're up to a girl like that?"

"By God's help," he said, "and Dad is giving me the farm someday."

"Well, yes," she agreed, "but I'm kind of surprised at this."

"I was hoping for it," he said, and with that, Sam firmly squared his shoulders. "I want to be a good man for her."

"Aren't you moving a little fast?" she asked.

"No," he said. "She's *writing* to me."

Nineteen

On Sunday morning, Hannah sat with Betty and the other women for the church services. This was simply a whim of hers for this one Sunday. It would hardly be considered proper for a girl her age to always sit with the married women. If she were an old maid, perhaps, but that time was not anywhere near.

For now, however, Hannah enjoyed the company of the older women. It took some of the awkwardness out of having to sit with girls much younger than she. The real reason, though, was that it removed her farther from the boys on the second row. Not that they were a threat, but she felt like she stuck out on the bench with the regular local girls.

Even sitting here with the women, she felt the eyes of one of the boys on her. Hannah had named him *Mr. Scarred Logger*. His real name was Ben Stoll. He came from a good family, she supposed. It was just that she felt no interest in him at all. That he had an interest in her was a foregone conclusion, given that his options were not that many.

No, this boy wasn't a problem…yet. But from the way he looked at her, he would soon get up enough nerve to ask if he could drive her home. The impression was so strong that she made a note to tell Betty her answer was "no" before he even asked. That would be if he approached either Steve or Betty to serve as an intermediary. But then he might just ask her instead of going through either of them.

Well, she would simply have to deal with it. She was already writing to someone. That would serve as a good enough excuse and prevent too many hurt feelings. Sam wasn't really that much of an attraction. In fact, why not drop the word around before any boy even asked? Maybe Betty could discretely make mention of this and pass it along the lines.

It was a good plan, and she would run it by Betty this afternoon.

At least she didn't have to deal with that fellow who had reminded her of Peter. Of course, he didn't *really* look like Peter. It must have been her imagination.

Since Sunday school was being held today instead of a main church service, the ministers were not upstairs in conference. Bishop Nisley stood up right after the singing ended and read a Scripture. After that he dismissed them for classes.

Hannah followed the youth as they moved upstairs to the open foyer area that served as their temporary classroom. All of the bedrooms had been designated for use by classes for the younger children.

Bishop Nisley was the youth teacher. This suited Hannah, especially because she was the only new girl. Although some bishops didn't make her feel all that comfortable, Bishop Nisley did.

The whole church, except the children's classes, followed the same text, and today the selection was the tenth chapter of Proverbs. It was read in High German, not in their common language of Pennsylvania Dutch. The first verse caught Hannah's attention. "A wise son maketh a glad father: but a foolish son is the heaviness of his mother."

Bishop Nisley went on to explain that this verse applied not just to sons but to daughters as well. Obedience to one's parents was a staple requirement of the Christian life. One should always honor one's mother and father.

Hannah drank it all in and resolved to apply this to her life. She would do what her mother wished. Betty would help her, and she would get it done. Wisdom was what she wanted very badly, and here was a chance to get it. Even if it might very well apply to Sam—as much as she wished it didn't.

Just before the class was dismissed, Bishop Nisley announced that a youth gathering was planned at his place for the next Saturday.

"We don't have many youth," he explained, "and only one hymn singing a month, though we have Hannah with us for the summer and Jake Byler every other Sunday. Since next Sunday is the planned hymn singing, we can have an extended youth weekend."

The locals smiled and nodded their heads. Hannah was sure she would appear quite pale if anyone had looked at her. Wasn't Jake the name of the boy she didn't want to see again? She was sure that was what Steve had said. So he would come every other week? That was not good news.

After Bishop Nisley dismissed the class, everyone gathered again. The whole group then went over the text one more time. Here in a mixed congregation, only the men spoke.

No lunch was served after such a Sunday-school Sunday, and the buzz of conversation filled the room while people got ready to leave. Betty tapped Hannah on the shoulder, and they gathered their shawls and bonnets in the front entryway. *Mr. Logger* stuck his head in from the main part of the house. Hannah gasped, but Betty just grinned and offered no help other than to dash back into the house after a tight squeeze past *Mr. Logger*.

"Hi," he said after Betty had left.

"Hi," Hannah said and offered a polite nod.

He stood there, towering over her by nearly a foot, 200 pounds of muscle and scars turned into blushing redness, his hat literally in his hands.

"Do you need a ride to the youth gathering on Saturday night?" he asked.

She had to do what she had to do. So she took a breath, offered her best smile, and said, "Not really. Betty and Steve can take me."

He cleared his throat. Obviously this tree wouldn't fall without the direct application of the saw. "I would like to take you."

"Oh, that's nice of you," she said and met his eyes, "but I'm already writing somebody."

"Ach." He drew in his breath, gathered his wits about him, and continued. "I'm sorry. I didn't know."

"That's okay," she said. "You couldn't have known."

"Well, then," he said, nodding in confusion. He put his hat on, reached for the doorknob, and was gone.

The women seated in the living room turned to catch a glimpse of him as he passed the window. "Do you think Ben had any success?" Bishop Nisley's wife, Elizabeth, asked the others.

"Not from the look on his face," Barbara Yoder, the wife of one of the younger men, said quickly.

"I could have told you," Betty spoke up sagely. "Hannah's already writing to someone, but I didn't want to say so for her."

"Oh, she is?" The disappointment was audible in the chorus of voices. "Who is he?"

"I've not seen him," Betty said, enjoying the attention on such an interesting matter. "His name's Sam Knepp. She received a letter from him this week already."

"They must be serious, then," Elizabeth said. "That's kind of soon."

"It sounds like it," Betty said. "Her mother is all for it."

On the buggy ride home, Betty spoke to Hannah from the front seat, "You did right today in turning down Ben, Hannah."

"I didn't want him," Hannah retorted.

"I know," Betty said, smiling. "Keep saying 'no,' to everyone else. You're writing, remember?"

"Would you stop talking in riddles?" Steve demanded. "What are you two talking about?"

"Oh, nothing," Betty said.

Steve raised his eyebrows and slapped the reins. Obviously there was little use digging deeper now. Hannah doubted if Betty would tell him in front of everyone anyway. He would probably inquire later. As likely as not, he'd conclude it was all just women's talk and forget the matter.

Jake had no way to know about the planned youth gathering when he arrived at Bishop Nisley's the following Saturday around three. He ambled in, relaxed and ready to be off the mountain for the weekend.

"It's at six o'clock," Elizabeth told him, "after supper, of course. We're having popcorn and cider and, of course, playing volleyball."

"A youth gathering?" Jake's eyes were big.

"*Jah*," she said, "John planned it last Sunday."

"Are there enough youth to make a team?"

"Probably not," she said, "but some of us married folk will come too. We have to, you know, with how many young people there are."

"Do you play too?" Jake asked dubiously.

"Now, now," she said, "don't be down on us old folks. We grew up playing volleyball."

"I guess you're not really too old," he ventured. "It's just that the bishop thing makes you think old."

"Well," Elizabeth said, "church does weigh John down sometimes, but we haven't had it too bad. The people around here are real nice. Of course, being a young church helps. People try harder to get along when there's only a few of us."

Jake nodded.

"There's also the Sunday night singing this weekend. Do you think you can stay for that?"

Jake thought about it. This was obviously an important question. If he stayed and joined in, the bishop's estimation of him would likely go up. Yet, how was he to get back to work by Monday morning?

"I'm not sure," he finally said. "I need to be back at the cabin for work by five the next morning."

"Maybe something can be worked out," Elizabeth suggested. "We rarely have visiting young people for the singings. It would be a real treat."

Jake still wasn't sure how he would be able to stay, but this definitely needed to be thought out. "I'll try," he said, finally agreeing. "I'll ask the bishop about transportation. He might have some ideas."

He could tell by her smile he had said the right thing.

A few minutes later, John appeared and asked if Jake would help him set up the volleyball net.

"Sure," Jake said and got up to follow John outside. This could also be his opportunity to approach the bishop about the Sunday night matter.

Together they pushed John's two buggies outside to use as end posts. They spread the net out on the ground to judge the distance and then parked the buggies, one on either side of the loose net. Next they tied the strings around the middle of the buggies. With the net tight, they placed pieces of logs under one side of the buggy wheels to raise the net to the proper height.

John's single buggy wasn't much of a problem to lift, but the surrey required both of them to lift each wheel while they pushed the log blocks in place with their feet. Once this had been done, they retightened the strings on the net and pulled the top of the net level with the top of the buggies. The result was Amish to the core—two tilted buggies on wood blocks holding a volleyball net taut.

As they examined their handiwork, Jake took his chance.

"Elizabeth says you're having a hymn singing this weekend."

"Yes," John said. "We'd really like to have you stay. There are so few youth here. We might as well make the most out of your summer with us."

"How can I get back in time for work on Monday?" Jake asked. "I usually use Sunday afternoons to get back up the mountain. I have to be there by five in the morning."

"We'll think of something," John assured him. "There are a few of the Mennonite people who come to our hymn sings. I will ask one of them to give you a ride. If that doesn't work, there are English drivers we can hire to take you back."

"That would be kind of expensive, wouldn't it?" Jake didn't make that much money to spend it on further taxi services.

"Yes," John said, "it would be. Let's just hope one of the Mennonites can do it."

Jake agreed. Apparently this was simply a risk he would have to take. Elizabeth then opened the kitchen door and called out, "Supper's ready."

"Well, we'd better go eat before the crowd gets here," John said with a quick laugh and headed for the house with Jake close behind him.

Twenty

It was a sunny Saturday afternoon back in Indiana when Sam went upstairs to write to Hannah. He sat on a chair by an old oak cabinet handed down from past generations and thought long and hard about what he should say. He felt that his next letter or two could be a watershed of sorts, and so they needed to be just right. Pen poised, he took his time to compose the words.

Confidently he began.

> Dear Hannah,
>
> Christian greetings in our Lord and Savior's name. I received your welcome letter. The news was very interesting. Things around here are about the same as always. The youth have their regular planned things, and I go. It's not the same, though, without you here.
>
> No really big news. No funerals or that sort of thing. Mom's busy downstairs and will have supper ready soon. I'm so glad we're writing. I guess it is second-best to seeing you. I look forward to that when you come back.
>
> My feelings are really strong about this. I see it as the right thing, the way our lives have crossed so many times before. I am still sorry for hurting you that night when we played the game at your place. Yet, as our preachers have always said, God works in mysterious ways, and I cannot but see the hand of God guiding us together.

*My joy is great that you see it also. I will wait for your next
welcome letter.*

> *Yours truly,*
> *Sam Knepp*

Sam sealed the envelope and set the letter on the cabinet, ready for
Monday's mail. He let his eyes skim over the address and her name one
more time. *It is all too much,* he told himself, *and yet it is so true.*

❖

Hannah stood in the yard with Prince, stroking his neck as both
enjoyed the sun's last afternoon rays. Prince lifted his head toward the
road as if he expected someone to pull in the driveway and require
him to take another run up the trail.

"It's over for the day," Hannah assured him. "You've done your
duty...and then some."

She had reveled in early summer weather all day. It was an absolute
delight—warm, yet without the humidity the East had.

The sun felt so good that Hannah couldn't bear to go inside yet.
Prince seemed reluctant to end his day too. Surely there would be time
for a quick ride before she had to leave for the youth gathering.

"How about we take just a short ride?" Hannah said as she ran her
hand across Prince's head.

He neighed, and she laughed. "I'll take that as a yes."

Quickly she tied him to the fence and ran inside. She stuck her head
through the kitchen doorway and told Betty, "I'm going for a ride."

"Be careful and be back in time for the youth gathering tonight."

"Yes, I will," Hannah shouted through the screen door.

She stroked Prince's long neck again before she mounted.

With the reins in her hand, Hannah said, "You're a wonderful
horse—a real beauty." She then placed her foot in the stirrup and
swung herself up onto the saddle.

Prince bounced his head, eager to start out.

She let him walk until they got to the river. There she stopped,
overcome again with the beauty and grandeur of this land. The water

of the Kootenai seemed to flow faster than it had the last time she was here, the ripples more pronounced even out in the middle of the wide body of water.

"It looks *wild*," she told Prince. "Of course, all of this country is wild."

She breathed in deeply, overcome with the joy that filled her. With a turn of the reins, she headed Prince north and reached the plateau along the river. There she let Prince have his head. They galloped, the wind rushing past her face, until she saw the end of the trail ahead and pulled back on his reins. As he slowed, she gave herself over to the joy of the ride and laughed heartily. Prince snorted loudly as if to echo her exuberance.

"You're a good horse," she said and turned him around. "Now, let's trot back. One run like that is enough for you. You've worked hard all day already and here I go making you work even harder."

On the way back, Hannah was fascinated by the clear blue sky above. It seemed to open into one giant expanse and go on and on forever. A few fluffy clouds hung on the horizon, but the rest was just blue and more blue.

"God is really something," she told Prince. "How did He make all of this? Then He made you and me, and He makes it all work together. Well, unless we mess it up, of course." Hannah patted the horse on the neck. "I don't mean *you*, Prince. You are just a horse. It's *people* who mess things up. Look at me and what I've done. But I will straighten it out, though, and be a good girl. Do you think I'll make a good wife for Sam, Prince?"

Prince simply trotted along and snorted again.

"That's what I think," Hannah said, laughing. "Sam? I guess it's a nice name, like Betty said, but doesn't it take more than a nice name? Doesn't there have to be love? See, Prince, there I go again—dreaming. Of course, Sam will love me. In the way that a farmer loves his wife, we will grow old together...work the land...with a dozen children probably. I'm sure Sam wants that many to help on the farm, of course. Little old me, I'll just be a farmer's wife. Do you think God wants that, Prince? He wants me to obey my parents, don't you think?"

This time Prince jerked his neck.

"I thought so," Hannah told him and urged him on a little faster lest they arrive at the house late.

Once they arrived at the barn, she pulled the saddle off of Prince's back and turned him out to the pasture behind the barn. "That's it for the week," she said. "Enjoy your break because it's back to work on Monday morning."

"Hannah, I need some help," Betty called to Hannah from the house.

"Coming," Hannah called back as she hurried into the house.

"Carry this out to the buggy for me, would you?" Betty pointed toward a plastic bucket. "Popcorn," she offered in answer to Hannah's look. "Everyone brings something. If there's too much, we just bring it back home."

"Okay," Hannah nodded. That wasn't unusual, but the fact that all these married folks were involved in the youth gatherings was different from the youth gatherings in Indiana. "Will there be a lot of the married people there?" she asked.

"No," Betty said, "only a few. Not everyone can come, of course. It's kind of informal, I suppose, but it suits our purposes. Maybe someday, when we have a lot of young people, things will be different." Her face brightened at the idea. "Maybe you and Sam want to move out here. You like the country, don't you?"

"You forget that he's to inherit his father's farm," Hannah said. "That kind of locks things in, I suppose."

"Yes, that would," Betty allowed. "It would be so nice, though, to have more young couples living here. We've never even had a wedding out here yet."

"Don't look at *me*," Hannah said. "Who's bringing the cider?" she asked, changing the subject.

"The Nisley's will supply that. We have to buy it in town, though, because none of the Amish have an orchard. That is, so far. We really need to look into it. They make some of the best fresh cider around here."

"Better than in Indiana?" Hannah asked.

"Without question, and that's speaking as one who is loyal to Indiana."

Hannah laughed. "It's hard to believe anyone can make better cider than we have in Indiana."

Outside, the sound of the driving horse being hitched reminded Hannah of the time. "We should go, shouldn't we?"

"I'm coming," Betty said. "I have to call the children."

"I'll wait for you," Hannah said. A few minutes later, they walked together to the buggy and rode to the Nisley's.

Jake lingered at the supper table with John, deep in conversation.

"So you enjoy your job up on the mountains?" John asked.

Jake grinned. "Even the loneliness suits me right now. The morning sunrise—it's like nothing I've ever seen. The pay is pretty good. It's as good as farmwork and certainly not as difficult."

John laughed. "I'd suppose that's so."

After a minute, he changed the subject and asked Jake, "Are you dating?"

"No," Jake said, gazing at his empty plate.

Elizabeth had just come into the kitchen to gather up the supper dishes and overheard the question.

"Are you sure that's your business?" she asked and laughed softly.

"I'm just curious," John said.

Jake's mind whirled. He wondered whether he should volunteer the information. Wrapped in the safe atmosphere of this home, he felt a pleasant sensation after the long hours alone on the mountain.

"There *was* someone," Jake finally said.

"Oh," Elizabeth stopped with the stack of dirty plates in her hands. "Was it serious?"

"Yes," Jake said, "very serious. Almost married. In fact, we were just three months from being married." The pain in his voice was obvious.

"*Ach,*" Elizabeth said, "that does hurt. But you want to be sure it's the right one."

"I thought it was," Jake told her.

"We can be wrong sometimes," she said. "The ways of God are not our ways."

John nodded. "That's right."

"I don't much trust girls now," Jake muttered. "She gave me no warning—none at all. Granted I was stupid, but it was because I trusted her. It was over just like that. Now she's dating my cousin... right there in front of me."

"You really loved her?" Elizabeth asked, sympathy in her voice.

Jake nodded.

"Still, it's better to find out now rather than later. That's what dating is for, I guess," Elizabeth offered.

"God has His ways," John repeated. "We must learn to trust Him... and not become bitter."

Jake numbly nodded but said no more.

The first of the buggies started to arrive, and the volleyball game was quickly organized. Until enough players came, it was a hit or miss scramble to knock the ball over the net. As more people arrived, the game soon turned into a fierce competition between opposing teams.

Hannah was uneasy when she noticed that boy, Jake. When he ended up on the opposite team from her, she felt more at ease.

Two games later, they broke for popcorn and cider. The women, headed up by Elizabeth and Betty, brought out the heaping bowls of white fluffy stuff.

"Bring up the picnic table," Elizabeth told John, who was still winded from the game. "If we set it up under the tree, it should be fine. There's no wind tonight."

John agreed with a nod and asked Steve to help him move the table. Together they carried the bench from the barn overhang to where Elizabeth wanted it.

Once the table was in place, she set the large bowls of popcorn down and scattered the smaller bowls around so that individual portions could be served. Betty went back into the house and returned with the cider jugs. These were then set up so cider could be poured into glasses as needed.

John saw that the women were ready and announced loudly, "Let's have prayer."

Everyone stopped what they were doing and gathered around. John then led out in thanks for the food and finished with a request for the grace and mercy of God to be on them during the rest of the evening.

The boys filled their bowls with popcorn first and then splashed cider into their glasses. They spilled generous amounts onto the picnic table, although no one seemed to mind. Hannah went next at Elizabeth's insistence.

"You are our honored guest," Elizabeth whispered. "It's not every day we have a girl your age visiting us for the summer."

"Is that good or bad?" Hannah asked with a chuckle.

"Good, of course, even if she's already writing to someone."

"How did you know that?" Hannah asked and looked quickly around to see who else had heard the comment. All the males seemed busy, and some of the boys were already knocking the ball back and forth over the net again, their bowls of popcorn and glasses abandoned in the grass.

"Oh, a little birdie told me," Elizabeth said, glancing in Betty's direction.

"You did not!" Hannah exclaimed in mock horror but partly serious. She reached over to pull on Betty's dress sleeve.

"I couldn't help it," Betty protested. "It just came out. It seemed like they should know. It *is* good news, after all, isn't it?"

Hannah wasn't sure what to say. They apparently took her hesitation as a sign of love's sweet work and turned the conversation quickly to other subjects to spare her any further embarrassment.

To comfort herself, Hannah took a deep swallow of her apple cider and was amazed. It *was* better than Indiana cider!

Twenty-one

Sam's dad, Enos Knepp, had wanted to talk with his son ever since his wife told him about the letters to Hannah. Tonight he got the chance when he and Sam were alone in the living room.

"Your mother tells me you're writing to Hannah Miller," Enos began.

Sam looked up from *The Old Farmers' Almanac* and nodded.

"You're serious, then?"

"Yes." Sam nodded again. "It's pretty serious, I would say." Then he asked, "Don't you like her, Dad?"

"No, no, it's not that," Enos said quickly. "She's a fine girl as far as I know. She comes from a good family. I was just wondering if Hannah's right for you. It seems to me that a real nice farm girl would be the better way to go."

"Hannah knows how to farm," Sam said.

"Well, maybe she does," Enos said, "but her father's only a part-time farmer. He doesn't seem to make enough of a living at it...to stay home full-time. He has that job at the factory now."

"What has that got to do with Hannah?"

Enos thought for a long moment before he responded. "It might reflect on her, that's all. I'm just concerned about you. When we leave you the farm," he said and motioned toward where Laura worked in the kitchen, "you'll need a wife who was raised on a farm. You'll need a wife who knows what it's like to get up early, milk cows, and put up

154

the hay...all in the hot sun sometimes. Farm life is hard. You know that, Sam. Just make sure you choose wisely. That's all I'm saying."

Sam nodded, his face sober. "I will think about it, but I really feel that this is the right thing to do. Maybe when Hannah comes home, she could come over to visit and maybe help out some here on the farm." Sam waved his hand around as if to indicate the more than two hundred acres surrounding them. "We can make sure then that she's comfortable with farm life."

"That would be wise," Enos allowed, "but you also need to keep your eyes open. Don't let feelings of love or her beauty blind your eyes. You will regret it—even if she is a decent girl."

"I will consider it," Sam assured his dad. "Maybe after you've seen more of her, you can tell me what you think."

"When is Hannah coming home?"

"I don't know for sure," Sam said. "I hope by the end of summer."

"There's another thing I want to talk with you about," Enos said. "I'm not quite ready to retire, but when I do, I've been thinking about building a smaller house down the road—on our acreage, of course—to eventually serve as our *daudy haus*. But until I'm ready to retire, you and your wife—whoever she is—could use it."

"How soon were you thinking of building this?" Sam asked with obvious interest.

"Are you in such a big hurry?" Enos said with a laugh.

"You never know how things work out," Sam said, his grin crooked. "I haven't asked Hannah yet, though I think it'll come to that. We're just writing now."

"It's serious then." Enos pondered the situation. "I don't think we can do anything for at least two years. If you should marry before that, I guess you could move in with us and take the large upstairs bedroom. That might work for six months or so. Not much more than that. They say two women in the house—no matter how well they like each other—never works for long. I hold to that opinion myself."

Sam nodded as if he thought this fair enough and went back to reading *The Old Farmers' Almanac*.

Enos hid his surprise, got up, and walked to the kitchen. He glanced back, making sure he was out of earshot, and then approached Laura. "Sam's really serious about this girl."

"I'm afraid so," Laura said.

"Do you think she's the right one?" he asked.

"Well," she said, "we never made decisions for any of our other children—other than they had to be in the church and all. They turned out all right. We'd better do the same for Sam, don't you think?"

"I suppose so," he agreed. "I guess I'm just getting jumpy in my old age."

"Ah," she said, chuckling, "you're still young."

"I am?" he said and grinned. "I wish I was, but I do need to trust God and place this into His hands. In that you are right." He playfully kissed her on the cheek.

"This is true," she said, grinning and lightly pushing him away.

As the sun was setting, another round of volleyball was beginning. This time Jake was on the same side as Hannah. She felt her heart thump and wondered if he'd end up placed close to her when the game began? What if she missed the ball, tripped, and tumbled down around his feet?

Since darkness threatened, Hannah had a quick hope the game might be canceled. Bishop Nisley crushed that hope when he came out of the house with two gas lanterns, lit them, and set one on top of each buggy. Perhaps they could play one more game but not much more. The lantern light simply wasn't strong enough.

The boy who had picked Hannah for his team was also in charge of the player lineup. He started off with a rapid boy-girl-boy-girl configuration, which left Hannah in-between Bishop Nisley and Jake. Her heart sank, but there was nothing that could be done about it. A protest would only reveal that she didn't want to stand beside Jake.

Self-consciously Hannah took her place. John was on her left and Jake on her right. As she stood closer to Jake, she could tell that her early impression that he looked like Peter had indeed been mistaken. Jake was a unique person.

From the corner of her eye, Jake appeared to be relaxed as he stood there. Taller than she was, yet he didn't tower over her. He had an air of calm assurance about him, but his face wasn't hardened. Perhaps he had his tender edges? He glanced toward her and briefly nodded and smiled. Hannah thought her return smile was perhaps tense, but his eyes didn't register a reaction. They looked sad, in fact. Perhaps he was lonesome for home or had some other reason for his sorrow. She took a deep breath and tried to relax.

Someone shouted, "Test!" and the game got underway. The ball came over the net in a clean arch, arriving in the second row. It was returned easily. The ball came right back to where Hannah stood in the front row between John and Jake. She expected a commotion of waving arms in her face as one or the other tried to reach for the ball but was surprised. Clearly both John and Jake had plans to stay in their places. This was to be her play. She gathered herself together, took a deep breath, and lifted both hands. A solid swat sent it solidly back over the net.

"Hey, how about setting me next time?" Jake said.

His words shocked Hannah out of her shyness. "Will you set for me too?"

"Of course not," he said. "You just set the ball for tall people."

"That's not fair," she retorted. "Girls want to play too."

"And I want to win," Jake said. "Is that fair?"

It was then that Hannah realized she had just spoken to him, and her good sense forsook her. "I guess so," she muttered.

Jake must have noticed her flustered state of mind and softened. "I do want girls to play—so don't pay any attention to me."

Hannah couldn't think of anything to say before the ball was served again. In a high arch, it passed over their heads.

"The next chance I have, I'll set for you," she said.

"Well, that's settled then," Jake said, smiling. "Now we can really play."

Well, indeed, Hannah thought. She had talked to this boy, and for some reason she felt her heart pounding. Now what did all that mean? *Stop imagining things,* she told herself firmly. *If he wants to talk to me, then I'll talk to him. It means nothing. I'm not going to dream again.*

So when he asked, "You're from Indiana?" she could answer him without any nervousness.

"I'm here for the summer, *jah*," she said. He had a nice self-assured, noninvasive attitude, and Hannah relaxed. He was also an excellent player, and she repeatedly set the ball for him, which he smacked over the net to the groans of the other team.

Eventually John grumbled that he didn't get to play, and so Hannah set the next ball she could reach for him. Hannah laughed when John fumbled her set, sending the volleyball into the net instead of over it.

"See, that's why she's setting them up for me," Jake announced loudly.

"You young people!" John protested. "You don't have to laugh about it."

"We're not," Jake told him. "We just want to win."

"Here it comes again," John announced. "Stop talking and play!"

They stood at the ready, and Hannah saw that the ball was coming her way again. She confidently lifted her hands and sent the volleyball sideways to Jake in a beautiful high arch.

Effortlessly Jake rose into the air and brought his arm into a round sweep that sent the volleyball just over the net and at a forty-five degree angle into the ground on the other side.

This action was greeted with howls of agony from the other side and smiles from Jake's side.

"We get him next game!" someone from across the net shouted.

"There will be no next game. It's too dark," John said. "If we don't hurry, this game won't get done."

As much as such a game can be hurried, they hurried. Hannah soon rotated into the back row and never made it back up front before the game point was called.

Apparently the interaction between Hannah and Jake had been so natural that no one thought anything of it—except one person.

On the way home, Betty said casually, "I saw you and Jake talking during the game. You seemed like old friends. Are you sure that you two don't know each other?"

"Never saw him until he was here the other Sunday," Hannah said.

"Well, I'm glad of that. I would hate to see your mother disappointed," Betty said from the front seat of the buggy.

"You women always imagine things," Steve said. "They seemed fine to me."

"It *did* seem like we knew each other," Hannah spoke up. She figured it might be best to say something, but she really didn't want to have to explain that Jake had reminded her of Peter.

Unbeknownst to Hannah, Jake received a similar inquiry inside the Nisley house. "Jake, you seem to know Hannah," Elizabeth commented while they sat at the kitchen table.

"No, I never saw her until I was here the other Sunday."

"That's interesting," John said. "You both seemed quite comfortable around each other."

Jake was going to say he didn't know why but stopped himself. He did know why. Hannah was very unlike Eliza.

"Hannah's a nice girl," he said aloud. He figured he should grant them something.

"That she is," Elizabeth agreed.

"I'll head for bed," Jake told them, "if that's okay."

"*Ach,*" Elizabeth said and laughed, "you don't have to stay up for us old people."

"Thanks for the wonderful evening," Jake said and got up to leave.

"Are you staying for the singing tomorrow night?" John asked.

"I think so," he said. "Hopefully someone can give me a ride back on Sunday night."

John nodded. "I will see what we can do."

⬧

Sunday arrived, and Jake pulled into the barnyard where church was held with the Nisley's, and Hannah arrived a few minutes later with the Masts. As Hannah got out of the buggy, she casually searched the line of boys by the barn for Jake. When she saw him, an unexpected thrill went through her, causing her to quickly glance the other way. Somehow she would have to keep her emotions under control. She simply couldn't allow things to get out of hand again, as they had with Peter.

Bishop Nisley gave the main sermon, which Hannah thought was good and helped her keep her mind off of Jake. The Bishop spoke about the life of Jesus and our need to accept Him as our Savior.

"It is a personal decision," the bishop explained. "Jesus doesn't look at us as numbers or as pages in a book. We are all individuals to Him. Each of us, as a person, has our own needs and faults. Yet Jesus cares about all of us and knows what our strengths and weaknesses are. We need to let Him into our lives beyond that one decisive moment—he needs to be part of every moment of every day of our lives. Daily we must take up our cross, deny ourselves, and follow Him."

His words made Hannah think about the baptism she still needed. Maybe she should ask for it here among Betty's mountains. The thought brightened her mood. That would be wonderful and something special to remember from her summer in the West. Practically speaking, however, Hannah wondered whether the baptism could be done. From the looks of things, six months of instruction classes could hardly be worked into the time she had left here.

On the off chance that it could, Hannah asked Betty, who then suggested Steve talk to Bishop Nisley. Word came back to Hannah that a summer instruction class had been organized and two of the local boys joined. Bishop Nisley told Hannah privately that the ministers were more than glad to make special provisions for her to start the class late and also complete it by the time she needed to return home. Hannah thanked him and eagerly accepted.

⬧

Jake found his attention drifting toward Hannah much more than he wished, especially in the evening when the hymn sing started. Maybe it was because the Amish church services felt so familiar or perhaps it happened because Hannah was a beautiful girl.

Hannah attracted him in a way no girl had before. It occurred to him that he had never before noticed this kind of girl. Eliza—the infamous one—had always been strong, and so he did little but follow. Hannah wasn't like that at all. She would draw on him to lead, and he liked the way that made him feel.

Stop it, Jake told himself. *I'm doing this because I'm trying to get away from the memory of Eliza.* Jake forced his attention back to the present and joined in the songs, his fine voice rising and falling in unison with the rest. Every now and then, the few attending Mennonites tried to sing the song's different parts. This practice was frowned upon where Jake came from and apparently here also because he heard none of the Amish youth doing it.

When the hymn sing closed with the arrival of nine o'clock, Jake saw John whisper to one of the Mennonite men. As the boys filed out, John came over to Jake and told him that he had a ride back that night to his cabin in the mountains.

Twenty-two

Sam's next letter arrived on Wednesday along with the monthly magazine *Young Companion* from Pathway Publishers, the Amish publishing house. Hannah decided to wait to read the letter until after supper, when she had time alone in her room. Whatever the letter contained, she hoped she had enough emotional energy left to deal with it.

The day had gone well. Riders arrived in a steady stream and filled most of the appointment slots. Hannah watched Prince do his part; gracefully walking up the trail with whomever Hannah had decided should ride him. The horse still moved her deeply. He was indeed a prince of a horse.

On her way upstairs, Hannah picked up the envelope on the living room table along with the copy of *Young Companion,* which Betty had clearly left for her. Apparently there was something she was supposed to read in it.

Settled into her room, Hannah laid the magazine on the dresser table and then opened the envelope. The shiny paper, as she pulled it out, seemed almost to glow in the light of her kerosene lamp.

As Hannah read the words, she could have cried from the weight of Sam's interest in her. He was so certain. If only she was.

Yet this was what seemed right. There certainly were no crazy dreams involved—as there had been with Peter—just the godly virtues of faithfulness and obedience. Surely that was enough.

Hannah glanced up and caught sight of the magazine on the dresser table, its plain white paper softened by the light. The drawing of a buggy and horse on the front cover outlined the title story, "Struggling to Know." She had always liked the magazine. Perhaps this story was the one Betty had hoped she'd read.

Hannah reached for the magazine. Quickly she scanned the story and found that it was about a young girl named Naomi who struggled to find the will of God in her courtship. As it turned out, Naomi wasn't a bad girl. In fact, she was a good girl who had joined the church two years earlier. Naomi's mistake in the story was to have yelled at a cow because its tail swished across her face as she was milking it. Her yell so scared the cow that it kicked over the milk bucket. Naomi knew she was in the wrong even though her face burned from the swish of the cow's muddy tail. The story went on to relate how sorry Naomi felt about this. Even though the spilled milk did not cost a huge amount of money, Naomi's father told her the real loss was the damage done to Naomi's character by lack of self-control.

"Well," Hannah muttered, "I wish that's all I'd done."

Naomi did have one other big problem. She was just sure she was not in love with Johnny, the boy she was dating.

Johnny was also a very good boy. He had never done much wrong. He drove his sisters regularly to the hymn sings, even when it was out of the way. He also saw that they had a ride home before he left for Naomi's house on Sunday nights.

Johnny's father wasn't rich. In fact, his family had to pinch and save for anything they wanted. This did not come from laziness on either Johnny's or his father's part. His father had been laid up for the past year with a back injury he sustained from their large Belgium horse. The horse was actually gentle, as most Belgiums are, but an unfortunate accident had occurred when the horse stumbled on winter ice.

Although Johnny's father was expected to recover fully, it would take some time. In the meantime, Johnny took the full responsibility for the family farm upon himself. He toiled to the best of his ability, but it was a lot of hard work and little income.

Naomi knew all of this and greatly admired Johnny for it. She also knew there couldn't be a better husband than Johnny anywhere.

Yet why did she feel the way she did? Or rather, why did she not feel what she was supposed to feel? Any girl would be glad to have Johnny interested in her.

But according to the story, Naomi had gotten hold of some English romance novels that led her to conclude there should be more feeling in her relationship with Johnny. Naomi's mother told her to throw the books away. She said that those people didn't live in the real world. People just wrote that stuff to make money off of other people's dreams. Naomi tried to the best of her ability to forget about what she had read, but it didn't help much. She would still remember the story and how the girls in love felt. Surely she was supposed to feel that way too.

Hannah was now fully into the story. How was Naomi going to sort this out? Was there really something wrong between her and Johnny? As she read on, it happened that Naomi became so worried about her lack of feelings for Johnny that she told him to no longer bring her home from the singings.

Johnny, of course, couldn't understand this and wanted to know what he had done wrong. Naomi was unable to explain it to him, which sadly caused hurt feelings to a heart that was already burdened down with life's duties.

Johnny waited until he was in his buggy before he showed his true feelings. Then he cried most of the way home. Yet the next morning, he got up at four o'clock to do the milking as usual. He had so collected himself by that time that his mother didn't even notice his tears when she served him breakfast at six.

All day and the week that followed, Johnny carried his burden alone and wondered if God had forsaken him. Happily, he did find peace before the next Sunday when he would have to see Naomi sitting across from him on the girls' benches. He decided that God could take care of even Naomi's heart, and that he, little Johnny, would leave the problem in the hands of a big God.

It was unclear how long these two young people might have been kept apart. Fortunately, the next week Naomi ran across her aunt who was visiting from a neighboring district. Naomi's aunt carefully explained everything to Naomi. She explained how love really works and that Naomi couldn't rely solely on feelings that come and go. Feelings, the aunt said, are fleeting, here one day but gone the next.

Hannah sighed as she read the conclusion. Naomi apologized to Johnny and began seeing his value as a person. It was then that her feelings for Johnny rushed back, and Naomi resolved to never let any romantic fantasy dictate how she must feel.

"Well," Hannah said as she put the magazine down, "why can't I be like that?"

She picked up Sam's letter and looked it over carefully again. Was he like Johnny? She supposed so. *I guess I should at least try*, she thought.

With fresh resolve Hannah found her writing tablet and started to write. For half an hour, she wrote to Sam, telling him all about the weekend, the volleyball game, the delicious cider, and the young people. The one thing she left out was a mention of Jake Byler, but Hannah figured he wasn't important. He was just the boy who made all the feelings go around in her heart.

For Jake Byler the days passed slowly. The mountains still awed him, yet he was bored. Looking out his window at the surroundings, he was sure they weren't the cause. Something else was the problem. Now even the silence and the slow passage of time weren't as enjoyable as they had been when he had first arrived.

Jake was determined to figure this out. He fidgeted on the chair by the kitchen table, his meager supper over. Perhaps his mother's cooking was what he missed. Jake laughed at the thought. Her food would taste good again, but it was something more than that.

Then it occurred to him that he had just laughed at himself. It had been a long time since he had been able to do that. Could it be that his laughter meant he was finally getting over his pain? Jake was sure that was what it was, and the more he thought about it, the more sure he became. Somewhere on this mountain and in this cabin, the pain had become less.

Jake found himself a little unnerved by the discovery that while he could still envision Eliza's face, the emotions no longer stirred him. Oh, there was still anger at the unfairness of it all, but somehow the healing must have begun. Now new emotions came over him with the realization that it was truly over.

A sense of calm settled in, a cessation of the roiling emotions he had endured for so long. He walked to the window and looked out. Full darkness was only half an hour away—the sun had already slipped below the horizon. Shadows were filling the valley, reaching out as if with long bands to hold the earth in their grip for the night.

Over the top of the mountain behind him, remnants of sunlight still streamed through the sky, highlighting the contrast between the sky and the darkness below. Jake sighed in resignation.

Jake turned away from the window, and a question occurred to him. Where was he to go from here? Was there another girl for him? The very thought, which would have seemed unthinkable not that long ago, now presented itself and demanded an honest answer.

He then realized he could ask this without feeling like he was committing a sin against something sacred. Was there to be another girl?

That question produced another question almost before the first was answered. Could she be Hannah? Hannah was so different from Eliza. Could it be possible that he should show some interest in Hannah?

No, perhaps not, he decided. It was simply not fair to Hannah. No, Jake wouldn't do it. A friend—now that was a possibility. Was that not what they experienced at the volleyball game on Saturday night when they felt so compatible, so much that even others noticed it?

Jake concluded that it was. They were a natural at it. He would keep it so. This new direction would not need to have the same goal as before—that of marriage—but simply something more manageable—a friendship with a girl.

Jake went to the kitchen table, picked up his dirty dishes, and took them to the sink. The summer lay before him. He would enjoy it freely and without regret. That was his decision, and next week would be a good time to start.

Twenty-three

More than a week later on a Saturday afternoon, Hannah was busy with the horse brush, taking long rapid strokes on Prince and Mandy's coats. She planned to turn the horses out to pasture for the weekend when she was done. The last riders for the day had just trotted up the trail on the other two horses.

It had been a long day. The first riders of the day brought their six-year-old son, Jared, with them. The sign at the end of the driveway now held the phrase, "Will Babysit While You Ride," written in small letters underneath "Horseback Riding," and so childcare was expected.

Jared, however, was *not* what Hannah was expecting. He wouldn't listen to anything she asked him to do. Instead, he ran all over the barn and into places that were dangerous for him. Everywhere he went, Hannah had to follow him.

"What's this?" he asked, sticking his hand into a feed bag of oats.

"It's a bag of oats," Hannah said. "The horses like oats a lot."

He then pulled out his hand and let a handful of fresh oats run through his fingers and onto the floor.

"It's for the horses," she said. "You can't waste their food."

"I never saw horses eat this stuff on TV," he said. "It must not be any good." Jared then deliberately tipped over the bag so the oats spilled out onto the floor.

"Don't do that!" Hannah protested. "Now I have to pick them all up."

"But if they're not good for the horses, you should throw them away."

"They *are* good for the horses," Hannah said. "Television doesn't show everything."

"Yes, it does," he said. "I watch it all the time."

So it went from one end of the barn to the other.

Finally when his parents returned, Hannah sighed in relief, only to see that the next couple also brought along their child.

This time it was little Louise, and although she was not nearly as much trouble as Jared, she did pull the cat's tail and manage to get herself scratched on the hand. This made Louise cry loudly, and she never completely subsided until her parents finally returned.

The incident also required Hannah to give Louise's mother an explanation that became more involved the longer Hannah talked. Her explanation didn't seem to have the same effect it would have for Amish mothers.

"Do you have some bandages?" the mother finally asked.

"Ah, yes," Hannah told her, "they're in the house." Since it was such a small scratch, she had not thought to bandage it but now went to get the kit Betty kept in the kitchen pantry.

With the hand bandaged, Louise's mother wanted to examine the offending cat. Hannah was afraid this demand would be hard to comply with now that kitty's tail had been pulled, but to her surprise, kitty proved amicable, even purring in Hannah's arms. Louise's mother thoroughly and carefully examined the cat. When she was satisfied, the mother petted the cat. The cat offered no resistance, even arching his neck for her hand.

"This cat is usually just fine," Hannah said and then thought about adding, *unless someone pulls his tail,* but decided against it.

"I guess everything will be okay," the mother finally ventured and gathered up Louise to go. "Maybe you ought to watch the cat in the future, though," she said.

Hannah nodded. What else was there to do? She would watch kitty in the future, if for no other reason than to keep him away from any future babysitting charges she might have.

So the day had gone, and now Hannah glanced up and was surprised to see another car drive up. *Not another customer*, Hannah thought.

The vehicle slowed, and someone got out, but not the driver. No, it was Jake Byler!

He got out of the car and waved to the driver, who then took off. Jake walked toward the barn. Hannah was uncertain how she'd react. She did have to admit he was an attractive boy. She quickly shoved *that* thought away before it triggered other unwanted thoughts.

Hannah tensed, prepared herself, and waited for his arrival. *What on earth could he want?* Surely Jake was not up to what he seemed to be. If he was, she would have nothing of it. There was simply no reason for this. Hannah had given Jake no encouragement of this sort, not even an indication at either the volleyball game or on Sunday night.

"Hi," Jake said when he got close enough for her to hear him. "How's your day going?"

Hannah shrugged and then said, "The last riders are on the trail."

"Do you have an opening for one more?" he asked.

When she hesitated, Jake said, "I know it probably sounds funny, but I get lonesome when I'm away from horses too long. I thought this would be a good way to get some riding in and some exercise too."

"You want to ride?" she asked, uncertain she had heard him right.

"Yes," he said, "how much is it for an hour?"

She told him.

"That sounds fine," Jake said.

Hannah, however, wasn't finished. "You—an Amish boy—are paying to ride a horse?"

"Why not?" Jake asked. "The Forest Service pays me well enough. Can't I spend some of it on a worthwhile cause?"

"I suppose so," Hannah said, unconvinced. She was sure there must be more to it than this and waited. Any moment now he would surely drop the other shoe.

"So, which horse will it be?" Jake asked.

She forced herself to think. "Prince, I guess. He's a wonderful horse."

"You like him?"

"Yes," she said, "very much."

"Then Prince it is," Jake said as if that ended the matter.

"I just got him brushed down, but I can do it again when you come back," Hannah said as she stroked the horse's neck.

"Don't worry. I'll do it. It's not like my Saturday afternoons are that full. Where's the saddle?" Jake asked, looking around.

Hannah pointed toward the barn. "I'll get it if you lead him over closer."

"No, you lead him," Jake said, his voice firm. "I'll get the saddle. Which one is it?"

Hannah took the reins from him and kept her eyes from his face. She did not want feelings to come at her again. There was just no way this could go anywhere. She was writing to Sam, and that's all there was to it. Another Peter was not on her list of things to do in life.

"It's the one on the first hook. The big leather one."

Jake headed toward the barn as Hannah followed with Prince. Expertly he threw the saddle on, fastened the cinches, mounted, and was off. "I'll be back in an hour," he called over his shoulder.

Hannah watched him ride up the trail, but Jake didn't look back. His hands expertly handled Prince's reins, and his body gently flowed with the rhythm of Prince's trot. Hannah was impressed. Jake did know how to ride a horse.

Just then Hannah became aware of Betty's presence behind her.

"What on earth is Jake Byler doing here on a Saturday afternoon?"

Hannah turned, her heart in her throat, and hoped Betty wouldn't notice.

"I don't know. He was just dropped off by his ride and then walked up to me and asked for a horse to ride."

Betty didn't look convinced.

"He's paying just like the rest," Hannah offered in an effort to make her case.

"He is?" Betty said but was still skeptical. "An Amish boy? He'd pay?"

"Jake said he needed to be around horses and that he wanted the exercise." Hannah put on her best smile. "He's paying for an hour."

Betty raised her eyebrows. "And there's nothing else? You know how your mother would feel if you were to quit Sam over another boy."

"I'm not doing that," Hannah replied, "and don't go telling Jake that I'm writing Sam. It would just insult him. He's not after me. I'm sure of that."

"Well, you might best let others be the judge of that," Betty said. Then, as an afterthought, she added, "Are you after *him*?"

"No, of course not!" Hannah said, her heart determined.

Betty seemed satisfied. "Well, it looked funny to me, is all." Then she changed subjects. "How did your day go?"

Hannah let out a breath of relief. "Not too well, actually."

"Really?" Betty seemed surprised.

Hannah started with Jared and then Louise until Betty had the whole story. Betty listened and nodded. "We all have days like that once in a while. Just be thankful, as I am, that God has given us protection for another day. Be extra careful with the children, though. Take whatever time it takes."

"Yes, I will," Hannah said. "And I *am* thankful. Louise's mother had me scared."

"God helped us," Betty was quick to say, "but we must also do our part—whatever way we can. I wouldn't let the children play with the pets anymore. "

Hannah nodded.

With that, Betty returned to the house. The last riders had returned and had just driven away when Jake came down the trail. "That's quite some horse you have here."

"He's wonderful," Hannah agreed, her joy overwhelming her caution. Prince had that effect on her.

"That he is," Jake said as he dismounted. He handed Hannah the reins, undid the cinches, and carried the saddle back into the barn. With a grin and a flourish, he pulled his wallet out to pay her.

"I'll have to do this more often," he declared as he handed her the money. "Oh, by the way, when are you returning to Indiana?"

"At the end of the summer—maybe the end of August," Hannah said. "What about you?"

"I don't know yet," he answered. "The fire season needs to end first. I guess that varies from year to year with how dry it is. When that's done, I'll be going back."

Jake cleared his throat and glanced at her.

Hannah stiffened. *Don't do it. The answer will be no.*

"I thought maybe the young people from the community could come up some Saturday morning for a hike past my station. It's quite a view from up there." Jake smiled sheepishly. "If it's on the Saturday when I come down, I could go back with you."

Hannah cleared her throat and avoided his eyes. The request seemed harmless enough, but she didn't trust herself. "I guess so. You would have to ask some of the others. I just do what they do."

"I suppose so," Jake allowed. "I'll see what Bishop Nisley says about the plan. He should know how to schedule something like that and if they would even be interested."

Hannah nodded, and then Jake was gone, his steps taking him quickly down the road. Apparently he planned to walk over to the Nisley's to get more exercise.

"There's a letter from Hannah on the living room table," Sam's mother said when he walked in for supper.

Sam headed for the letter, but his mom stopped him. "Clean up first, and if your father is still not in, you can look at it then."

He hesitated, offering a frown before heading for the sink in the laundry entrance.

Laura watched him go. *My, they all grow up so fast, especially the last ones.* She sighed, and her eyes misted over. *This one is going to be hard to let go of. And this Hannah thing—is she really right for my son?*

Getting jumpy, like Enos said, in my old age. Maybe that's why I'm worrying about him so much. What if he gets the wrong girl, though? The question made her catch her breath. Surely Sam would have better sense than that. But it worried her. Once married there was no longer any question of whether it was wrong or not. Now was the time to ask questions.

When Sam returned, cleaner now, she asked, "How's it going with Hannah?"

After stepping back to toss the towel into the laundry room, he turned toward her. The glow on his face said it all.

"She writes wonderful letters," he said.

"When's she coming home?"

"She hasn't said," he replied and headed for the living room to read the letter since there was no sign of his father yet.

Laura heard Sam tear open the envelope as Enos slammed the door.

"Supper ready?" he shouted from the laundry room.

"As soon as you wash up," she said.

Sam was in his place at the kitchen table before his father had finished cleaning up, and the smile on his face lasted all through suppertime.

I sure hope he knows what he's doing. Laura thought as supper proceeded in silence.

Twenty-four

Bishop Nisley agreed readily with Jake that the youth would have a great time hiking into the mountains. He said such a thing could be arranged for the young people in the near future. On Sunday morning he would ask several of the men about the matter. Elizabeth would make inquires among the women, and he would let Jake know.

The next time Jake came down, Bishop Nisley had his answer. There had been no negative reactions, and the announcement was to be made that Sunday during his youth Sunday school class. The news was greeted with enthusiasm, and Jake congratulated himself. After all, it had been his idea.

"When will it be?" Ben Stoll asked.

"How about the first Saturday in July?" Bishop Nisley said. "If it doesn't suit someone, let me know today after church, and maybe we can move the date."

That was not necessary, it turned out, and so at eight o'clock on the first Saturday in July, Hannah waited for her ride into the mountains. Originally, they had talked about using the buggies to get to the Cabinet Mountains, which were within sight of the Amish community. That was until Ben Stoll received an offer from the English boy he worked with on the logging crew. The boy offered his driving services and his pickup truck on the condition he could go along.

"It's an Amish youth group," Ben told him.

174

"No problem," Scott said. "Hey, I work with the Amish, right?"

"You're not after one of our girls, are you?" Ben teased.

Scott laughed. "Like I would do that? They're *Amish*. Besides, I already have a girlfriend."

"Well, then bring her along," Ben suggested.

"We'll see," Scott told him. "I'll have to ask."

Hannah watched from the living room window and saw the pickup truck pull into the driveway. An English boy, who she assumed was Scott, drove with a girl in the seat beside him.

"There are only Amish boys in the back," Hannah protested to Betty. "I don't want to be the only girl!"

"John and Elizabeth are going along," Betty said. "They probably haven't picked them up yet."

"Are you sure about that?" Hannah asked.

"I'm sure," Betty said.

Bales of hay were stacked in the bed of the pickup to be used as make-do seats. Hannah was offered a comfortable spot toward the back as well as nods of "good morning" from the seated boys.

Settled in, Hannah hung on tightly as Scott turned left at the end of the driveway toward Bishop Nisley's place. Not used to riding in the back of trucks, she soon learned to face backward. The wind took her breath away once Scott got up to his cruising speed.

John and Elizabeth waited at the end of their driveway, and Hannah made room for them beside her on the straw bale.

Scott made a U-turn, headed back to Troy, and then turned south in town toward the Cabinet Mountains. When he came to where the road started to climb, he stopped and hollered out of his window, "How far are we driving up?"

"To Jake's cabin," John said. "We'll get out and hike the rest of the way from there."

"You know where the cabin is?" Scott called back. The truck jerked as he found the low gear.

"Jake said it was about three quarters of the way up. It's the only outpost on this side, so we should be able to find it easily."

"Good enough," Scott nodded.

They drove slowly. The pickup started to groan under its load as the grade became steeper.

"Going to make it?" John hollered forward.

Scott didn't hear him or else decided to keep his mind on his driving.

The truck made its way with deep groans up another grade to where the road leveled off, a steep bank on the right. Here the view opened up to the sweep of the valley below. Scott hugged the cliff's edge for a few hundred yards before the road turned and went up again.

Hannah barely had time to enjoy the view or catch her breath. Still the sight below them was the first good view of the valley and the town of Libby in the background.

"Beautiful," John said, his hands tightly gripping the truck's sides.

"It is nice," Elizabeth agreed, turning on the straw bale for a better view. "I'd enjoy it more, though, if I didn't think we'd fall off this mountain."

John laughed. "It's a good truck, and Scott's a good driver. Just enjoy God's handiwork. He really did some of His best work in these mountains."

Hannah looked when she could stand it. At the next turn, the scene was repeated, only higher up and enhanced by the freshness of the morning mountain air. *This view makes my senses come alive,* Hannah thought, *that and the thrill of danger.* They rode on in silence, watching for fresh views of the valley until a cabin and an obvious lookout tower came into sight.

"We're here," Scott announced as he pulled the truck into the designated parking space.

John unlatched the tailgate before he jumped down and then offered to help the others. Hannah brushed straw from her dress as Elizabeth did the same.

Hannah tried not to appear too eager to see Jake. After all, he only caused her trouble with the way he made her feel.

The door to the cabin opened, and Jake stepped out. He grinned, waved, and asked John, "Are you driving all the way to the top?"

"No," John told him, "we want to hike from here."

"You want to climb the tower first?" he asked.

Hannah found this agreeable as did the others. She could stay with the group, sort of out of sight, as Jake led the way to the tower. There was a momentary wait until another group came back down.

"I am off work all day," Jake said. "Another ranger will take my place. I guess they don't have this many friends come up every day."

Hannah watched Jake's face and thought she saw more than he had explained. Likely this gave him a chance to avoid the English uniform she heard he wore. Bishop Nisley had approved it, but Jake might not want to take the chance of letting them actually see him in it.

Jake seemed intense as he waited for the younger couple to make their way down the winding staircase, past the Amish group that waited to enter the observation platform.

"Girls first," Jake announced when they were past. He motioned with his hand, and Elizabeth and John went first.

"You next," he told Hannah with a quick smile and then followed her up.

She felt no nervousness at this public display. Not that Jake had made a big deal, but her friendly relationship with Jake was already well established with the others. If they only knew what her feelings toward Jake sometimes were, they might actually conjure up a few ideas. Hannah felt very thankful that no one but God could know her thoughts. To the others Jake was her friend—almost like a brother.

Hannah glanced back at Jake who was still following closely behind.

"Some view, huh?" he said brightly.

Indeed it was, and Hannah nodded. She wished her heart wouldn't beat as hard as it did, but perhaps that was from the climb. With a glance out over the valley, she asked, "They pay you to work here?"

"It doesn't seem right," he said, laughing, "but they do."

When they reached the top, Hannah stood with the others, taking in the full impact of the view. "It's so beautiful," she said, her voice expressing the awe she felt.

Jake nodded silently beside her.

"Time to go down," he said a few moments later. "We have to keep it moving. Lots of people come through on a Saturday."

Halfway down Hannah glanced over her shoulder toward Jake. For the first time, she caught a gleam in his eye that she had never seen before. Her heart leaped, and this time Hannah couldn't blame it on the climb. Hannah only hoped she wasn't bright red.

By the time she reached the bottom of the stairs, she had somehow collected herself. She made sure to keep her eyes away from Jake's face as she walked over to the railing to look at the valley again. The other half of the group headed up the metal stairs above her.

"Have you thought about moving out here?" Elizabeth asked from beside her. Hannah had been too distracted to notice Elizabeth's approach.

"It's a wonderful area," she replied as soon as she could think of what to say. "But moving...I'm not sure. I'm still an Indiana girl at heart."

"We're always looking for new people," Elizabeth said, "young couples especially. It seems like they are more resilient than older people to new things."

Hannah decided it was time to re-establish things as quickly as possible. "Sam will inherit the farm on the home place," she said.

"Oh, you're that serious, then?" Elizabeth said.

Now Hannah did blush. "Well, we're writing."

"He must be a nice boy," Elizabeth said hopefully.

Hannah nodded. She didn't trust further words. Sam was nice. At least her mom thought so. She might agree if his mouth didn't fall open all the time.

Moments later the group got underway again and reached the top of the mountain an hour later. Going back down was much quicker. Jake seemed to make a point of staying out of Hannah's way the rest of the afternoon. Even on the way home, he sat on the back end of the pickup. Hannah sat on a hay bale close to the cab.

The truck stopped at the end of Betty and Steve's driveway to drop Hannah off first. After her brief goodbyes, she walked into the kitchen where Betty cheerfully asked, "Did you have a good time?"

"Wonderful," Hannah said. "The valley looks lovely from up there."

"Any problems?"

"No," Hannah said, wondering if the way Jake looked at her that once in the tower might actually become a problem. She resolved, quite firmly, to keep her dreams in check.

Twenty-five

That evening after she retired to her room upstairs, Hannah made a valiant effort to stem the tide of her uncertain feelings. They seemed to come in waves out of nowhere. In desperation she shut her eyes in an attempt to block them out. But then they would come again—those same desires the poem and Peter had awakened in her.

Perhaps action would help. Hannah took out paper and a pen to write. Surely a letter to Sam would help her focus again. It was worth the attempt because something needed to be done.

"Dear Sam," she wrote on the fresh sheet of paper and then continued.

> *We hiked up the mountain today during a youth outing.*
> *The view of the valley was really something.*

Hannah lifted her pen, considered what else to write, and then decided to include more details of the day and tidbits about her past week handling riders. When she came to the end, Hannah told Sam:

> *I know it's only the first part of July, but already my*
> *thoughts are about coming home at the end of August. As*
> *fast as the time has been going out here, it will come soon*
> *enough.*

She thought for a second and then closed with, "I will see you then, I guess. Love, Hannah."

She slipped the letter into an envelope and sealed it for Monday's mail.

"There," she said out loud, "that's done."

Now no more dreaming! Hannah told herself as she got ready for bed.

But once her eyes closed, Hannah drifted between sleep and awakening and then *did* dream. It was Peter's car again she rode in, gravel crunching under its tires. They were traveling at a fast rate, but she couldn't see who drove the car. Somehow she sensed in her dream that it was not Peter at the wheel.

They passed rapidly through the darkness and then under the yard light of some residence along the road. She caught a glimpse of the driver's face. It was Jake Byler. The face was focused and intent. And then the light from the yard light was gone, and she couldn't see anymore. In the darkness she hung on to the handle as horror swept over her. She was disobeying again, and now she was back in the car. How had this happened without her consent, or had she consented and didn't know it?

Scenes flashed in front of her eyes as the car slowed and finally stopped. She glanced outside the window but wasn't sure where she was. A flash of light came through the car and revealed the driver's face again. It *was* Jake.

As darkness filled the car again, the first notes of the praise song began. Jake was singing them loudly, confidently, just like he had done at church. Its melody rose and fell in the night air. Never had she heard such a haunted and out of place sound.

Hannah reached deep within her for the strength to awaken. Her muscles strained with the efforts, and it seemed as if nothing moved. Her left arm was pasted to her side, and the other clutched the handle by the window and wouldn't let go.

She filled her mouth with air and screamed. At least she thought she did. Finally awake, she heard no sound. Her body was covered in sweat under the covers and chilled. The whole house was silent. Hannah waited for footsteps in the hall, expecting someone to come and see what the problem was. There was still only silence.

If she had screamed, wouldn't she have awakened someone? Hannah waited, trembled, and listened in the dim starlit room. Still, no one seemed to stir anywhere else in the house.

Finally her breathing slowed, and she relaxed enough to think about going back to sleep. Hannah's last thought before dropping off was a fresh resolution to hold her heart's dreams in check. *I must stay away from Jake Byler.* That much was clear. How could such a nice boy do such awful things? But then hadn't Peter also been nice? Her heart obviously couldn't be trusted to do the right thing.

In the morning, Betty said nothing about any screams in the night, and so Hannah figured that must also have been a dream.

At church the next morning, Hannah kept her eyes on the floor whenever Jake Byler was in her line of vision. Sunday night at the hymn singing, she made a point to sit on the second bench even though the younger girls sat there. She had to avoid Jake no matter how great the effort.

Hannah crawled into bed that evening, impressed with her own efforts to still her heart, yet had a vague suspicion she might have made matters worse. How that could be, she wasn't sure. A brief glimpse of Jake's face toward the end of hymn singing didn't bode well.

By the end of the week, Sam received his letter from Hannah. He was close to the barn door when the letter carrier stopped at the mailbox. In a dash out the lane, he was the one who got to the mailbox first. He read the letter, one page dangling in the air on the walk back to the house.

What he read couldn't have pleased him more. Hannah's hard work with the horse stable at Steve and Betty's continued to impress him. Perhaps she was quite the businesswoman. This couldn't help but improve his parents' opinions of her.

Also, Hannah had said she would come home soon and would be seeing him then. Not that they had ever said it in so many words, but it had been somehow implied. Now it was official—of this Sam was sure. Hannah would be his steady in the true sense of the word—not just in letters but in his buggy on Sunday nights for the ride home.

The whole world would know that he, Sam Knepp, had done well for himself. Gone would be the stigma he had often felt since the last few years of Amish grade school. Now, with such a girl as Hannah by his side, all would be set right.

Sam held his chin firm as he walked up the lane toward the house, his letter still in his hand. This was a moment to savor. Full of joy, he remembered to keep his mouth shut. He was almost a man, and such habits now seemed to belong to childhood days.

"Another letter?" his mother asked when he stuck his head through the kitchen doorway to deliver the rest of the mail.

He grinned, and his face revealed the answer before he shut the door.

She watched him walk toward the barn, his step high, but she couldn't help the worried look on her face.

❖

The next week a letter arrived from Sam. Hannah stuck it in her drawer after she read it, intending to read it again later, but time seemed to get away from her.

This was Jake's scheduled weekend down from the mountain, and against all her protests, Hannah knew she wanted to see him.

On Saturday the regular number of riders arrived throughout the day, keeping her busy. As of yet, there had been no unruly children, but her nerves were on edge for another reason. How was she to deal with Jake if he came down today for another of his rides?

No amount of worrying about it seemed to provide a solution, nor did her resolution to keep her feelings in check give her much comfort. By three o'clock, she had gotten the last group of riders ready and had just sent them off down the trail when a car slowed down and then stopped by the road.

She turned to look but knew who it was before she could see him. Jake Byler climbed out, waved, and while she stood there, her heart rattling, he came right toward her, his form tall and confident.

Hannah was sure he looked like Peter, only different in every other way. But after that dream the other night, she wasn't so sure. He *seemed* so much more mature, conscientious, clean, wholesome, and even godly. Surely her dream had deceived her about him. Jake would never drive a car, let alone try to steal a kiss from her.

Please, God, help me, she prayed silently. *I'm not a strong person like I need to be. You will have to save me.*

"Hi," Jake said as he approached her. "Are your riders about done?"

Hannah took a deep breath and thought, *So far so good.* He seemed like he always had before. Maybe she had just imagined things in her *dummkopf* ways. That was what it was she decided. She had jumped to conclusions when there really were none to jump to.

"The last ones for the day, I hope," she said as their eyes met. His eyes looked like they always did—gentle and friendly. She relaxed. "Do you want Prince again?"

"Yes," he said. He paused momentarily before asking softly, "Would you come riding with me today?"

She froze, unable to find her voice.

Jake looked at her with a question on his face. "You love to ride," Jake said. "I thought we might go together."

Hannah fumbled for the right answer. "I...I guess we could."

"Then it suits," he said. "Is Prince in?"

"Yes," Hannah said, "both he and Mandy are in the barn."

"So you were waiting for me?" he asked and grinned.

"No...Yes...I mean, I expected you to come. You often stop by on your Saturdays."

"Well," he said, "let's get going, or do you have to wait for your riders to come back?"

"Someone has to," she said. It occurred to her that if Betty were told about the ride with Jake now, this would be much easier than when

she came back. Why not ask her to take care of the returning group
and break the news that way?

"I'll ask Betty," Hannah said and turned toward the house.

Hannah entered the house and found Betty folding laundry. As
casually as she could, Hannah said, "Would you mind taking care of
the last group of riders when they come back?"

Betty looked questioningly at her. "You're not going to be here?"

"Well…Jake asked me to ride with him," she said, sure her cheeks
were red.

"No," Betty said firmly, "you can't do that. You're writing."

"But it's not like that," Hannah assured her. "If Jake asks for anything
such as bringing me home on Sunday night, I'll say 'no' right away.
This is just a ride. I think it would be rude not to go with him."

Betty didn't look convinced.

Hannah couldn't help the flow of words from her mouth. "I can't
hurt Jake's feelings. He's down here by himself…away from his family.
He's not been untoward at all. He'll think I have something against
him if I don't go."

Betty thought for a long moment while Hannah held her breath.

"Well, I guess," she said finally. "You have both behaved yourselves. Yes,
I'll take care of your riders, but don't get any ideas about Jake. Okay?"

Hannah nodded and quickly went out before Betty could change
her mind.

Jake had both horses ready as she approached. He gave Mandy's
reins to her and then climbed onto Prince. Hannah mounted Mandy,
careful to keep her eyes away from Jake.

Together they rode in the direction of the river with Jake leading
the way.

At the river they met the other riders on their way back. Hannah
told them about the arrangement with Betty, to which they readily
agreed.

Both had grins on their faces as if they knew more went on between
the couple than what Hannah admitted to. Hannah told herself they
were wrong. She wished to speak the protestation out loud, but figured
that would just make matters worse.

With a press of her reins she followed Jake, who was already heading down to the river. The riders would just have to think what they wanted to. She had plans to be good girl. Of this, she was determined.

"Let's go," Jake yelled over his shoulder as he approached the open stretch by the river. He waited momentarily until Hannah caught up, and then he let the reins out on Prince. With only a brief backward glance, Jake rode Prince in a wide-open gallop.

Jake assumed a lot, Hannah thought as they raced along the river. How did he know she could ride this well? She had never ridden with him before, nor mentioned her ability. Yet, the fact that he felt she was that good was obvious by his actions. Her heart throbbed with the pleasure of his confidence in her.

Hannah kicked Mandy lightly in the ribs and thrills ran up and down her spine. It wasn't just the speed she quickly achieved or the rhythm of a horse under her. She knew it was more than the wind whistling through her hair. It was Jake, bent over on his horse, his legs firm in the stirrups. He *was* a dream, after all, in so many ways. Yet Hannah knew she could never admit this—not to herself, not to God, and especially not to Jake himself. Jake was forbidden to her by forces beyond her control. There was a line between them that could never be crossed.

When Jake pulled Prince in, Hannah did the same with Mandy and came to a stop just behind him.

"Wow, that was something!" he exclaimed. "You do know how to ride."

Hannah shrugged. "Of course, I do. We have horses in Indiana."

"Is that where you learned to ride like that?" Jake asked.

"Yes. I've had a pony since I was small," she said. Then she added, "I fell off of him shortly before I came here...broke my collarbone. Things like that help you learn."

"How did it happen?"

"Honey, my horse, stepped into a groundhog hole," Hannah said and almost added, "Sam was there." But that wouldn't do. Jake wouldn't understand. She was to be married to Sam, the same Sam who had stood there by the fence with his mouth open and watched her. She

was to be Sam's wife someday, but now—here as she rode with Jake—
her heart was beating furiously. Things were strange, indeed, in how
they worked out. Hannah supposed it would all be okay once she was
married. It seemed to be so for others once they said yes to the bishop's
questions. Maybe then all these silly love dreams would cease, and
she could be what she was supposed to be—obedient to her parents
and a good wife to Sam.

"Did it hurt the horse?" Jake had apparently asked the question
already, but she hadn't noticed.

"Oh, no," Hannah said, her face blushing. Why did she have to be
so clumsy? What if he knew what she'd been thinking?

"How did he keep from breaking his leg?" Jake asked.

Hannah willed her brain to stop its spin and tried to form words
that made sense. "He...I don't know. It happened so fast. I suppose
we were going slowly enough that he had time to pull it out."

"Still he was going fast enough to break your collarbone?"

"Yes," she said. "He threw me against a fence post. It doesn't take
much speed when you add in the fall."

"I'm glad you weren't hurt worse."

Hannah nodded her thanks.

They rode on in silence for a while, just admiring the surrounding
beauty.

Finally Jake said, "I suppose we should head back now?"

Hannah nodded, and they rode back to the barn in silence.

Betty said nothing about the subject that night, and Hannah did
her best to ignore Jake in church the next morning. Hannah again
got the distinct feeling that ignoring him might just have made things
worse, but there seemed to be little she could do about it.

Twenty-six

As July quickly faded, Hannah realized there were only a few more weeks left of her stay in Montana. Her baptism would take place on the last Sunday she was here.

She'd miss this place with its beautiful mountains, peace, brisk air, and, of course, the people she had met. At the bottom of it all, she admitted—just once and then quickly shoved the thought away— she'd be sad not to see Jake anymore.

There were two Saturdays yet when he would likely stop in for a ride. If he didn't, that would certainly solve her problem. But deep down, in spite of the potential for pain, she hoped he would drop by again.

Turning her mind where it belonged—to Sam—she sat down on Friday night to write him a letter. She told him all the news she could think of—the riders, the horses, how beautiful the approach of fall weather was here, and of her planned trip home.

In the morning Hannah got up early to start the day, but the riders made a slow start of things. Few showed.

"It's getting toward the end of summer, and the weather is beginning to cool," Betty said when Hannah came back into the house at ten o'clock. "We always slow down about this time of the year."

Hannah had little to do after lunch and was glad to see that Jake was indeed coming by today. This time he rode out alone on Prince. She watched him go, and emotions throbbed through her. Why hadn't he invited her along? Was he mad at her? Had she offended him? Then she realized what she was thinking and spoke harshly to herself,

"Stop it right now. It doesn't matter. It's none of my business how he's feeling. It could just be his work or something. And I'll be leaving soon…very soon."

Startled to hear the kitchen door open, Hannah glanced up. It was just Betty, who waved and then went back inside. The gesture was unmistakable. Betty had just checked up on her. *She doesn't trust me anymore. She thinks I am going riding with Jake again and am up to something.*

Hannah pressed her hand against her head. To distract herself, she went into the barn and brushed Mandy down and then released her into the pasture. She didn't want to go inside yet, and so she waited out of Betty's sight until the sound of Prince's hooves came back down the trail.

"It's getting a little chilly," Jake commented as he dismounted. "Fall comes early in this country." He didn't look at her.

"That's what Betty said," Hannah said as a feeling of desperation flowed through her. She wished he would look at her. How would she stand it if Jake was mad at her for some reason?

"Well, I should be going," he muttered. "John has some work for me to do yet before dark."

Hannah tried to think of what she could say and came up with nothing. Jake nodded and was gone. She watched his back retreat slowly down the lane and then down the road. It was a full ten minutes before Hannah could move again. Her face ashen, she found her way to the house.

Betty couldn't help but notice Hannah's composure when she came in. "Are you okay?" she asked.

Hannah nodded, apparently unconvincingly.

"Was there a problem with the horses?" Betty probed.

Hannah shook her head, "No, they're fine."

"What is it then? You look positively white."

Hannah didn't trust her voice, and so she simply flopped down on the couch. The house was silent as Betty looked at her.

"I guess it's that Jake," Betty finally concluded. "You haven't agreed to see him, have you?"

Hannah shook her head.

"Did he ask?"

"No," Hannah managed to say.

"This isn't turning into something it shouldn't be, is it?" Betty's eyes bored into Hannah's.

"I don't think so," Hannah ventured.

Betty raised her eyebrows. "I think your heart is straying again. That's really what's happening. You must stop this, Hannah. You know that, don't you?"

Hannah nodded numbly. She *did* know it, but she was helpless to do anything about it.

"Well, I'm glad to hear you say it." Betty's voice reached her as if from a great distance. "Thankfully, there are only two more weeks, and then this thing will be over. I want to get you safely home to your mother."

Hannah tried to smile, but the effort wasn't very successful. It seemed to satisfy Betty. She patted Hannah on the head as if she were a five-year-old.

"I'll try real hard," Hannah said. "And I'm looking forward to getting back home. I will miss this place, though, and the people out here."

Betty smiled now. "We will miss you too, and maybe that's part of your problem. Leaving and going home like this. Well, you can always come back for a visit."

"It's pretty far," Hannah said. "It's expensive too."

"That it is, but we will just have to see. Well, I must get busy. Sunday's coming on fast." She then headed for the kitchen and her work. Hannah soon followed her, tackling the day's stack of dishes without being told. The splash of the water and the slush of the soap soon joined her thoughts of Jake in one mixed-up, jumbled mess.

After supper Hannah went to bed early. She could see that Betty approved of this because the whole family liked an early bedtime on a Saturday night. Hannah had tried to comply once she understood the custom. And tonight it was no sacrifice. She was ready for sleep.

Thankfully no dreams came, and she woke refreshed. That morning at church, Hannah sat on the church bench facing the line of teenage boys as usual. Jake sat all the way over on the end. To her dismay, Hannah couldn't keep from looking in Jake's direction. All her resolve to control her feelings and to obey her parents waved around like a stalk of dry wheat blowing in the wind.

When Jake finally looked at her, the dam broke. She could hide it no longer. Hannah let him see every feeling she had for him. Every desire that her dream had inspired passed from her eyes to his. And she knew it could never be taken back. Jake now knew.

What she expected the next time she looked in his direction, she wasn't certain. Feelings of guilt rushed over her, but she couldn't help herself. Jake would now ask her home, of that she was sure. When or how didn't matter. Hannah also knew her answer would be, "Yes."

That would involve so many things, confessions to Betty and to her mother topped the list. It would also mean a letter to Sam, or perhaps she would wait and tell him when she got home. The thought of his mouth dropping open in shock and disbelief caused her no joy. Instead her sorrow increased. How could one do something one knew wasn't right and still be unable to stop it?

Maybe God will help me yet, Hannah thought. That brightened her spirits a little. He always had before, had He not? Yes, that's what she would do. She would pray and ask for help. Surely the Almighty God in heaven, who knew so much and could run the whole world, could figure this all out.

But does He have time? The thought startled her. Hannah had no idea what the answer was. *Suppose He doesn't and I'm on my own?* Panic struck her, and she prayed all the more for God to help her— somehow.

Around her, the church service continued. Bishop John had the main sermon, and Hannah tried to focus her attention. The desire to look at Jake was somehow gone now that she knew he knew.

Whether or not Jake paid her any attention, she felt no desire to know. It was only a matter of time now when she would say yes. Beyond that the world looked far more fearful than she would ever have thought possible. Her future would have to rest with what God would do for her.

When there was no sign of Jake after the service, peace still stayed with her. God would surely supply help in some way.

◆

At his cabin and surrounded by the presence of the Cabinet Mountains, Jake went through his plans. His time to leave was approaching, but the looming question was what to do about Hannah? She cared for him—a lot—he now knew for certain.

But what could he do about it? Could he ask Hannah for a relationship? He wasn't sure. For all his efforts to the contrary, there remained a residue of anger for what Eliza had done to his emotions. No doubt by now, she and his cousin were even talking of marriage. His cousin was now the one who looked into the blue eyes that Jake had once thought he would spend a lifetime gazing into. The two of them would marry and live out their happiness right in front of him.

No, his pain was not as sharp as it once was. Likely Hannah was responsible for that. She had given him a completely new vision of what a girl could be, and he admitted that he liked that vision better.

Jake started getting some of his things together, but he wouldn't pack until Thursday of the next week. There was little to pack, and most of his things could be easily thrown into his duffel bag. On Friday he would hitch a ride down to town for his final paycheck.

That left the question of whether he should stay at the Nisley's for one more weekend or return home right away. The Nisleys would think nothing of his early departure, and his parents would be glad to see him.

Jake decided without too much thought that he would go back to church for one more weekend, and he would ask Hannah about their new relationship. That thought brought a smile to his face. How wonderful God was, and His ways were truly mysterious. Here he had thought the world had ended when Eliza betrayed him, but, instead, it had just begun in a completely fresh and new way.

Visions of a letter writing relationship with Hannah and perhaps visits to her community arose in Jake's mind. Suddenly he remembered that he wasn't quite certain where she lived. He knew she grew up somewhere in Indiana, but the Indiana Amish community was vast. He would have to ask her this along with the many other things that he was now curious about.

With the matter decided, he squared his shoulders, walked out to highway 2, and raised his thumb to hitch a ride. The second car pulled over, and twenty minutes later, he stood beneath the sign with the words "Horse Rides" printed above the phrase "Will Take Care of Children" in smaller letters.

Twenty-seven

From her seat in the living room, Hannah saw Jake arrive. There had been no riders all day except for one at eleven. Now that the Saturday housework was caught up, she and Betty were resting for a moment and savoring their last few hours together. Sunday would be the baptism, and Monday morning would find Hannah on the Greyhound bus to Indiana.

"It's Jake," Hannah said, startling Betty who had her back to the window.

"I was wondering if he'd stop by," Betty said dryly. "It's his last weekend also, isn't it?"

"Yes. He probably wants to ride Prince for one last time," Hannah said. She avoided Betty's eyes. Whatever miracle the Lord planned to do, He needed to do it fast.

"Let him get Prince by himself," Betty told her. "He's capable."

"I should be out there," Hannah insisted. "It's the last weekend."

Betty shrugged but didn't look very happy. "I guess it can do no harm now."

Hannah was out the door in a flash, much too fast she knew, but she couldn't help herself.

"Hi," Hannah said. Jake was standing by the barn door as if waiting for her.

"Hi." Jake turned and met her eyes. They were as warm and soft as Hannah had ever seen them.

Hannah felt her insides soften and looked quickly at the ground.

Her guess had been right. He was going to ask her before he left. Wasn't that why he was here? The confirmation came quickly.

"You want to ride with me?" Jake asked, his smile steady.

She nodded, glancing quickly up at him before she went to get the horses.

"I'll saddle both horses." Jake's voice stopped her.

"I can do at least one of them," Hannah protested.

Jake smiled but shook his head. He then took her hand off of the saddle and let it drop gently. She blushed, feeling awkward and bumbling as she stood there doing nothing. And yet, she enjoyed this moment. She was delighted to watch Jake swing the saddles into position, see the strength of his arms when he tightened the stirrups, and glimpse his smile when he noticed her watching him.

Later would come the guilty feelings, Hannah reasoned. They would just have to come because it was simply out of her power to do anything about it.

They mounted the horses and rode up the trail. Hannah turned and noticed without surprise that Betty was watching from the kitchen door.

When they reached the river, Jake turned to her. "One last good gallop for the summer?" he asked.

Hannah nodded and her heart swelled with emotion. What a boy he was—so alive and full of life! She bent slightly forward over her saddle and made ready to follow his lead. He laughed out loud as he urged Prince forward. The sound of his laughter was so musical and manly all at the same time that she could hardly believe such a sound existed.

Together they raced along the river plain, their horses' hooves beating in rhythm. The mountains filled Hannah's vision as the wind stung her eyes. It was all a little too much, and she was afraid there really would be a flow of tears, but somehow she managed to control her emotions.

Jake pulled Prince up and threw his head back in sheer joy. "Whee! That was something. I sure will miss it."

Hannah stopped Mandy beside him but didn't say anything. The moment had come, she was sure. Beside her, Jake sat on Prince, looking off into the distance as if considering the deeper things of life.

Hannah was just ready to say something to break into his thoughts when they both heard an unearthly piercing sound from the woods just to the west of them. Both horses reared and neighed in panic, their nostrils flaring in fear. Jake kept his mount, but Hannah slid off backward. She managed to use the saddle and Mandy's haunch to keep herself upright before hitting the ground and falling.

Jake yelled in anger when Hannah hit the ground. He waved his arms at the source of the awful sound—a large mountain lion that now stood in plain view in front of them. Jake tried to move Prince toward it but had to dismount when Prince jerked his head violently back and forth in refusal. He grabbed Mandy's reins and held both in one hand.

Reaching down, Jake found the rock he wanted and hurled it in the direction of the cat. The animal hissed as the stone flew past and into the woods. It then backed off a few paces, turned, and then vanished as suddenly as it had appeared.

With the horses in tow, Jake went to where Hannah still lay on the ground. "Are you hurt?" he asked.

She moved what body parts she could feel and then slowly rose to her feet. "Everything works," she commented without much confidence.

"There's blood on your foot," he said.

Hannah quickly found the spot just above the ankle where a small gash had been cut. "I probably cut it on a stone," she said.

"It needs to be looked at," Jake said. "It needs to be disinfected if nothing else."

Hannah nodded in agreement, dazed.

"Can you ride?" Jake asked.

"I think so," she said as she balanced herself against Mandy. The climb onto the saddle proved no problem, and they were soon on their way. They rode in silence all the way down the riverbank and then toward the house. Betty saw them coming. She noticed something amiss, raced out of the house, and met them halfway across the lawn. "What happened? Are you hurt?" She held on to Mandy's reins, her other hand on Hannah's leg.

"It was a mountain lion," Jake said. "It screamed at us, and the horses reared. Mandy threw Hannah off."

"Are you hurt?" Betty repeated, noticing the blood. "Come down off that horse right away so I can check."

"I think it's just a little scratch on my foot," Hannah volunteered.

"Let's look at your foot, then. Come down, and we can go into the house."

Hannah complied, swung her good leg across, and slowly slid off the saddle.

"I'll put the horses away and then check on her," Jake said. "I think I know where things go."

Betty nodded. "I'll tell Steve about this tonight," she said on the way into the house with Hannah in tow. "He'll get the game warden on this right away. We can't allow a big cat to wander around here."

Hannah didn't pay much attention to Betty's fussing about her foot. Her mind was on Jake and the interruption. How could Jake possibly restart the conversation now that Betty was present? Once inside, Betty grabbed the first aid packet and led Hannah upstairs. After she was certain Hannah could move all her limbs without pain, Betty concluded there really was nothing more serious than the cut on Hannah's leg. With that bandaged up, Betty went back downstairs, leaving Hannah to change.

Hannah heard Jake come in and the low murmur of voices. She rushed to finish changing, afraid that Betty might ask Jake to leave and let her rest or something. The least she could do, Hannah figured, was walk him to the barn. Perhaps away from the house, they could pick up where they left off.

Before she was done, the downstairs front door slammed sharply. Hannah couldn't see across the yard from her window, and so she tiptoed down the hall to look through the front bedroom window. Jake was walking purposefully across the yard without a backward glance. He soon turned to walk down the road. Betty had chased him off. Hannah sighed. Perhaps tomorrow they could patch things up. She no longer cared what people thought.

Hannah found Betty on the living room couch.

"So Jake left?" she asked.

"Yes. I just did what needed to be done," Betty said.

"I'll talk to him tomorrow," Hannah said. "I should have done this a long time ago."

"I don't think so." Betty pointed toward the small lamp stand beside the couch.

Hannah looked where Betty pointed. She had left one of her letters from Sam lying there, unread, from the morning's mail.

"I let him look at it," Betty said, her face determined.

Hannah's face went white. "He saw one of Sam's letters?" She barely got the words out.

"*Jah*," Betty said, "I told him you two have been writing all summer, that I thought you had been sweet on each other since your school days, and that your mother was really for it."

Hannah felt the world go round and round and had to sit down.

"I'm sorry," Betty said, "but you should have told him yourself."

"Maybe," Hannah said.

Later that night as the twinkling stars filled her window and the house was quiet and still, Hannah cried like a baby, her sobs muffled by her pillow.

Sunday morning—the day of Hannah's baptism—arrived with wonderful weather. But the joy of the occasion was diminished by Hannah's knowledge that after hearing about the letters between her and Sam, Jake would not be at church. He might even have already left for home.

It's for the best, Hannah tried to tell herself, knowing full well that her mind would not be able to convince her heart. Apparently God had intervened and answered her prayers. She just had no idea the answer would be so painful.

Hannah had woken up with a splitting headache, dressed, and made her way slowly downstairs. She knew her face must still be tearstained, but she didn't care.

"What on earth? What's happened to you, Hannah? You look awful," Betty said when Hannah entered the kitchen.

"I've messed everything up," she wailed.

"Sit down," Betty ordered. "Not so loud—you'll wake the rest of the children."

"Now it's my baptismal day, and Mom and Dad aren't even here."

"You knew that wasn't possible," Betty said, sympathy in her voice. "It's too far for them to travel, and everything moved so fast."

"I could have asked Bishop Nisley if I could be baptized at home." Hannah felt the tears come again, her insides in knots.

"That's a little late to think about now," Betty said. "You knew it would have been hard to move your baptism into Indiana since your instruction class was out here. Just be happy with what you have. It's a beautiful day for a baptism. And you have your problem with Jake solved—not the best way possible but taken care of. And you'll be baptized out here under our beautiful mountains."

Hannah felt the tears stop but not because of Betty's words. It was the thought that Jake wouldn't be in church that turned her heart cold and made her tears dry.

"It will be beautiful," Hannah agreed with a weak smile.

"That's a good girl." Betty patted her on the arm. "Now let's get ready around here."

Hannah nodded, helped with breakfast, and then got the younger girls up. They ate mostly in silence, but on the way to church, her heart pounded again. *What if Jake hadn't left yet at all? What if he had pondered the question long and hard and figured out that I would never look at him that way if my heart truly belonged to another. Jake surely understands me, trusts me, and will at least stay for my baptism. Perhaps we can talk this afternoon and get this matter straightened out.*

"God has been so good to you," Betty said from the front seat as they left for church.

"I know," Hannah said, gazing at the nearby mountains.

She then turned her eyes to the buggies in the line ahead, and her heart caught in her throat at the sight of the Nisley's buggy. Dizzyingly she watched, almost certain it was Jake's dress shoes and pant legs appearing in the doorway of the buggy.

"Well, we're here," Betty said.

Distracted, Hannah glanced away and hoped her cheeks weren't flushed. When Betty turned back around, Hannah looked toward the Nisley's buggy again, but there was no Jake. It must have been one of Nisley's young boys because there was no place for Jake to have disappeared to so quickly.

Numbly she climbed down from the buggy, helped Betty's girls down, and then followed them inside. In the washroom she smiled the best she could and hoped it was good enough.

During her last instruction class, which was held upstairs, the sober-faced ministers didn't seem to notice anything wrong with her. If they did, they wrote it off to baptismal jitters. With the class done, they all filed downstairs again and took seats on the front bench. Hannah felt a great nervousness sweep over her at this sudden exposure. Never would she have sat in front of the church by her own choice. Was this how it was when one got married? If Jake were beside her, Hannah figured her emotions could have been much more manageable. Even if he was in the boy's row, it would have helped.

Since he wasn't, she bit her lip and hoped the tears wouldn't come. How foolish she had been—so caught up in her own world again—and now her parents weren't even here for her baptism.

The ministers filed down from upstairs, and the local minister, Mose Chupp, stood up to speak. What he said, Hannah thought was nice, but she wished he was finished. Bishop Nisley had the main sermon, and she tried to listen more carefully.

Bishop Nisley had just finished with a story of a shepherd who went out to look for the sheep he had lost.

"All of us were lost sheep," he said, "lost on the mountains of sin and bound for destruction. If God hadn't come looking for us, there would have been no hope. We could never have found our way home on our own. The mountains were too rough, the path too steep, and the road too hard to travel. Only the loving care of the Shepherd saved us. Jesus shed His blood so that as many who wished could be carried home in His arms.

"Today we are here to witness several of our young people who have made that choice. They have chosen to forsake the world and all it has to offer and follow Jesus and His commandments. They have also made themselves open to the voice of His church and to receive counsel and instructions for the new life they have entered into.

"And make no mistake about it—new life in God begins before baptism. We are to believe in God and then to seal our inward renewal with an outward confession and sign. Baptism is that sign of water—not that it can wash away sins, only the blood of Jesus can do that."

Bishop Nisley paused and let his gaze move up and down the line of young people. "As many of you, then, who still desire baptism, would you please kneel?"

Hannah and the others moved slowly to their knees on the hard floor. She felt like every eye must be looking at her, but somehow she kept on breathing.

"Do you confess before God and the church that you have forsaken the world, sin, and the devil, and all their evil works?" Bishop Nisley asked and quickly heard the answers from those kneeling.

Hannah's mouth felt dry, but somehow "*jah*" came out.

"Do you believe that Jesus Christ is the only begotten Son of God, sent to take away the sins of the world, and have you accepted His salvation?"

This time Hannah's answer came a little easier.

Then he asked, "Do you confess that you will continue to submit to the Word of God and to the counsel of the church in your Christian journey through life?"

Hannah said, "*Jah*," and relief flooded her. She would begin this new life and forsake the old. How appropriate it was that all this was coming together in one place. Even if her parents weren't here, she would see them soon. Once back home she could forget about Jake and teach her heart to behave.

The tears stung her eyes again, but resolution gripped her. She *would* behave.

The bishop's voice was distinct as he came down the line, but soon both of his hands gently touched her *kapp*.

"I baptize you on your confession, in the name of the Father, the Son, and the Holy Spirit," he said, and Hannah felt water from the deacon's pitcher wet her hair and then trickle down her cheeks.

Moments later, he was done with the girl beside her and had gone back to lift the first boy from his knees with a handshake and a kiss. When Bishop Nisley got to Hannah, he offered his hand and then turned her over to his wife Elizabeth, who kissed her on the cheek. Hannah wiped the water off her face and tried to smile. Elizabeth touched her gently on the shoulder and then greeted the girl beside her.

Hannah took a deep breath as the service came to a close. While the meal was served, she wished again that Jake was seated in his familiar place at the long table but pushed the thought away. She really needed to begin now to live her new life away from such foolish dreams.

As the Greyhound bus drove through Billings, after the all-night drive, Jake ached from his seat's tight quarters. Other things hurt a lot worse, things like the pain in his heart—pain tempered only by his anger at Hannah.

So, all girls are the same, after all. Now I know for sure. Even girls that don't look the same are treacherous beings who smile while they cut your heart out and throw it away. So Hannah had been writing to her boyfriend all summer. She was writing to someone while she led me on with those deep brown eyes. How could I have fallen for this again? Jake hit the seat in front of him out of sheer frustration, glad no one sat in it.

"Would you quit beating the seat?" a voice protested. A twenty-something girl stuck her frowning face around the back of her seat. When she caught sight of his face, she brightened. "Oh, I didn't know it was you. I'm sorry. I didn't intend to snap at you." Her blue eyes sparkled. "My name's Clara. What's yours?"

Why not? Jake asked himself. *Just talk to her. Sure she's English, but maybe English girls are somehow different, maybe better than Amish girls. They couldn't be worse, that's for sure.*

"Hi," he said, returning her smile. "It's Jake."

"Well, hi, Jake," Clara said. "Are you heading home?"

"Yes, I am," he said, surprised that she should guess. "Where are you going?"

"Nowhere in particular at the moment."

That's a strange answer, Jake thought. *Everyone is going somewhere.*

"Really?" He went along with her. "Well, I'm going home after being gone all summer. Home to the farm and working the soil I guess. I've always been a farmer, and I guess I always will be."

"Ugh," Clara said and made a face. "Dirt. Who wants dirt and soil and working in the sun?" Her face disappeared around the edge of the seat. From the sounds that followed, there was no doubt she wouldn't turn around in her seat again.

So, they are the same, Jake thought.

The girl got off at the next stop, and Jake was glad. He resolved that when he got back home he would never trust girls again, good-looking or otherwise.

Twenty-eight

Hannah was dropped off at the Greyhound station only to discover her bus was running late. To pass the half hour or so, she decided to take a walk across the street to what seemed to be a small bookshop.

Inside, she browsed for a few minutes and found the religion section. Most of the titles and authors were unfamiliar to her until she saw a copy of a book she had loved in school a few years ago. She picked up the paperback copy of *Pilgrim's Progress* by John Bunyan and opened it to read a few lines. Then, as she started to return it to the shelf, she thought of Sam. She had loved this book so much and thought perhaps he would too. Maybe it would give them something to talk about together.

She took the book to the counter, paid the clerk, and walked back to the bus station with renewed hope.

At first, the whine of the Greyhound bus helped soothe Hannah's nerves. It was only later on the long trip home that the drone bothered her. It had been some time since anything had seemed so endless to her. Town after town, stop after stop, and still the bus moved on slowly.

Finally, by dusk on the third day, the bus approached Nappanee from the west on highway 6, where the sight of Amish Acres sharply brought back the fact that Hannah was home. For much of the long trip, Hannah had thought about Jake and the fresh pain in her heart. But now she would have to push that aside.

She was home now. She was back where the land was semi-flat and houses could be seen everywhere, certainly not Montana. Yet, here was where her problem with unrealistic dreams started, and perhaps here she could end it once and for all. Surely Sam looked forward to her return, and she would just be happy for that.

Hannah saw her mother before the bus came completely to a halt. Kathy stood outside the station, her white head covering and plain dress clearly distinguished her in the small crowd that stood waiting.

At the sight of her mother, Hannah felt the first stir of joy rise up in her. Thankfully Sam wasn't here at the station to spoil the moment. His mouth hanging wide open at her appearance wasn't a sight she wished to see just yet. The time would come for that all too soon, she supposed.

Hannah stepped off the bus and saw her mother's face light up. She waved and then rushed over to embrace her mother.

"It's so good to see you!" Kathy exclaimed. "How was the trip?"

"Whiny," Hannah said and laughed. "It was okay for a while, but three days of it is a lot to bear."

"*Jah*, I remember how it was," Kathy said. "Well, now, tell me how everything is at Betty's." Hannah hardly knew where to begin.

"Let's see," Hannah said, taking a deep breath, "Betty said to tell you 'hi,' and that they are really happy you let me come out for the summer."

"Did it go well with the horse riding?" Kathy asked.

Hannah grinned. "I think so. I enjoyed it, and I think they made gobs of money. Betty never said how much, but it must have been more than they expected."

"Well, we're glad to help," Kathy said. "They can certainly use it. In the West it's harder to make money than here in the industrial East."

"But it's so beautiful out there!" Hannah gushed. "The mountains, the rivers, and even the air are all wonderful."

"It sounds like you fell in love with the country," Kathy said, "and I hear you fell in love with someone else too."

Hannah was sure she turned white. How had Betty so quickly passed the news on of Jake?

"It's not that terrible. Sam's a nice boy," Kathy said.

Oh, she means Sam —not Jake! Hannah collected herself. "Well, we've been writing all summer."

"So how does it stand by now?"

Hannah felt her face grow even paler. She must not disappoint her mother now, not after all she had been through. God had helped her out, and she must now do her part. "Well," she said quietly, "I've not seen him since I've been away. It's hard to say."

"I guess that will change now that you're back," her mother said. "Has Sam asked to see you?"

Hannah nodded. "He wants me to be his steady."

"And?" Kathy seemed positive about Hannah's prospects with Sam.

"I said yes."

"Well, Sam's a nice boy," Kathy said. "Your dad has always liked him, and so I'm glad to hear it."

Hannah nodded again and tried not to look too glum.

When they arrived home, there was the flurry of greetings from her siblings, and then she got settled into her room again.

Her dad was pleased to see her and asked for details about Steve's logging in Montana. He was even more pleased when Hannah told him that Sam had asked her to be his steady.

"I'm glad to hear you are going with such a solid boy," Roy said. "If it comes to something more serious, Sam is well placed financially and comes from a good family."

Now Hannah did blush, which apparently was the response both Kathy and Roy were waiting for. They appeared glad to see her on solid ground after the Peter episode.

After supper she went upstairs, claiming to be tired from her trip. She walked over to the familiar window, the very one she had climbed out of to be with Peter. Much had happened since that sad night. Now the new moon hung just above the horizon to the west. The little sliver glittered in the sky, the rest of the circle appearing as only a faint outline.

Hannah noticed that the long tree limb that had hung over the roof was gone. For this she was glad.

It reminded her of how her old life seemed to her—gone. Peter was no more, and even her memory of him was fading. Now, God had helped her get away from Jake when her own strength had failed her. From here on out, she would be free from dreams and take the opportunity of a life with Sam Knepp while she had it.

Safe. That's what she considered Sam, and making the choice to see him wasn't even such a hard choice to make, now that she was home. Sam was a good boy, a hard worker, and he would inherit the farm. Why not take the blessings God offered her and be happy? Many girls would jump at the chance. Mary Troyer, for one, had always been nice to Sam. But then Mary was nice to everyone.

God had helped her, and she would now help herself. And with that, she climbed into bed and slept soundly all night long.

Hannah got up in the morning ready for the day, eager to get back into the swing of things. But right after breakfast, her mother pulled her aside and said, "Before we begin the day's work, we need to talk about something."

Hannah wasn't sure what it could be but sat down on the kitchen table bench to listen.

Kathy sat down across from her. "I want to talk about Sam," Kathy began.

Hannah waited.

"I just want to make sure that you understand…that we're not pushing you into anything with him just because of your mistake with Peter."

Hannah wasn't sure what to say, and so she simply nodded.

"This should be your own decision. Even though your father likes Sam a lot—as do I—you're the one who has to live with him."

"Yes," Hannah said, "but I *have* made up my own mind."

"Well," Kathy said, "then I wouldn't want to interfere. But you shouldn't do this just because you might think someone else wants you to."

Surprised at her mother's words, Hannah said, "I went through a lot out in Montana, and this seems to be the right thing to do."

"I'm sure you did."

"Now the way seems clear. I want to follow God and His direction."

"And His direction is Sam?" Kathy asked.

"Yes," she said, her voice firm, "the way that I am to go seems to be clear."

"Then I hope for the best," Kathy said. "If that's settled, let's get to work."

Hannah was relieved that this discussion and this decision of hers were over. Now life could go on the way it was supposed to. She would see Sam on Sunday, and God would be with her, she was sure.

Jake arrived home in time to help with the oat shocking, which was already in full swing. The teams of Amish men and boys moved from place to place in preparation for the fall threshing season. They took turns, a few days at each place, depending on the grain's ripeness and the weather.

Jake pitched in and was glad even for his itchy arms after the long days in the fields. He threw and stacked with great vigor the bundles the binder dropped. Behind him he left little shocks that resembled miniature tents across the fields. He did them right so the wind or gravity wouldn't pull them down.

He began to notice that many of the boys were eying him with admiration. Apparently they thought his trip out West had done him a lot of good. *If they only knew,* Jake thought but said nothing.

At lunchtime a huge meal was served at whatever place they happened to be that day, and Jake ate with abandonment. The work made him hungry and compensated for his otherwise lack of desire for food.

Jake was glad to be back home during the hardworking days, but the evenings and nights were another matter. Hannah always came to his mind, and, yet, that was a hopeless cause. She had a boyfriend and had written to him all summer. That was just the way it was. He would have to find a way to forget that part of his time in Montana.

Being home was also hard when he heard the news that Eliza and his cousin were to be married in November. His mother had made the announcement on his first day back.

"I thought someone should tell you," she said, her voice gentle.

Jake nodded and took shelter in silence. It was safer there. Whenever someone wanted to talk about his summer in Montana, he gave the simple basics, no more, and, of course, never a mention of Hannah.

Bishop Andy talked to Jake after church the second Sunday he was home, wanting to know more about his stay in Montana. What he really wanted to find out, Jake knew, was whether or not he had found a community there to become a part of. Jake told him about Bishop Nisley and even gave him the address in case he wanted to ask Bishop Nisley anything. And he knew that letters between the two bishops would indeed flow back and forth. There would be no secrets about his time in Montana. That's just the way it was.

Twenty-nine

On her first Saturday night home, Hannah heard the sound of buggy wheels on the driveway just before dark. She suspected who it was, and her mother confirmed it with a look out the window by saying, "Look who's here!"

Hannah knew she'd have to face him sooner or later. *Might as well be now*, she thought. Remembering the book she had purchased for Sam, she ran upstairs to get it and then walked out to the porch and waited for Sam to swing around to the hitching post. After he had his horse tied, she walked out to meet him.

Unable to believe his good fortune, he still wore an astonished look on his face, but his mouth stayed shut. For this Hannah was thankful. Had he finally overcome that habit? Hannah hoped so.

"Good evening," she said. "I thought you might stop by."

Sam seemed at a loss for words. Here at long last was Hannah, back again. *His* Hannah.

She smiled to encourage him, which seemed to make things worse.

"Good evening," he finally managed. "I just thought I'd stop by and see you before Sunday."

She nodded, not certain how she could help him become comfortable around her.

"Those were awful nice letters," Sam ventured. "Thank you."

Hannah gave him a smile in return.

He then spoke awkwardly, "I just wanted to check, to make sure I understood you right. Can I take you home on Sunday evening?" He searched her face. "I know we said so in the letters, but I wanted to be sure."

"I understand," Hannah said. "*Jah*, that will be fine. Sunday night."

"Okay, then." Sam smiled now and seemed a little less embarrassed.

"I'll see you, then," he said, climbing back into the buggy. "I really have to be going. There are still chores to do at the farm. I just took a few minutes to come over to see you."

"Oh wait," she said, almost forgetting the book in her hand. "I have something for you. I hope you like it." With that she handed him the book.

He looked pleased but again at a loss for words. "Thanks," he finally mustered. "That was nice of you."

"Oh, it isn't much. Well, have a good evening, Sam," Hannah said as she stepped aside so he could swing his buggy around and out the lane again. When he was on the main road, she stood still and watched his buggy drive away, a queasy feeling in her stomach. *Well, he's already improving his manners at least. Surely God is giving me signs to point the way.*

Slightly comforted, Hannah walked back inside the house.

"Seeing him on Sunday night?" Kathy asked.

Hannah nodded and went up to her room. Morning would come soon enough, and her new life would begin in earnest. It would take a lot of rest, she thought, to keep up with it all.

Just the sight of Sam smelled of hard work, and she knew she would be expected to keep up. Why she hadn't noticed before, she wasn't sure, but hard work was good for everyone, she believed. *And with God's help,* she told herself as she fell asleep, *I can do it.*

On Sunday morning Mary Troyer, Hannah's friend from school

days, found time to talk with Hannah in the entrance to the house where the meeting was to be held.

"How was Montana?" she asked.

"Beautiful," Hannah whispered. This one-word explanation truly captured it all for her. Jake had best be kept out of the picture.

"I haven't seen your Aunt Betty in years," Mary said, "ever since they moved out there."

"She's doing fine," Hannah said. "Their little group has their struggles, but they'll make it. And they were all very nice to me."

"Was there a large young people's group?" Mary asked.

"No," Hannah said, "and just boys."

Mary grinned. "I'm surprised you didn't find one out there...instead of writing to Sam. You surprise me, Hannah."

"I guess it was just meant to be. So what about you and Laverne. Is that still on?"

"I guess you could say so," Mary said. "We're going to marry."

"When's the date?" Hannah asked.

"I can't tell you," Mary said slyly, "but Laverne will be helping on the new construction crew out at Miller's. I can tell you that much."

"So it's soon, then?" Hannah said, visions of the good-looking Laverne flashing in her mind.

Mary demurred. "You know how it is. It takes money nowadays to run a household. A good job helps."

"So when is it?" Hannah insisted, forcing herself to stay with the subject at hand.

"I can't tell you," Mary repeated and laughed. "But don't be surprised. I can tell you that much."

"Ah, so it's soon, then?" Hannah concluded.

Mary laughed again. "We should join the others," she said and motioned toward the other women. "It's just you and Sam that surprises me. Even back in eighth grade, I could never figure it out when you picked him, but I guess he does need a good wife."

Hannah said nothing as they walked over to the others.

As church started, Hannah could clearly see the line of boys. Sam didn't pay her much attention during the service, keeping his eyes on the preacher, which was fine with her. Not like Jake, it occurred to her.

After church she rode home with her parents. Hannah spent the afternoon in her room with a book, not looking forward to the evening's date with Sam.

After supper she rode to the hymn sing with Isaac and Miriam, wondering what she and Sam would talk about later. *Will Sam stay till twelve? Should I mention anything about what time might be appropriate? What time would that be?* Hannah sighed and decided that things would just have to be taken as they happened.

She was not as afraid that the relationship might fail as she supposed she ought to be. She would care for Sam eventually, and for now, she just needed to stop worrying about what *could* be and think about what *was*.

Certainly Sam wouldn't stop the relationship. Would she stop it? *Could* she stop it? That was the question she couldn't ask. The road was simply too clear—too certain. The signposts were too obvious to be mistaken. Life was not meant to be lived in a dream world, but with real people. Yes, that was what it was, and Hannah would do her part to make it work.

The start of the hymn sing arrived soon enough and with it the familiar songs. It was good to be back among so many young people. Most of the faces were familiar to her. Those that weren't, she assumed, came from neighboring districts. With such a large settlement, such back and forth visits were common enough.

After the last song had been sung, Hannah stepped outside and realized that it was harder than she had anticipated to figure out which buggy was Sam's. It wouldn't be right to ask someone, so she had to make the selection on her own. In the just-fallen dusk, she headed down the walks, hoping against hope some strange boy wouldn't be sitting behind the buggy door she was about to open. With Jake—though she had never seen his buggy—she would have known his buggy at first sight. She seemed sure of that and then scolded herself for even thinking about Jake.

It was Sam's freckled face that greeted her, lit dimly by the lantern light from the kitchen window. She couldn't have missed because his red hair glowed softly. Her feelings of relief at the correct choice soon translated into a comfortable silence as they headed out the driveway. Sam said little until they arrived at her place, and she left it at that. A farmer's wife spoke little anyway, and it might as well begin in like manner.

Hannah offered Sam a glass of orange juice, a fit gesture, she figured, to a healthy start to their relationship.

Sam still proved to have little to say, and so Hannah filled in the blanks with talk mostly about Montana. Sam joined in but only on subjects that involved work and business. Even when she talked about her trip, his questions were about the amount Betty had charged for rides, how many rides were given each day, and how much profit they made.

Her answers caused Sam to lapse into silence and then mutter calculations, which were followed by expressions of delight. "That was pretty good money," he said.

"I suppose so," Hannah allowed, although that hadn't been the point of her story.

"I wonder if someone could do something like that around here?" Sam wondered out loud.

"There are no mountains," she said. "That seems to be what really drew the people."

"Tourists, in other words," Sam stated.

She nodded.

"Then tourists are tourists," he said. "They are really all the same. They all want to see things. In Montana they want to see the countryside, but here they want to see us." Sam had suddenly become quite the conversationalist.

"I suppose," Hannah agreed but didn't entirely like the idea. A horseback ride in Montana was one thing. A trail ride in Indiana was something else entirely.

"It's really good." Sam was fully enthusiastic now. "That's valuable experience you gained. I never thought people out West could teach us anything." He shrugged his shoulders in sympathy and dismissal.

"We are much more industrialized in the East. We have the factories, the hotels, the big lumberyards, and Amish Acres. But I guess it goes to prove that we learn something new every day."

"I think people around here probably already know about giving horseback rides," Hannah said with a smile.

"Could be," Sam allowed. "I just had never heard of it. Anyway," he said, brightening again, "you still have had the experience of doing it. That's very valuable. Not too many women can do that."

"I think they can," Hannah objected. "It wasn't that hard."

"Well," Sam said, blushing a little, "I think it's good that you can. About the others, I don't know. I know my mother can, and it's important that you can."

Hannah got the distinct feeling that she had passed some kind of test. But it was okay, she decided. She needed to learn to be the proper wife, and this was how she would learn it, that's all. It certainly never happened that way in dreams, though. Of that she was sure.

"I'm glad you like it," Hannah said out loud.

Sam grinned from ear to ear, and his mouth stayed shut, which Hannah took as a sign from God to continue on this journey. Maybe she was having a positive influence on Sam.

"You should have seen the countryside down by the river," she started to tell him in the silence that followed. "The land stretched out in a long, flat plateau beside the river. There were mountains all around, and the wind blew across the water. We used to gallop—" She caught herself in horror, but the words couldn't be taken back. What if Sam asked who she meant by "we"? Hannah continued, hoping he had missed it, "along the riverbank, mostly in the evenings." Sam didn't say anything one way or the other. He just seemed to be listening.

Hannah quickly continued, "Sometimes there were sunsets. You couldn't see them too well because of the mountains, but it's so amazing when the sun just drops behind them. And one night…Well, it was just so beautiful!"

Hannah glanced at Sam. He looked at her but showed no signs of interest. "That's an interesting story," he said.

Hannah was ready to tell him about the encounter with the

mountain lion, but decided to save her breath. Apparently farmer's wives weren't supposed to enjoy mountains or have wild adventures with mountain lions—just hay bales, cows, and wheat shocks.

"Well, I had better be going," Sam announced, glancing at the clock. "We have to be up early to do the milking, and then the fall plowing starts right after the oats are shocked."

So he would leave early. In a way Hannah was glad, but aloud she said, "You can't stay any later?"

"Maybe next time, although I doubt it. I don't like staying up too late." Sam then cleared his throat, a slightly embarrassed smile crossing his face. Just to make sure, he said, "I guess there will be another time?"

"If you want to," Hannah said, already knowing his answer.

"I do," he said, and thankfully his mouth stayed shut. "Until next Sunday then. Maybe we can see each other on Sunday afternoon after a while?"

"Would you like that better?" Hannah asked.

"I think so," Sam said. "Not always, maybe, but sometimes. I could take you over to our place on those Sundays."

"But you do the chores then, don't you?" she asked.

Sam nodded. "I could take you straight home from church, we could talk some in the afternoon, and you could help chore. I would take you back to the hymn sing, then."

"Not every Sunday, though."

"No," Sam allowed, "not every Sunday."

"Okay then. We'll decide as we go along. Next Sunday at the hymn sing, right?"

"Right," Sam said and disappeared out the door. The sound of his buggy wheels soon sounded on the gravel, and he was gone.

"My first date," Hannah said aloud with a frown. "My first real, legal date, and I'm not dreaming. That's good—just good, old, practical, sensible human living. That's a good girl."

She climbed the stairs slowly and went to her window before she climbed in bed. A momentary sadness passed over her at the thought of Jake somewhere all alone. Had he arrived back home safely? Did his parents accept him again? Had he already met someone to care for? She hoped he had.

"I am a new person now," Hannah whispered. "It is a new and a better start. This will make me happy. I know it will."

Thirty

"So how did your evening with Sam go?" Kathy asked the next morning.

"Okay, I guess," Hannah said to the rattle of dishes in the kitchen sink. "Sam's a farmer. He wants to have me over to his place on a Sunday afternoon sometime."

"Likely to help chore, right?"

"I think that's the plan," Hannah said. "He probably wants to see if I meet the grade."

Kathy wrinkled her face and said, "Maybe you shouldn't jump to conclusions too quickly. Sam seems quite smitten with you. I doubt if you doing chores has anything to do with it."

"Whether I can do them or not may have," Hannah said and kept her eyes on the dishes.

Kathy laughed.

"It's not funny, Mom. I shouldn't have to prove myself. It makes no sense at all. I thought love was supposed to just come all by itself."

"Now, Hannah," Kathy said, "first of all you don't know if that is what this is, and even if it is, that's not too unusual. You can't blame Sam, can you? He does have to keep that farm up, the one he's getting from his father."

"I guess," Hannah said, sighing in resignation. "I'll try. Not that I don't like cows, but it just doesn't seem right."

"There's still time to say no," Kathy said. "That's what courtship is all about."

"I can't do that," Hannah said. "It would be like walking away simply because it's too hard. I don't want to do that."

"Well, love *is* hard sometimes," Kathy said. "Life throws all kinds of things at us, and some aren't too pleasant."

"So I'm learning," Hannah said as she lifted the last of the dishes out of the soapy water, rinsed them, and then placed them on the rack. She jerked a towel out of the drawer and started to wipe the plates dry.

"It'll all work out for the best," Kathy assured her. "It always does when we trust God. He knows what is best."

Hannah nodded and hoped against hope her mother was right.

✦

On Sunday night, as expected, Sam raised the question about whether or not Hannah could come over the following Sunday afternoon.

"*Jah,*" she said and hoped her smile was sincere, "I can come."

Sam was delighted, and a week later, she got into Sam's buggy after church at two thirty.

"Did you get a chance to read the book I gave you," Hannah asked, hoping to start a nice conversation because he hadn't said anything beyond his usual "hi" since she'd climbed in.

"I tried to," he said, "but I didn't get very far. It's pretty heavy stuff."

"Not really," Hannah said. From her school days, she remembered that he didn't read much. "Perhaps it will do you good."

"I got as far as Christian falling into the swamp," Sam told her, a silly grin forming on his face. "I thought that was pretty stupid of him. If he had just stopped to look, there was a perfectly good set of steps to use. That evangelist, whoever he was, pointed this out to Christian after pulling him out of the mire."

"It's supposed to teach a lesson—" Hannah said, "a spiritual lesson about what happens when we have sin strapped to our shoulders."

"So why doesn't the story just come out and say that?"

"Because it's more interesting this way."

"It wasn't to me," he told her. "That's the problem with books. They don't just say what they want to say. You have to think and figure it out for yourself. It makes no sense to me to even bother. If I have to figure it out anyway, why not just figure it out without the books?"

If it had been dark, Hannah would have looked at him, but because it wasn't, she kept her eyes straight ahead. Her look of dismay would have been too obvious. Clearly another tact was needed to encourage him to read books.

"Have you ever read any books that you liked?" Hannah asked.

Sam shook his head, his freckles moving with his face.

"Have you heard of *The Adventures of Tom Sawyer* or *The Adventures of Huckleberry Finn*?" she asked.

"No," he said, pulling up on the horse's reins as they approached the Knepp driveway.

"I'll give them to you next Sunday night," Hannah said, her determination resolute. "Every boy ought to love those. Not that they have as much value as *Pilgrim's Progress*, but they are interesting."

"Are they fit for married men to read?" Sam asked.

"But you're not married," Hannah said.

Sam blushed. "That's what Dad says is a good standard," he explained. "He never said it about books but about other things. If a married man should do it, then it's probably okay."

Hannah shrugged in despair. "I've never heard that one before. Anyway, let's see what you think about *Tom Sawyer,* okay?"

"Was it in the school library?" Sam asked.

"No," Hannah said, "it wasn't. Why do you ask?"

"I can't remember seeing anything like that," he said. "I looked at all the books there once. None of them interested me."

"Well, maybe these will," Hannah said.

Sam pulled up to the barn and got out to unhitch. Hannah helped him undo the traces and then waited while he went into the barn with the horse.

They walked together toward the house. Sam reached ahead of her to open the kitchen door so she could enter first. "We can go into the living room," he said as he shut the door behind him.

She took off her bonnet but was uncertain as to where to put it, and so she carried it with her. Both of his parents were in the living room. Enos nodded at her from where he was seated on the couch. "Hi, Hannah," he said. He had *The Budget* open in his hands, the pages dangling down the side of his lap.

Hannah nodded in return and looked back over her shoulder to see where Sam was.

Laura got up from her rocker and set her crocheting on the floor. "Sam said you were coming," she said, reaching for the bonnet Hannah still held in her hand. "Let me take that for you."

Hannah wondered where Sam was and glanced back toward the kitchen again.

"He's probably looking to see if the popcorn's ready," Laura offered as explanation. "Just take a seat. He'll be out when he finds it's not made yet."

True to her word, Sam appeared at the kitchen doorway. "Where's the popcorn?" he asked.

"It's not made yet," Laura said. "So, what are you two going to be doing this afternoon?"

Sam grinned. "Why don't we play a game of backgammon with you and Dad? You can make the popcorn later."

"But only two can play," Laura said.

"We can take turns," Sam insisted. "Two watch and two play."

"Are you up to it, Enos?" Laura asked her husband.

"I guess," he said with a grunt and scooted forward on the couch. "I haven't played it in a while."

"It has been a while, but you and I used to play it a lot," Laura reminded him. "Get your old bones up here and try your hand again."

Enos laughed. "Well, where are we playing?"

"Out in the kitchen," Laura said and stood to look for the game. The others followed her.

"Who goes first?" Enos asked as they took seats around the table.

"You and Mom," Sam announced. "Then Hannah and me. The winners play winners."

"Sounds good," Enos said. "We need to get this done before the chores, though."

"And the popcorn," Sam said.

"Let's start, then." Laura opened the playing board as the brown and tan checkers slid across the table.

Enos made the first move once the checkers were arranged in their proper places.

Hannah noticed that Sam watched the game intently, easily offering advice to his mother.

"You just be quiet," she finally said. "I usually beat you anyway."

"Not always," Sam said with a boyish grin. "Just sometimes."

The match was a close one with Laura ahead at first, and then Enos pulled off a string of double sixes right at the end.

"That's not fair," Laura protested.

"It's just a game," Enos said. "Enjoy your defeat."

"It's still not fair," she complained as he moved his last piece home.

"Now I get to play the winner of you two," Enos pronounced triumphantly to Sam and Hannah.

Sam led out first, and Hannah followed with a careful throw of her dice. They were even till the bottom of the board, and then Sam threw a couple of twos, and Hannah pulled ahead. It wasn't even close when she finally brought her last checker home.

"That's good, Hannah," Laura said. "Really good." Sam didn't look too happy, but Hannah figured it was just a game. He'd have to get used to it. Games could turn out either way.

"Okay, now it's us two," Enos said to Hannah. "You seem to know what you're doing."

"Just throw the row of sixes again," Laura said sarcastically, "just to be fair, you know."

"I'll try," Enos assured her.

This time Hannah led. Again, as with Sam, it wasn't even close beyond the bottom of the board.

"Where are your sixes?" Laura had started to rub it in halfway through the game. "Hannah is beating you."

"She must have played this a lot," Enos suggested with a laugh.

"Not really," Hannah said. "Maybe it's just luck."

Enos grunted as Laura set up the board again. Then she glanced at the clock and announced that there was still just enough time for popcorn before chores if she started right now.

"I hope so," Sam said. "I wouldn't want to miss that on a Sunday afternoon."

Hannah mentally noted that Sam liked his popcorn. Obviously this would be expected in the future after they were married.

At four, Enos and Sam left for the barn to get the cows in. Hannah went into the bedroom to change into some old clothing Laura offered her. When Laura announced that it was time for them to go, they walked outside together to the barn. Hannah figured it would often be this way in her future as part of this family.

The cows were already lined up in their stanchions, licking at the little dash of feed in front of them.

"You'll just watch," Laura said, "since you've probably never milked before."

"I've milked by hand," Hannah said in an attempt to redeem herself.

"This is different," Laura said. "Here we milk with *milkers* as you can see."

"Is there something I can do?" Hannah glanced around. There didn't seem to be.

Laura thought for a moment and then suggested that Hannah wash the cow's udders. "Not a pleasant job," Laura said, puckering up her face, "but it's something you could do."

Hannah figured the moment of truth had come and that she had better jump to it if she was to survive Sam's way of life. "Sure, I'll try," she said.

Laura offered her the bucket of water and gave her instructions.

Hannah leaned carefully against the first cow's hindquarters with the cloth in hand. A sharp kick would do her in, she figured, but the task had to be done. Bent over, Hannah closely followed the instructions she had been given. She used the washcloth to clean the entire area the *milkers* would touch. Despite slipping on something slimy, she scrubbed pieces of dirt and manure from the cow. When she finished the first cow, she knew it had been done right.

Laura confirmed the point. "That's right," she said, nodding. "Now just move on to the next one."

Twenty cows later, Hannah had fully mastered the technique. She also now smelled like a cow.

Sam passed by and seemed satisfied. "Looks like she's doing real well," he said to his mother.

Hannah straightened her back, causing Sam to probably wonder if she was up to it. Disappointment filled her, but Hannah continued on to the twenty-first cow.

When the chores were done, Hannah walked to the house with Laura before the men came in. She had time to change and help with the family's supper before she and Sam left together to attend the hymn sing. Sam seemed in high spirits, humming to himself in the buggy. That was another thing he would need to work on, Hannah decided. One didn't hum in other people's presence. It wasn't good manners. But that would all come later. The day had been full enough already.

"We're doing the last of the shocking next week," Sam said, interrupting her thoughts.

"Yes," Hannah said, assuming he meant the threshing crew.

"I was wondering if you could come over, perhaps in the afternoon, to help."

She looked at him in bewilderment. "But the threshing crew does that."

"Oh," Sam said, "they were already there. This is just a small field that wasn't ready. We have to do it ourselves. All the help we can get would be appreciated."

Hannah's head spun. Would Sam pick her up, or was she supposed to drive over herself? Would he think it a weakness to ask for a ride? Finally she simply asked, "What time?"

"After lunch on Thursday," Sam said.

"Okay, I'll be there if Mom doesn't object," Hannah said.

Sam nodded, slapped the reins, and hummed softly.

After the hymn sing, he took her home and dropped her off at her front door.

"See you next week," he said and drove down the driveway.

Hannah listened to his buggy wheels fade into the night. So this was the way life would be. Well, it might not be too bad. At least he knew how to play games. She would have to work hard, but there were worse things. Softly she tiptoed into the house and upstairs to bed.

She took *The Adventures of Tom Sawyer* off her little bookshelf and laid it on the dresser.

"He'd better like it," she muttered before she fell asleep.

Thirty-one

Kathy had no objections to Hannah helping Sam's family. "They probably do need the extra hand," she offered as explanation to the surprised look on Hannah's face.

"They're just making it hard on me," Hannah insisted. "I just hope they decide I'm capable of being a good farm wife before too long."

"It might just be what life is like with him," Kathy said. "You can't say you aren't being warned."

"I can make it," Hannah said, squaring her chin. "I'm capable and strong enough for anything a farmer's wife is supposed to be. They'll see."

"How are you getting over there?"

"Will you let me drive your horse?"

"I guess so. Just be back before too late because your dad might want it for the evening."

So after lunch on the following Thursday, Hannah hitched the horse and headed down the road. It was a beautiful day as she drove along. The nice weather reminded her of Montana. *What a distant place that has become*, she mused.

Already Montana seemed so far away, and even the thought of Jake didn't really bring a reaction. She hadn't thought of him in several days. That was surely a good sign, wasn't it? Hannah slapped the reins and assured herself that it was. And now she was off to Sam's place to prove herself a capable farm woman. But she considered that if he knew all her sins, it might take more than just a day in the fields to convince them. She settled back into the buggy seat and let the memories of that far away place flood through her—Betty and Steve, the horses, the mountains, the plain by the river, and the rides with Jake. She had come so close to saying "yes" to Jake. She could hardly believe it now. Where would that have led her? No doubt someplace wrong, and so God had intervened when she couldn't have helped herself. He had sent the mountain lion for one thing. And then, if that wasn't enough, He had Betty tell Jake that she had been writing to Sam all summer.

Now she would live the life He had planned for her. She had to admit, though, that she couldn't help but wish there was more excitement in being a farmer's wife. But then, wasn't her dream of excitement what had gotten her into trouble before? Yes, it was. No more of that.

Hannah slapped the reins again and urged the old driving horse on. When she reached sight of the Knepp place, already a small cloud of straw dust was in the air, light puffs beside the barn. The afternoon threshing had started before she got here.

Laura waved to her as she drove in. After she tied the horse, Hannah headed toward Laura, wondering exactly what her duties would be. Laura solved that question by offering her a pitchfork.

"Come up and help me," Laura hollered above the racket.

Hannah looked in horror at the great rugged tractor that was attached to the threshing machine by a wide flap of belt. Both looked like mortal danger, but Laura smiled and waved her up.

Hannah gripped tightly as she climbed up the front of the wagon with its tiered sideboards and stood shakily on the top.

"Don't fall off," Laura hollered. "Grab the fork. Use that to keep your balance."

Hannah followed Laura's directions but wondered how she would be able to do anything else.

"Have you ever done this before?" Laura asked.

Hannah shook her head.

"Be careful, then," Laura said. "Pick up the bundles one at a time and throw them into the hopper."

Hannah looked down over the edge of the wagon at the hopper. Its great mouth stared back at her. Out of the hole came rotating sets of iron teeth that reached toward her as if to grab her and suck her in. Hannah shuddered at the thought.

"We need bundles," a voice hollered from around the corner of the threshing machine.

Hannah didn't recognize the voice above the roar of the machinery.

"We'd better get to work," Laura said, her face grim. "Hang on tight and throw when you're ready." She demonstrated how it was done, and Hannah followed her lead. One by one, the bundles of oats hit the spinning iron teeth, causing the threshing machine to roar and groan.

Hannah was scared about missing the hopper on her first try, but she succeeded to her own great pleasure.

"That's good," Laura said from beside her.

Hannah threw her next one. Laura followed, and they cast down the bundles one after the other until the wagon was empty.

When they had finished, they noticed another full wagon waiting. Sam was the driver. He looked sweaty and dirty—the same condition Hannah assumed she was in.

"I would have offered to help," he hollered above all the racket, "but you're already done."

"Hang on," Laura hollered back. "I'm moving the wagon."

Hannah balanced herself on the empty wagon bed as it lurched forward. Sam immediately pulled his wagon into place in front of the threshing machine and began to throw bundles into the hopper.

"We'd better take over," Laura told Hannah. "He needs to go back for another load."

She nodded and followed Laura up the side of the wagon.

"Hi," Sam said when she got to the top. "How's it going?"

"Okay, I guess," she said and forced a smile. "It's dusty work."

"She's doing just great," Laura said. That answer seemed to please him.

"Two more loads," Sam said before he headed down the side of the wagon. "We should be done before dark."

"I can't stay too late," Hannah told Laura as Sam's wagon bounced noisily down the lane toward the back fields. "Dad might need the horse tonight."

"You just go when you need to," Laura said. "I think we'll be done before Sam thinks. He always overestimates the time it takes."

Hannah and Laura swung away at the bundles until the wagon was empty again. Laura offered her a glass of water while they waited for Sam to return from the field. As Hannah wiped her brow, Laura smiled her approval, and Hannah felt perhaps she *could* be a farmer's wife.

"Only another half a load," Sam announced when he returned. "We'll have it loaded in no time."

"What about unloading it?" Laura said with a groan. "The life of a farmer's wife," she said, turning to look at Hannah, "what do you think of it?"

"I think I can do it," Hannah said without much effort.

"Just thought I'd warn you," Laura said.

Hannah nodded. It seemed that her mother had said something like that not too long ago. *I can do it*, she told herself firmly, grabbing the fork again and swinging the bundles into the hopper.

"You're good at this," Laura said, "for never having done it before."

"I'm trying," Hannah answered as she heaved another bundle into the air.

By the time the next load was finished, she excused herself, happy that she had lasted until the end. At her buggy she retrieved the copy of *The Adventures of Tom Sawyer* for Sam, gave it to Laura, and asked her to see that Sam got it.

Laura looked amused but accepted the book. With a last wave, Hannah climbed into the buggy and headed home.

As she fell into bed that night, barely after supper, she said aloud, "I *can* make it. Life as a farmer's wife is a good life."

Apparently Sam agreed because several weeks later, with the advent of winter, he proposed. It was one of those early winter, Sunday afternoons with a blizzard threatening from the west. Talk had been of calling off the hymn sing, but the young folks had braved it. Now with still no snow in the air, Sam sat in Hannah's living room. He had seemed nervous all evening. Now he cleared his throat, squirmed on the couch, and simply asked, "You will marry me, won't you? That's what these past few months have been about, haven't they?"

"Well, *jah*," Hannah said slowly, startled now that she was confronted by the expected question. She thought herself ready, but it still took her breath away.

You have stopped dreaming, she told herself, but there was still one more sign she needed. "Did you ever get around to reading that book about Tom Sawyer that I gave you?" Hannah asked.

Sam looked as if he wondered what that had to do with anything. He finally found the answer he thought was best and said, "My dad said it wasn't worth reading. But I told him I'd read it anyway because you gave it to me." He laughed. "It was funny."

"So you liked it?"

"*Jah*, I think it's the first book I have ever really liked."

"Well." Hannah was pleased and felt a sense of accomplishment. Perhaps this wouldn't be as bad as she imagined. "Then the answer is yes."

"Yes to what?" Sam asked, apparently puzzled.

"To *marrying* you," Hannah said.

"You *will*?" he asked, astonishment gripping his voice. "That's wonderful." He stared at her, his mouth shut, but a tear threatened one eye.

"So when will it be?" Hannah asked, embarrassed that he was so touched.

He thought for a moment, as if contemplating whether or not to answer, and then his face became certain again, as if he had arrived at a firm conclusion. "How about in spring?"

"That soon?" she asked, her mind spinning. "How do we make plans that fast?"

"It can be done if you want to," Sam assured her. "Dad already started the *daudy haus*. It might be done in time. If not, we can stay upstairs in the big house until Mom and Dad leave."

"Oh," Hannah said, catching her breath, "why not." The signs were right, and the way was clear. She knew her smile was crooked, but it was the best she could manage.

"Spring it will be, then," Sam said triumphantly. His hand trembled as he reached for her hand.

How pure, she thought. *He is so much better than Peter and my foolish dreams.* She just wished her heart would be a little more excited.

The winter passed quickly, and spring came before Hannah wanted it to. The day of the wedding arrived with perfect weather. Kathy had been in a tizzy at first when she heard the planned date, but now it was finally going to happen. The pies were baked, the potatoes done, the casseroles stirred, and the fruit set out.

Roy's cousin lent them his place—the large house for the ceremony and the pole barn for the reception afterward. The Miller home simply wasn't large enough for an Amish wedding. Hannah picked out her color—dark blue for a wedding dress and a lighter shade of blue for her attendants.

Rows and rows of tables were set up in the pole barn. They were covered with white paper tablecloths and matching silverware, all set out in marvelous perfection. Betty had arrived by Greyhound on Monday. Steve was unable to come, but Betty said she would not have missed this for the world because she had a hand, of sorts, in the matter.

Relatives came in from the neighboring states, most arriving the day prior and were put up in whatever homes were available. Kathy had people in every room of the house, stacked in it seemed, but at least all had some place to sleep.

Laura insisted that their entire upstairs be kept empty out of respect for the soon-to-be couple who were planning to spend their first night together there as well as the weeks ahead.

Bishop Knepp from Holmes County would preside over the ceremony. He was more than just an uncle to the family. Apparently he was also someone who was pretty important. Although the exact reason had never been made entirely clear, Hannah accepted that and understood an important bishop must be respected—whoever he was.

At nine sharp they all filed in to take their seats. Hannah and Sam sat up front, very prim and proper in their starched wedding outfits. Sam wore a brand new black suit Laura had ordered from a top seamstress who lived in the Goshen area.

It was when the men filed in that Hannah felt a stab of pain in her heart. Where it came from, she couldn't understand. But it was suddenly there, just out of the blue and with the force of a hurricane. Terror gripped her. *After all this waiting and all this pain, what if this is the wrong thing to do?*

Stop, dummkopf, *you can't doubt this now.* Although Hannah told herself this firmly, she was sure her face grew white against the blue wedding dress. She glanced at Sam although she knew it wasn't proper. Amish brides-to-be were supposed to keep their eyes on the floor. But Hannah had to know if Sam noticed her sudden distress.

Sam hadn't noticed. He seemed wrapped up in his own world, his eyes gazing calmly in the minister's direction as if he didn't have a care in the world.

If he's okay, I'm okay, Hannah told herself and calmed down a bit.

The singing started, and with it her breathing fully returned to normal. Sam and Hannah then followed the ministers upstairs to receive their final instructions. Hannah managed that without embarrassment and then followed Sam quietly back downstairs when the instruction time was over.

Ten minutes later the ministers themselves came back down, and the preaching started. What then seemed like only ten minutes later—although she knew it was more like at least an hour and a half—she heard the voice of Bishop Knepp faintly reach her.

The moment had arrived.

"If these, our beloved brother and sister, still desire to be united in holy matrimony, would they rise to their feet."

Hannah rose after Sam had stood up. It was then that the hurricane returned in full force. Her heart pounded so hard she was sure others could hear, but even so, she knew the ceremony must go on.

Bishop Knepp turned to Sam and asked him, "Do you confess before God and the church that this, our beloved sister Hannah, is given to you in marriage by the will of God?"

Sam answered in a loud and clear voice, "Yes."

Bishop Knepp turned to Hannah, his hand already prepared to reach out and join the two of theirs together. "Do you confess before God and the church that this, our beloved brother Sam, is given to you in marriage by the will of God?"

Hannah couldn't have gotten a sound out if she had tried, and she didn't try.

By the will of God? Horror flooded her. *What am I doing?* In desperation she reached for sanity and resolution but found none. The air seemed empty around her as if there wasn't enough to fill the words let alone her lungs.

Bishop Knepp looked at her, a kind expression on his face. No doubt he had seen fright-stricken Amish brides before and was sympathetic to her plight. It crossed Hannah's mind that all she had to do was nod, and Bishop Knepp would accept it.

Instead, to her own surprise, she shook her head.

"Die schwester sagt nein?" the Bishop asked out loud in sheer astonishment.

Hannah nodded and replied with surprising clarity. "Yes, the sister says no."

She suddenly knew.

Bishop Knepp seemed rooted to his spot. Clearly this was out of the routine. Finally he simply motioned to Sam to seat himself and signaled for the service to proceed. The song leader led out in the final hymn. All around her Hannah could see people looking at each other with shock in their eyes. She had embarrassed not only herself but her whole family. She looked at Sam, seated at her side, his mouth closed and eyes dazed.

Truly she was the community *dummkopf* now.

Thirty-two

Hannah felt the song end more than she heard it. The congregation around her was obviously uncertain as to what to do when the last notes of the song died away. Hannah could have burst out in sobs right then and there, but it wouldn't do to lose control in public. What was going to happen next, she had no idea.

In front of her, someone shuffled their feet, and a man cleared his throat. Hannah hardly dared look when she heard the voice of her father. "The meal is already prepared and will proceed as normal," he said simply and sat down.

Apparently that was all the direction that was needed. A frightened bride might have ruined her wedding day, but they would all discuss that later. Food was prepared and must be eaten. That much could easily be understood and followed.

One problem remained. The bridal party was to lead the way. Custom was ingrained deeply, and Sam didn't move, his face tight and turned toward the floor. Neither did anyone else make that first move.

Hannah dared not move a muscle. Sheer numbness had overtaken her body. She was now much more than a *dummkopf* in the eyes of everyone. She was likely a mental case in everyone's mind. The pity and compassion could almost be felt.

Kathy solved the problem when she rose to her feet. Hannah could have cried with relief, but she withheld even that emotion. Even though her mom might rebuke her, Kathy was still her mother. Kathy walked to the front and stood where everyone could see her—where the bridal party was seated. She placed her hand on Hannah's shoulder and shook it gently.

Hannah lifted her head slightly, and Kathy motioned for her to come. She took Hannah by the hand and led her into the kitchen. From there they walked into the small sewing room off to the side. No one followed except Betty, but the problem was now solved. Hannah could hear people getting to their feet.

Hannah thought about Sam and how he must feel. She didn't notice him as she and her mother and Betty made their way past the food and into the bathroom for some privacy. Later someone would tell her that he had gone straight to the barn, found his horse, and, with the help of several of the sympathetic younger boys, was on his way by the time the yard began to fill with people. None of the adults stared as he drove out the lane. A man must be given his privacy, even in public, for his time of grief.

In the bathroom, Hannah had dissolved into uncontrollable sobs. Lest her cries extend beyond the door, Kathy pressed one of the towels against Hannah's face. Betty stood there helplessly, quietly repeating, "*Oh, Gott im Himmel. Oh, Gott im Himmel, helfen Sie uns.*"

Hannah sensed Kathy and Betty looking at each other and wondering how they could take her home. Her outburst couldn't be hidden for long. Hannah wished she could stop sobbing, but she simply couldn't. She didn't know how they would get her out of the house without a scene, and at the moment, she no longer cared.

"Tell Roy to get the buggy," Kathy whispered to Betty. "Have him pull it up to the end of the walks."

Betty whispered something and then was gone, the door pulled gently shut behind her. In the long moments of silence that followed, Kathy simply held Hannah tightly as the hurricane inside had its way. Then Hannah heard the door open behind them.

"I told Roy to bring the buggy around," Betty whispered, "but he said he's not leaving because there are people who must be taken care of."

"Then I'll go talk to him," Kathy said. "You stay with her."

"I wasn't finished," Betty whispered, obviously out of breath. "I told him there were others around who could help. Quite a few have volunteered. Someone's bringing up the buggy now."

"What about the food and managing the meal?" Kathy asked.

"There are plenty of cooks around," Betty told her. "They can manage."

"I guess so." Kathy's hands gripped Hannah's shoulders.

"Roy wanted to know what's wrong with Hannah. I told him I didn't know."

"We'll talk to her later," Kathy whispered as if Hannah wasn't there, "when we get home."

"He said he may do more than that," Betty said. "He said the whole family has been embarrassed in front of everyone. No one can hide this."

"I know," Kathy whispered back, "but we'll talk about that later."

"The buggy's here." Betty moved to help with the despondent girl.

Kathy and Betty lifted Hannah together and took her out the door. Hannah kept her eyes on the floor as the circle of women parted to let them through. Outside she felt as if everyone in the whole yard was staring at her. People turned and looked, and a low astonished murmur swept through the crowd. Kathy and Betty said nothing as they stepped quickly down the sidewalk.

"Up we go," Betty whispered as they helped Hannah inside the buggy.

"You drive," Kathy said as Betty climbed in the other side.

"I'll take it from here," she told Roy, who held the horse's bridle. He simply nodded and stepped aside. Betty drove out the driveway and onto the blacktop. Hannah broke out into fresh sobs of sorrow.

When they arrived home, Kathy marched Hannah into the house while Betty tied the horse. Hannah felt herself set down hard on the couch, but her mom said nothing, waiting for Betty to come in. Hannah wiped her eyes and blew her nose.

A few moments later, Betty quietly came in through the front door and took a seat on the rocker.

"So what are you trying to prove?" Kathy stood in front of Hannah, her arms on her hips. "That was quite a show to put on for nothing. Now your father has all that wedding to pay for, and you're not even married."

Hannah felt fresh tears fill her eyes. She tried hard to gather her thoughts together. "You wanted me to marry him, and…I just couldn't," she said numbly.

"Wanted you to marry him?" Kathy was incredulous. "What has that got to do with it?"

"After Peter I wanted to be a good girl," Hannah muttered.

Kathy was still. "Hannah, I never said I wanted you to marry Sam. Where did that come from? You said you were making up your own mind. I told you to do *that*."

"Betty said you did." Hannah nodded toward her aunt.

"Betty did?" Kathy waited. "Betty told you I wanted you to marry Sam?"

"Yes," Hannah said, "she did."

"It's still your own fault," Kathy said. "It was your choice."

"I know," Hannah wailed.

Betty spoke up. "I did assume you wanted Hannah to marry Sam, Kathy. I kind of put two and two together and thought that was why you sent her out there to be with me. I figured she was trying to get away from Sam, and you wanted her to be with him. Wasn't that why he wrote right after she arrived in Montana? Your letter said you gave him Hannah's address."

Kathy took a deep breath and sat on the couch. "Maybe you had better start at the beginning and tell me everything."

So Betty did. She started with the day Hannah arrived and finished when she chased Jake off with the revelation that Hannah was writing to Sam.

Hannah listened with as much interest as her mother.

"Now it's your turn," Betty said to Kathy. "What was really going on?"

"I guess it is," Kathy said. "What a mess. I just wish we had done this sooner."

"I'm waiting," Betty said, looking impatient. "You made me tell everything."

Kathy took another deep breath. "There was Peter..." she began and wrapped up minutes later with the funeral and their decision to send Hannah out West.

Betty could hardly believe what she was hearing.

Hannah was close to a fresh set of tears but just lamented, "Oh, my life is all messed up now—completely messed up!"

"I would say so," Kathy agreed. "How are we going to get it all untangled? Now you've walked out at your own wedding. You know people are never going to forget that. What are we going to do?"

"I suppose this is all my fault—entirely my fault," Betty said mostly to herself as if she was stuck on that one thought.

"I'm ruined," Hannah cried. "No one will marry me now. I had planned to tell Jake about Sam...Now it's too late forever." She covered her face in her hands in total despair.

"So what do you think?" Kathy asked Betty. "Where do we go from here? The rest of the family will be home soon."

"I've messed things up so badly. I don't know," Betty admitted. "Maybe Hannah should come back out West with me. We could leave tomorrow. We can tell people she is going with me to get well out there, which she is, of course. That will make sense to everyone, and with a little time, this thing will blow over."

"It won't blow over for me," Hannah muttered, "not ever."

Kathy ignored Hannah and spoke to Betty, "That does make sense. Let me tell Roy about it when he comes home, and we'll go from there. For now, Hannah, go up to your room, get out of that dress, and start packing as if you're going. I'll bring your supper up. You can say goodbye to your sisters in the morning."

Hannah nodded, her face glum, her steps hollow on the stairs.

◈

Kathy recounted the entire story to Roy that evening, and Betty filled in the details Kathy left out.

"I've not heard of anything so stupid in a long time!" he proclaimed. "I guess now we have to see how things can be straightened out."

"Can Hannah go with Betty, then?" Kathy asked.

"*Jah*," Roy allowed a moment later, "but she's paying for her next wedding herself."

"Just be thankful if there is another one," Kathy said.

"Oh, there will be one," he said. "You can count on that."

"That will take God's help," Kathy said.

Roy nodded. Apparently his anger had run its course.

◈

The whine of the Greyhound bus got on Hannah's nerves again. She wished a thousand times she could be somewhere else. At least Montana was at the end of this noise. In between her occasional outbursts of tears and Betty's silence, Hannah comforted herself. Her normally talkative aunt was saying little, but at least there hadn't been further lectures.

Somewhere on the plains of Nebraska, Hannah finally got up the nerve to ask, "How did I go so wrong? I was just trying to stop dreaming and do the right thing."

Betty continued to gaze out the window until Hannah was sure there would be no answer. *She's mad,* Hannah thought. *The whole world hates me now, and I've lost any hope of love—ever.*

Betty shifted on her seat and turned from the window toward Hannah. "It's this way," she finally said. "Dreams are just to show us the way, to give us courage when the road gets hard, and to give us hope when we find the thorns on the rosebush. Dreams are neither evil nor to be rejected."

"But I did reject my dream," Hannah said, tears filling her eyes again, "and can I ever trust dreams again?"

"Yes, you can open your heart again," Betty said. "Don't keep on with what is wrong. Look ahead, not behind."

"But it hurts." Hannah stifled a sob.

"I know," Betty said, "but that hurt is where God will walk with you."

Hannah couldn't find her voice and simply let the tears flow.

They switched buses in Sioux Falls at about five that evening. The new bus was a connecting bus, and some passengers were already aboard, their dim silhouettes visible through the high windows.

Betty led the way onto the bus. Hannah followed close behind, her mind elsewhere. Betty stopped abruptly midway back, and Hannah almost bumped into her.

"Jake!" Betty exclaimed. "Jake Byler, what are you doing here?"

Jake stared at them, his face dark and expressionless. Hannah felt all the blood leave her body, her knees trembled, and she gripped the sides of the seats with both hands.

"I've left home again. Not sure where I'll end up this time," Jake said without emotion, remembering the hurt he had received from his attraction to Hannah. "Not that it should matter to you—or your niece."

To Hannah's great surprise, Betty moved toward the empty seat behind Jake, motioning Hannah in first. Hannah kept her eyes on the floor, unwilling to say anything.

"I suppose you have the right to feel that way," Betty said, her voice surprisingly cheerful. "Who would have thought we'd meet you here like this? Now I have a chance to make things right, and I will start right here."

Hannah was too frightened to make a sound.

A white-haired older lady seated in front of Jake, her head visible when she turned toward the window, caught Hannah's attention. Behind them was a younger couple with sandwiches they must have purchased during the stopover. Surely Betty would know enough to speak in Pennsylvania Dutch, whatever she planned to say.

Betty launched into her side of the entire story in her native tongue. Hannah listened, shocked herself at how clumsy she had been. Jake would never forgive her no matter what Betty said.

Betty concluded with Hannah's botched wedding and then folded her hands. "So, that's my story."

Jake was silent, taking it all in. There was still hurt in his eyes, but he seemed to soften a bit after hearing Betty's story.

"Now it's your turn, Hannah," Betty said, turning to her niece.

Hannah froze, her blood like ice, but she knew it was now or never. With slow words she told Jake about Peter, his death, and why she had agreed to write to Sam. She told him how she had planned to tell him about Sam that evening the mountain lion had screamed at them. She explained how she took his departure as a sign from God that she was supposed to stop dreaming and marry Sam. And then she said, "I'm so sorry for how this has all turned out."

Hannah was astonished to see an even softer glow in Jake's eyes. Could he possibly have a heart that would understand—after such a story?

"I guess I have some things to say too," he finally said. Then for the next twenty minutes, he told them his own story. "See, I have done some things I shouldn't have. My bishop thinks I'm making a mistake by leaving again."

When Jake was done, the older lady in front of him turned around in her seat and stuck her head around the corner. "Oh, that was the sweetest thing I have heard in a long time. You people sure make a mess of things, but it looks like God is looking out for you."

Betty was aghast and said, "But we were speaking in German. How did you understand?"

"*Ach,*" she said, chuckling, "*Ich bin Deutscher.* You were speaking some dialect, but I understood it. It's such a wonderful story."

"I see," Betty said, seeming to recover herself rather quickly. Turning to Jake, she asked, "And now you're wondering again, is that it? Still trying to get over the pain?"

"I guess that's it," Jake said, his face sheepish. "I have a thirty-day ticket. Maybe I would have stopped in Montana. If I do and if Bishop

Nisley will give a good report, perhaps I can get back home before my bishop gets upset."

"Especially if you have some news," Betty said with a smile.

Jake grinned at her and nodded.

"What about it, Hannah?" he asked. "Can we start over—all fresh and new?"

Hannah looked at him, her eyes growing misty, her heart pounding hard. Could God—and Jake—really be giving her another chance at happiness, even after she had messed things up so badly?

"I think we can," Hannah said through her tears. But now they were tears of happiness not sorrow.

"Oh," Betty said, ecstatic, "is it too much too hope for—a wedding in Montana, perhaps? Maybe you'll even *live* there!"

Jake and Hannah said nothing but simply looked at each other. Betty beamed and said, "Oh! This is really happening. I'm not dreaming."

"Let's not mention anything about dreaming right now," Hannah said.

"That's because we don't have to," Jake said. "We're living it."

"By God's grace. *Jah,* by God's grace we are," Betty repeated herself.

"That's right," Jake agreed, still gazing at Hannah.

She simply nodded.

It was a moonless Indiana Sunday night and fifteen minutes after the hymn sing had been dismissed. Girls stood around the front door, watchful and ready for their rides. The group stiffened when Annie Bontrager walked out. Her brother's buggy was not next in line—Sam Knepp's was.

Annie stepped forward and one girl whispered, "So soon?" to the others. Another one answered with, "Someone's sure in a hurry," and the buzz began.

"Good evening," Annie simply said to Sam as she gracefully hopped into the buggy, her dress not even brushing the buggy wheel.

"Good evening," he responded, letting out the reins of his horse. They drove quickly out of the driveway in silence.

She gathered herself to say it, her hands clasped tightly in her lap. The quiet of the night gave her strength. No more was she the clumsy, blushing girl from her school days. Years of waiting and sorrow had tempered her soul. Now she would take the chance given to her and not let it slip away. Annie cleared her throat and said, "What Hannah did to you was not nice, Sam. You know that."

Sam said nothing but held onto the reins as his horse pulled hard.

"I'm glad it happened, though," she said into the darkness.

"Really, Annie?" he asked, and his voice trembled.

She said nothing for a long moment and then said "I think God has kept you. You don't know how thankful I am for that. The day of the wedding was really a miracle for me—and maybe for us."

No light penetrated the buggy at the moment, and nothing much could be seen, the darkness heavy around them. If there had been a little light, one could have seen that while his hands were still on the reins, Sam's mouth hung wide open.

Hannah stood on Betty's front porch holding a letter in her hand, her cheeks flushed rosy.

"Well, can I see it?" Betty asked, her voice a tease.

"*Nee*, you can't," Hannah said. "You know better than that."

"Then at least tell me what it says."

"Some of it." Hannah held the letter away from Betty. "Let's see. He's home, and there was no trouble with his bishop. His parents thought him a little reckless when he told them about us, but they settled down when they heard we already knew each other from last summer. No news has gotten there about my disastrous wedding day. I know I'll never be able to be married in Nappanee," Hannah said. "But Jake thinks I should stay out here for the summer anyway. It would do me some good, he thinks."

"He sounds like a husband already," Betty said and grabbed for the letter.

Hannah laughed and kept it out of her reach.

"Did he, at least, ask the question?" Betty asked, barely able to contain herself.

"He asked while he was here," Hannah said as a blush came to her face. "You know he wouldn't ask in a letter."

"No, I don't know that," Betty retorted. "The way you two do things!"

"Well, he *did* ask, and we'll wait till next year to let things settle down and get to know each other better."

"You're staying the summer, then? You'll run the riding stable again?"

"If Mom and Dad don't object, I'd love to."

"They won't," Betty said, her voice grim, "or I'll have something to say about that."

Hannah laughed and said, "Just think—all summer in Montana and letters from Jake."

"When the time comes, is there a chance for a Montana wedding?" Betty pleaded. "We so need one out here. Don't you see how lonely we are?"

"We *might*," Hannah teased. "As much as I would like to have it at home, I guess I have to take into account what my dreams have cost me. Plus Dad will have calmed down by then and be ready for the trip out here."

"A real wedding," Betty said, her eyes glowing, "in the mountains of Montana. Won't that be something?"

"*My* wedding," Hannah said, and the tears stung her eyes.

"Now don't you get started," Betty said. "We had best drop it for now and get the noon meal started."

Hannah nodded as she focused, once again, on her letter.

That evening, upstairs in her room, she reread the letter again and then gently folded it and put it in her drawer.

She then sat at her desk, opened her tablet, and by the light of the kerosene lamp began to write.

> *My dear Jake,*
>
> *I received your letter today. It was so very welcomed. I can't tell you how much I love you, but perhaps you already know. Betty wants me to stay all summer again, and I think I will. When can I see you in Iowa? I suppose I should visit your family before the wedding. I will leave that up to you and how it can be arranged.*
>
> *Tonight my heart is so full of joy and with many other things that concern you, but I will leave them unsaid. It's best that way…so love and kisses. I'll dash this note off tomorrow and send more detailed news later. For tonight, I just wanted to let you know how I love you and how thankful I am to God for you.*
>
> *Hannah Miller*
>
> *P.S. You are a dream come true.*

The months passed quickly with a flurry of letters between Iowa and Montana.

"If I see one more, I'll throw it in the trash myself," Betty teased when another arrived in the mail.

"If you do…" Hannah said, glaring at her aunt and tearing open the letter.

"Hopeless cases you two are," Betty said and sighed deeply. "It's going to be a long, long winter."

"Do you think Dad will let us marry in the spring?" Hannah asked.

"How would I know that?" Betty said. "I'm not sure I would let you. Both of you could use a little more maturity."

"That's what I thought," Hannah said, her eyes quickly back on her letter. "He's coming to Indiana this winter."

"Just one visit?"

"Of course not," Hannah replied, glowering. "He's coming for a whole month, and I'm coming back to Montana next year again."

"Does it say that in the letter?" Betty asked. "Is Jake already deciding those things for you?"

"Don't be such a tease. Of course not. Mom said so in her last letter."

"Then no spring wedding."

"One can always hope," Hannah said, "but I really don't think so. Dad agrees with you on the maturing thing. Mom said so."

"At least we're on the same page now," Betty said triumphantly.

Betty wasn't surprised, though, when later that winter a wedding date was announced. A flurry of letters set the plans in motion, and then in early May, Hannah returned to Montana. To Betty's delight, the couple decided they would, after all, be married in Montana.

Jake visited in June and stayed for two weeks.

The night before he left, he and Hannah rode back to the river. Memories of a less fortunate time returned to Hannah as they rode along the rushing water.

"Do you remember another evening…when things didn't turn out too well?" she asked.

"I was trying to forget that," Jake said with a somber smile.

The mountains lay all around them as they rode quietly. Hannah's heart beat faster as she savored this time alone with Jake away from the bustle of the house.

"Come," Jake said, motioning with his hand. He dismounted, keeping hold of the reins.

He approached her horse as she swung slowly down. She faced him, so close she was certain he could hear her heart pounding.

"Our wedding's soon," he said, and his fingers searched for her face in the falling dusk.

She nodded, unable to speak. Never had she felt so close to him. He was a vision to behold against the backdrop of the strong majestic mountains—and he was all hers now. The pain of the past was just a memory.

He brought both of his hands up to her face and came closer. She closed her eyes as he kissed her for the first time. She could scarcely breathe—so much joy filled the moment.

"Jake," she whispered and clung to him, "you really do want to marry me?"

"Of course, silly," he said, laughing and letting her go, "I do love you so."

They walked a bit farther, and then he said, "I have to leave tomorrow, and I want the memory of us here by the river to stay in my mind until I see you again—just the two of us, alive and so in love."

He kissed her again and then they saddled up to go back.

"Jake," Hannah said, "let's have a good gallop on our way back."

"Okay, let's do," Jake agreed. They both let their horses have their head. Hannah bent low over the saddle to cut the wind, the tears stinging her eyes. Jake pulled ahead slightly and waved his arm over his head. *So unlike an Amish boy*, she thought as their horses kept neck to neck all the way back to the barn.

As they led their horses to their stalls, Hannah felt her cheeks still burning like fire—but not from the wind. Jake unsaddled the horses and kissed Hannah again before he left. She watched him walk out the driveway, thinking she had never seen a more handsome boy in all her life.

Jake returned two weeks before the wedding date, and they sat up half the night talking of their plans. Kathy and Roy arrived a week after that.

"What that girl doesn't put a man through," Roy said, grumbling and settling himself onto Betty's couch. Hannah heard him but took hope from the smile that played around the edges of his mouth.

The morning of the wedding had finally arrived. Hannah came downstairs in her blue dress, which had been packed away since that fateful day when she last wore it. Her step was uncertain as she lowered herself from the final stair, not sure how Jake would react. From the expression on Jake's face, as he stood by the window all dressed up in his new black shiny suit, she needn't have worried.

"Cast me over the *odel*," he said, unable to take his eyes off of her.

"I love you," she whispered.

Kathy and Betty must have heard the couple because they then rushed into the room from the kitchen.

"Don't get used to it, Jake," Betty teased. "She won't always look this good."

"And neither will he," Kathy added, thinking of her Roy. "Now get back upstairs until it's time to go out. There will be people in and out of the house who might see you."

At five till nine, Jake walked out the door with Hannah following behind him. The two pairs of witnesses followed them across the yard to the barn where the ceremony would be held.

In front of such a small group of people, Hannah could breathe with ease. With Jake beside her, it wasn't nearly as hard to endure as that sad day back in Nappanee. Here in Montana only a few of the invited relatives could attend due to the distance involved. That also left only the home ministers to perform the ceremony.

Minister Mose Chupp spoke first, and then Bishop Nisley gave the main sermon. Figuring it was her day, Hannah paid little attention to what they said as she kept a demure watch on Jake.

"And now will this brother and sister please come forward if they still desire to be joined together as man and wife," Bishop Nisley said at the conclusion of his sermon as he motioned with his hand.

Jake rose first, and then Hannah followed him. She said "*jah*" at all the right places, unable to believe this was really happening and not just a dream.

Then Bishop Nisley took both of their hands in his and smiled. She was certain it wasn't a dream as she heard his voice proclaim, "And now I pronounce you man and wife by the will of God and the authority of the state of Montana."

He let go of their hands, and Hannah clung to Jake's hand lest he disappear before her eyes. When he moved back to sit down, she followed. Someone from the back announced the last song number.

As the music began for the last song, tears swelled in Hannah's eyes. She dared to take a quick glance at Jake only to find tears streaking his face too. Then he turned to her and smiled.

And he wasn't a dream at all. He was very real.

Discussion Questions

1. Was Hannah wrong in becoming so starry-eyed when she first found the love poem?

2. Is the pressure Hannah felt in grade school to have a boyfriend universal, or is it only a Western phenomenon?

3. Are there better ways in which Hannah could have resisted Peter's charms?

4. What additional methods could Kathy and Roy have used to help Hannah overcome her guilt at Peter's death?

5. Have you ever considered a trip to Montana and its combination of big sky country and mountains?

6. Hannah experienced emotional healing while working around Betty's horses. Do you know of anyone in pain who could benefit from a similar experience?

7. Jake struggles with his own hurts from being rejected, and it played a large part in his misunderstanding of Hannah. Are there better ways of dealing with hurts, so that overreactions can be avoided?

8. What caused Hannah to believe that because she found a suitor unattractive, it was possibly closer to God's will?

9. Betty makes a lot of assumptions about her sister Kathy's desires for Hannah's future. Was she just a poor communicator, or too wrapped up in her own world?

10. Do you think Jake would have gotten over his bitterness and wanderings, if Hannah and Betty had not met him on the bus?

About Jerry Eicher...

As a boy, **Jerry Eicher** spent eight years in Honduras where his grandfather helped found an Amish community outreach. As an adult, Jerry taught for two terms in parochial Amish and Mennonite schools in Ohio and Illinois. He has been involved in church renewal for 14 years and has preached in churches and conducted weekend meetings of in-depth Bible teaching. Jerry lives with his wife, Tina, and their four children in Virginia.

If you enjoyed A Dream for Hannah, *be sure to look for the sequel,* A Hope for Hannah.

One

from A Hope for Hannah

Hannah Byler awoke with a start. She sat upright in bed and listened. The wind outside the small cabin stirred in the pine trees. The moon, already high in the sky when she and Jake went to bed, shone brightly through the log cabin window.

Beside her she heard Jake's deep, even breathing. She had grown accustomed to the comforting sound in the few short months since they'd been married. She laid her head back on the pillow. Perhaps it was just her imagination. There was no sound—nothing to indicate something might be wrong.

But now her heart beat faster—and fearfully. Something *was* wrong—but *what*?

"Jake," she whispered, her hand gently shaking his shoulder. "Jake, *vagh uff*."

"What is it?" he asked groggily. He spoke louder than she wished he would at the moment.

"I don't know," she whispered again and hoped he would get the hint. "I think there's something outside."

Jake listened and sat up in bed with his arms braced on the mattress.

"I don't hear anything," he said, a little quieter this time. "There are all kinds of noises in the mountains at night."

"I think something is outside," she insisted.

They both were silent a moment…waiting. Hannah half expected Jake to lower his head back to his pillow, tell her the fears were a bad dream, and go back to sleep. Instead he pushed back the covers and pivoted his feet to the floor.

Just then a loud snuff outside the log wall stopped him. They both froze. Hannah didn't recognize the sound. No animal she knew ever made such a noise.

"It sounds like a pig," Jake said, his voice low. "What are pigs doing out here at nighttime?"

"It's not a pig," Hannah whispered back. No stray pig, even in the nighttime, could create such tension. "It's something else."

"But what?" Jake asked, the sound coming again, seemingly right against the log wall.

Hannah lay rigid, filled with an overpowering sense that something large and fierce stood outside.

"I'm going to see." Jake had made up his mind, and Hannah made no objection.

Jake felt under the bed for his flashlight and then moved toward the door. Somehow Hannah found the courage to follow but stayed close to Jake.

Their steps made the wooden floor creak, the only sound to be heard.

Jake slowly pulled open the wooden front door, his flashlight piercing the darkness as he moved it slowly left and then right.

"Nothing here," he said quietly and then stepped outside.

Hannah looked around Jake toward the edge of the porch. "It was around the corner," she whispered.

Jake walked slowly toward the corner of the house, but Hannah stayed on the porch near the front door.

Jake stopped momentarily and then stepped around the corner of the house. Hannah could only see a low glow from the flashlight. In the distance, by the light of the moon, the misty line of the Cabinet Mountains accented the utter ruggedness of this country. During the day, the sight still thrilled her, but now that same view loomed dangerously.

For the first time since they'd moved into the cabin after their wedding, Hannah wondered whether this place was a little too much for the two of them. Was a remote cabin, a mile off the main road, and up this dirt path into the foothills of the Cabinet Mountains, really what she wanted?

"It's a bear!" Jake's voice came from around the corner. "Come take a look—quick—before he's gone."

"Gone," she whispered.

"Come see!" Jake's urgent voice came again.

Again Hannah found courage from somewhere. She stepped around the corner of the house and let her gaze follow the beam of Jake's flashlight, which now pierced the edge of the clearing around their cabin. At the end of the beam, a furry long-haired bear—as large as the one she'd seen once at the zoo—stood looking back at them, its raised head sniffing the air.

"It's a grizzly," Jake said, excitement in his voice. "See its hump?"

"Then why are we out here?" Hannah asked, nearly overcome with the urge to run, desperate for solid walls between her and this huge creature.

"The men at the lumberyard said there aren't many around," Jake said in her ear. "Mostly black bears down in this area."

"Shouldn't we be inside?" she asked the question another way, pulling on his arm. "It's not going away."

"It will leave sooner if we stay in sight rather than go inside," he told her, his light playing on the creature whose head was still in the air and turned in their direction.

"Well, I'm going inside," she said, her courage now wholly depleted.

"It's going," Jake announced, so she paused. They watched, fascinated, as the great creature bobbed its head and disappeared into the woods.

"It's gone," Jake said, a bit disappointed. "That was a grizzly."

They turned back to the cabin, Hannah following Jake's lead. As they stepped onto the porch, Hannah considered their front door. Suddenly the solid slat door—so bulky before—now looked thin, an unlikely protection against the hulk that had just disappeared into the dark tree line.

"What if it comes back?" she asked.

"It won't. It's just passing through," he assured her. "They don't like humans. They're wanderers anyway. It'll probably not come this way again. Ever."

Not reassured, Hannah shut the door tightly behind them and pushed the latch firmly into place.

"Bears hang around," she told him. "This one could come back."

"Then we'll deal with it. Maybe the game warden can help. I doubt it will return, though." Jake was fast losing interest and ready for his bed again.

Jake snuggled under the covers, pulling them tight up to his chin. "These are cold nights," he commented. "Winter's just around the corner. I have to get some sleep."

Hannah agreed and pulled her own covers up tight. Jake's job on the logging crew involved hard manual labor that required a good night's sleep. She didn't begrudge him his desire for sleep.

"I sure hope it doesn't come back," she said finally.

"I doubt it will," he muttered, but Hannah could tell he was already nearly asleep.

To the sounds of Jake's breathing, she lay awake and unable to stop her thoughts. Home, where she had grown up in Indiana, now seemed far away, a hazy blur against the fast pace of the past few months.

What is Mom doing? she wondered. *No doubt she's comfortably asleep in their white two-story home, secure another night just like the night before and ready to face another day just like the day before.*

Thoughts of her earlier summers in Montana—tending to Aunt Betty's riding stable—pushed into her mind. This country had seemed so glorious then, and she had dreamed of her return.

First had come the wedding—she smiled in the darkness. After a flurry of letters and Jake's visits as often as he could, Betty had received her wish for a wedding in Montana. Hannah's mother realized it was for the best. After the plans for Hannah's wedding to Sam Knepp ended in a disaster back home in Indiana, there was no way either Roy or Kathy would go through that embarrassment again. Even Jake was in favor of the wedding in Montana—here where they had met.

Their hearts were here in Montana now—close to the land and the small Amish community just off the shadow of the Cabinet Mountains. But now Hannah asked herself if living out here in the middle of nowhere was really for their best. Then she was thankful that at least she was with Jake—better here with Jake than anywhere else without him.

But as she lay in the darkness unable to sleep, she found herself wishing for close neighbors. She wished she could get up now and walk to the front door, knowing that someone else lived within calling distance—or at least within running distance if it came to that. Now, with a bear around, a night wanderer with mischief on his mind, there was nowhere to go. She shuddered.

She wondered if she could outrun a bear, even if a neighbor's house stood close by. She pictured herself lifting her skirt for greater speed. How fast could bears run? Could they see well at night to scout out their prey?

Hannah shivered in the darkness and listened to Jake's even breathing, wondering how he could sleep after what they had just seen. A grizzly! Jake had been sure of it. A grizzly sniffing around their cabin, outside their bedroom wall. Why was Jake not more alarmed? He had even seemed fascinated...as if it didn't bother him at all.

She had always thought she was the courageous one, the one who wanted adventure. After all, she had come out to Montana on her own that first summer. The mountains had fascinated her, drawn her in, and given her strength. Now tonight those same mountains had turned on her and given her a bear for a gift—a *grizzly*. Even the stately pine trees, with their whispers that soothed her before, now seemed to talk of dark things she knew nothing about, things too awful to say out loud.

She turned in the bed, hoping she wouldn't disturb Jake. She thought of his job on the logging crew, really a job of last resort. Yes, at first it was a blessing because they needed the income, but now it had become more and more of a burden. Jake didn't complain, but the burden was apparent in the stoop of his shoulders when he came home at night. It revealed itself in his descriptions of how he operated the cutter, navigated the steep slopes, and worked with logs that rolled down the sides of the mountains. She also heard it in his descriptions of Mr. Wesley, his boss. She had met Mr. Wesley once when he had stopped by the house to interview Jake for the job. He operated the largest timber company in Libby, and his huge, burly form matched his position, nearly filling their cabin door that day. She had been too glad Jake had gotten the job to worry much about Mr. Wesley, but after he left she was glad she wouldn't see him every day.

Hannah shivered again, feeling the sharp chill that seeped into the log house—the same one that seemed so wonderful in summer. But now winter would come soon to this strange land, and neither she nor Jake had ever been through one here.

Hannah willed herself to stop thinking. Now she knew for certain. There had been something she wanted to tell Jake but had wanted to wait until she was sure. Now on this night—the night the bear came—she was certain. The strangeness puzzled her. How could a bear's unexpected visit and this wonderful news have anything to do with each other?

The Adams County Triology
by Jerry Eicher

Rebecca's Promise

Rebecca Keim has just declared her love to John Miller and agreed to become his wife. But she's haunted by her schoolgirl memories of a long ago love—and a promise made and a ring given. Is that memory just a fantasy come back to destroy the beautiful present...or was it real?

When Rebecca's mother sends her back to the old home community in Milroy to be with her aunt during and after her childbirth, Rebecca determines to find answers that will resolve her conflicted feelings. Faith, love, and tradition all play a part in Rebecca's divine destiny.

Rebecca's Return

Rebecca Keim returns to Wheat Ridge full of resolve to make her relationship with John Miller work. But in her absence, John has become suspicious of the woman he loves. Before their conflict can be resolved, John is badly injured and Rebecca is sent back to Milroy to aid her seriously ill Aunt Leona.

In Milroy, Rebecca once again visits the old covered bridge over the Flatrock River, the source of her past memories and of her promise made so long ago.

Where will Rebecca find happiness? In Wheat Ridge with John, the man she has agreed to marry, or should she stake her future on the memory that persists...and the ring she has never forgotten? Does God have a perfect will for Rebecca—and if so how can she know that will?

Rebecca's Choice

Popular Amish fiction author Jerry Eicher finishes the Adam's County Trilogy with an intriguing story of a young couple's love, a community of faith, and devotion to truth. Rebecca Keim is now engaged to John Miller, and they are looking forward to life together. When Rebecca goes to Milroy to attend her beloved teacher's funeral, John receives a mysterious letter accusing Rebecca of scheming to marry him for money.

Determined to forsake his past jealousies and suspicions, John tries hard to push the accusations from his mind. Upon Rebecca's return, disturbing news quickly follows. She is named as the sole heir to her teacher's three farms. But there's a condition—she must marry an Amish man. When John confronts Rebecca, she claims to know nothing. Soon Rachel Byler, the vengeful but rightful heir to the property, arrives and reveals secrets from the past. Now the whole community is reeling!

Rachel's Secret
BJ Hoff

Bestselling author BJ Hoff promises to delight you with her compelling new series, *The Riverhaven Years*. With the first book, *Rachel's Secret*, Hoff introduces a new community of unforgettable characters and adds the elements you have come to expect from her novels: a tender love story, the faith journeys of people we grow to know and love, and enough suspense to keep the pages turning quickly.

When the wounded Irish American riverboat captain, Jeremiah Gant, bursts into the rural Amish setting of Riverhaven, he brings chaos and conflict to the community—especially for young widow Rachel Brenneman. The unwelcome "outsider" needs a safe place to recuperate before continuing his secret role as an Underground Railroad conductor. Neither he nor Rachel is prepared for the forbidden love that threatens to endanger a man's mission, a woman's heart, and a way of life for an entire people.

Where Grace Abides
BJ Hoff

In the compelling second book in the series, Hoff offers you an even closer look at the Amish community of Riverhaven and the people who live and love and work there. Secrets, treachery, and persecution are only a few of the challenges that test Rachel's faith and her love for the forbidden "outsider," while Gant's own hopes and dreams are dealt a life-changing blow, rendering the vow he made to Rachel seemingly impossible to honor.

Many of the other characters first introduced in *Rachel's Secret* now find their gentle, unassuming lives of faith jeopardized by a malicious outside influence. At the same time, those striving to help runaway slaves escape to freedom through the Underground Railroad face deception and the danger of discovery.

All the elements you have come to expect from author BJ Hoff (romance, drama, great characters) join together in *Where Grace Abides* to fill the pages with a tender, endearing love story and a bold, inspiring journey of faith.

Shadows of Lancaster County
Mindy Starns Clark

Following up on her extremely popular Gothic thriller, *Whispers of the Bayou,* Mindy Starns Clark offers another suspenseful stand-alone mystery full of Amish simplicity, dark shadows, and the light of God's amazing grace.

Anna thought she left the tragedies of the past behind when she moved from Pennsylvania to California, but when her brother vanishes from the genetics lab where he works, Anna has no choice but to head back home. Using skills well-honed in Silicon Valley, she follows the high-tech trail her brother left behind, a trail that leads from the simple world of Amish farming to the cutting edge of DNA research and gene mapping.

Anna knows she must depend on her instincts, her faith in God, and the help of the Amish community to find her brother. She also must finally face her own shadows—and pray that she's stronger than the grief that threatens to overwhelm them all.

The Homestyle Amish Kitchen Cookbook: Plainly Delicious Recipes from the Simple Life
by Georgia Varozza

Just about everyone is fascinated by the Amish—their simple, family-centered lifestyle, colorful quilts, and hearty, homemade meals. Straight from the heart of Amish country, this celebration of hearth and home will delight you with the pleasures of the family table as you take a peek at the Amish way of life—a life filled with the self-reliance and peace of mind that many long for.

You will appreciate the tasty, easy-to-prepare recipes such as Scrapple, Graham "Nuts" Cereal, Potato Rivvel Soup, Amish Dressing, and Snitz Pie. At the same time you'll learn a bit about the Amish, savor interesting tidbits from the "Amish Kitchen Wisdom" sections, find out just how much food it takes to feed the large number of folks attending preaching services, barn raisings, weddings, work frolics, and much more.

The Homestyle Amish Kitchen Cookbook is filled with good, old-fashioned family meal ideas to help bring the simple life home!

Shoo-Fly Pie
2 8-inch unbaked pie crusts

SYRUP:
1 cup molasses
½ cup brown sugar
2 eggs, beaten
1 cup hot water
1 tsp. baking soda, dissolved in hot water

CRUMB TOPPING:
2 cups flour

¾ cup brown sugar
⅓ cup butter
½ tsp. cinnamon

Mix syrup ingredients thoroughly together. Divide mixture in half and pour into the two unbaked pie shells. Thoroughly mix together the ingredients for the crumb topping. Divide and sprinkle crumb topping onto the two pies.

Bake at 450° for 10 minutes and then reduce heat to 350° and continue baking until done, about another 30 minutes. Enjoy!